Strip

Strip

Delta Dupree

APHRODISIA
KENSINGTON BOOKS
http://www.kensingtonbooks.com

APHRODISIA BOOKS are published by

Kensington Publishing Corp.
850 Third Avenue
New York, NY 10022

All Kensington Titles, Imprints, and Distributed Lines are available at special quantity discounts for bulk purchases for sales promotions, premiums, fund-raising, and educational or institutional use.

Special book excerpts or customized printings can also be created to fit specific needs. For details, write or phone the office of the Kensington special sales manager: Kensington Publishing Corp., 850 Third Avenue, New York, NY 10022, attn: Special Sales Department, Phone: 1-800-221-2647.

Aphrodisia and the A logo Reg. U.S. Pat & TM Off.

ISBN-13: 978-0-7582-2702-7
ISBN-10: 0-7582-2702-7

First Kensington Trade Paperback Printing: November 2008

10 9 8 7 6 5 4 3 2 1

Printed in the United States of America

As one of the lucky souls to become published, I could easily fill pages with family and friends' names who have offered help and encouragement to keep me from veering off the winding road to success. I'll use the short list instead.

To the AAW ladies—Donnell, Julie, Marie—thank you for your genuine friendship, critiques, and gentle pushes when my writing slipped by the wayside. Pam and Stephanie, we're all published now. Tell me we didn't trudge down a long, muddy road to get to where we are. Longtime girlfriend Dianne read parts of my very first manuscript and loved it for some crazy reason. Luv ya, Di. And my good friend Liz gave that outside encouragement I will always treasure.

To my dad, my oldest brother, and my children, we've been through a lot over the years and we'll enjoy many more together. Love you guys all the time.

Forever love to my romantic husband who stood by me when my pride nosedived. We'll always soar together, hand in hand.

Most of all, I dedicate this book to Momma, who passed away in 1981, and my youngest brother, who followed her recently. Neither doubted I would find success in all endeavors. I miss you both terribly.

1

"Ooh-*ooh*. Girl, I'll need to change my panties when this is over. He chose the perfect tune to turn us out. 'Jamaica Funk' was the baddest hit on record," Galaxeé said. She swayed to the hip-hop song's downbeat, snapping her fingers as loudly as she popped gum. "He's hot, isn't he?"

"No doubt." Rio Saunders shifted, sat straighter on the barstool at Killer Bods. The male strip club she and Galaxeé Barnett owned wasn't open for business until eight tonight, but the current dance applicant . . . mercy.

For a youngster he was a prime specimen, one of Denver, Colorado's finest. With a sable mane hanging well down his thick neck and a startling pair of slate-gray eyes, this tall honey paraded his attributes. He was God's blessed gift to women.

He swaggered toward the stage's edge. Under bright spotlights in the darkened theater, his view was nowhere near as good as hers. He flaunted all his finery. With broad shoulders, acutely defined pecs with just enough dark hair and a rippling six-pack, his body was a temple built for some lucky girl's loving.

"Mm, mm, mm," Rio purred quietly. And he had rhythm. Hiding a smile, she sipped from the glass of lemon water the bartender had set down.

"What do you think? Yes? Can't imagine otherwise," Galaxeé insisted.

They'd judged all sorts of wannabes for three hours—lean, stout, cute, plus a few sure-goners. Bryce Sullivan was the last performer applying for one soon-to-be vacant position.

No one else had danced so well. No one else had boasted his hard-body physique.

No one else looked this darn good.

Except Dallas Cooper, a.k.a. Panther Man. He—rather, his twenty-two-year-old hussy, Shannon Fields—decided to hang up his G-string for marriage. Dallas was Killer Bods' shining star. At twenty-eight, with smooth skin blacker than obsidian, he moved effortlessly during his performances, flexing his bulging muscles. Had he been a dozen years older, closer to Rio's age, she'd gladly let him turn her inside out. Welcome it.

"Let's think about it a couple days," she finally replied. "This is an African American revue."

Galaxeé's huffs would deflate most people's lungs. "Girl, time is running out. Panther's last night is next week. So what if this guy's white? As good as he looks, not to mention how well he boogies, he'll draw more chicks to the club. From Silk's."

Killer's dancers loved their sistahs, although a variety of women, single and married, looking for outstanding action frequented the nightclub. Quality advertisement was a must in this business. "White women."

"Blacks, too. And Latinas, Thais, hell, Egyptians. He is fine. You know it. I know it. Why wait? He could start tomorrow night. We can break him in for the Christmas rush, ready by . . ."

"Slow—" Rio clamped her mouth shut, shaking her head.

Galaxeé talked faster than any auctioneer's banter during a hot sale.

"... We've booked four private parties so far, all between now and New Year's. He could work them. Shit, he'd clean up and so would we. Think of how much money we'd have coming in for only three real working days a week."

She shook her head again. "I don't think so."

Two deep frown lines creased Galaxeé's forehead and her lips thinned flatter than the straw Rio had chewed on. "Why not?"

"You know the sisters hosting these parties. They want chocolate, not vanilla."

She stared at Sullivan as he moved across the stage. He halted, struck a sexy pose. Every lean muscle rippled.

Jesus.

He unzipped his pants, stroked the length of his ... Rio sucked in a tank full of air, held it.

Slowly, sensuously, the denim slid down narrow hips, displaying powerful thighs and strong calves. When he kicked the garments aside, Sullivan straightened to his full height—a towering statue of regal flair fit for any queen's fantasy.

Breathing again, Rio lowered her gaze.

Good night!

Brazilian G-string. Miniature. Bulging flame-red against bronzed skin. Unblinking as he gyrated, she wasn't sure the fabric would hold together or hold all it carried inside the thin material. Barely enough to cover ... She drew in the next breath between her teeth and sat straighter on the stool.

"Ooh, gir-irl," Galaxeé breathed, fanning her face twice as fast as the music's rhythm. "He's exactly what you need."

Air flowed from Rio's lungs in a long, unsteady rush. "You mean us. Killer Bods."

"I mean *you*," her partner qualified. "You need a good fucking by a young buck just like him to fry your brains senseless. You've been going without way too long."

"Shut up."

Water and ice spilled over her hand as she set the glass down, splashing on the wooden bar top. An instant later, Luanne the bartender wiped away the puddle and handed Rio a fresh white towel.

"You do. That's why you've been so evil." Smoothing her hand down the length of her auburn dreadlocks, threaded beads clicked together. Galaxeé flicked the thick mass over her shoulder, still staring at Sullivan, mesmerized.

Rio tsked. The nerve of this woman. She folded the towel neatly into quarters and laid it across the curved bar. Yeah, maybe she had been evil, but she'd never shown bad manners to anyone other than her best friend and, of course, her ex-husband Devon, the midlife-crisis hound.

Arching one eyebrow a fraction, Galaxeé said, "You're getting another pimple, too, right there in the center of your forehead. At your age, any fuckable age, lack of weenie action always launches a round of zits."

"Shut up. Where do you come up with this mess?" She stole another glance at Sullivan. This man wasn't lacking anything from what she could tell.

Galaxeé leaned back, dangling her arms behind the chair, cackling. "It's true, especially after wrestling the monthly blues. I used to get them." She'd hooked up with a new honey, an older man who, after four months, still lavished her with expensive gifts, bombarding her with boyish love. "Besides, I can tell you really like the way this guy looks, the way he moves. Your aura's melting, on the verge of disintegrating. And it's the first time I've seen your eyes glaze over in almost two decades."

Aura. And glaze? She tsked again. Sometimes Galaxeé talked too much smack. No one caused Rio Saunders to glaze over, especially youngsters. "Bar lights, disco lights—"

"Bullshit. Admit it. He's hot."

He was hot—*is* hot—and far too young for her. Plus, he was

nowhere near *right* for her. "Why do you think he came here for a job? Why not apply at Silk's?"

Smoothly Silk, Killer's sole competition, employed two African American dancers Rio and Galaxeé had disqualified from their league of performers a month before their own club opened. The guys were physically unsuitable for near-naked entertainment.

"Maybe he did," Galaxeé replied as the music died away. "We need to interview him anyway. Ask him."

Bryce collected his clothes and went backstage. After stripping out of the G-string, he struggled into a pair of tight stonewashed jeans. Luckily, his navy knit pullover soaked up sweat. It was freezing outside.

Snow—big flakes—had begun to fall by the time he'd arrived here. Winter had settled on Denver on Halloween night as usual, and continued a blustery rampage.

This was the stupidest plan on record. Galaxeé and whoever the hell this Rio broad is will never hire me. Should've come up with a better scheme and left Dallas out of the mix. If he ever finds out, our friendship is history.

His half sister, Angelina Berardi, owned Killer's competition and Bryce was her silent partner. Silk's was headed straight to hell as long as Killer Bods kept its doors open.

The club's downward spiral had stretched his cash thinner than ice after a first hard freeze, compounded by Thorobred Computers lacking a new contract over the last seven months. Banking on a few still in the till, he hadn't exactly wanted to strip to please a bunch of frenzied chicks. But, he also had a second working program: boxing in Jason Simmons, one of Killer's dancers, who needed somebody to knock the arrogant chip off his shoulders. Simmons dated Angelina—as in, walked all over her.

Armed with a fail-safe plot backed by his computer expertise, Bryce had pretended he'd met Rio Saunders. Dallas had fallen for the in-lust ruse.

"If you want her," Coop had said, "you got to get close to her. I'll tell you what, my man. She is not easy meat. The woman's got soul and determination, along with much class. This club means everything to her. Everything, dude. Nothing and nobody gets in her way when it comes to Killer Bods. As for Galaxeé Barnett, don't try to get slick—nothing gets by her. Some of the guys nicknamed her 'Loose Lips' for good reason, and she knows everything that goes on, somehow. But the owners are professionals, all business."

At the time, Bryce needed Dallas's foot-in-the-door help. "She must have an old man or sugar daddy." Not many chicks had their own business without financial help—like Angelina.

"Not. Unless she's got him under lock and key, hogtied and gagged. She dates. Saw her with a couple older dudes, fifty-ish maybe. I've never seen her with a youngster like you, and never any guy tinted on the color scale's lighter side, especially one with hair longer than Cher's. I'll get you an application, drop a heads-up, but you gotta lose those damned Coke-bottle glasses. Makes your eyes look bigger than E.T.'s peepers. Might want to think about waxing, too." Laughing, Dallas said, "Hurts like hell."

Testily conforming, Bryce permitted a beautician to chop off his locks to near-respectable length. Lasik surgery corrected the crappy vision he'd had since childhood. Horn-rimmed glasses had been a pain in his . . . on the bridge of his nose. Fuck waxing.

The new look had earned him lots more attention when he had little time for play. Work kept him busy, kept his libido in check most of the time.

He tucked the pullover inside his jeans, slung his black leather jacket over his shoulder and went out the dressing room's door. Unfamiliar with Killer's layout, he strode back across the stage and down the stairs, his gaze directed at the floor. Through a collection of tables stacked with hardwood chairs, he wove his way to the bar where Killer's owners sat. Dancing was the easy part.

"Very nice."

He recognized Galaxeé's business tone from the call for try-outs.

"Exceptionally provocative."

That sultry voice, chilly as a winter pond, floated through his senses, heating his skin unnaturally. Bryce looked up. The partner?

Exotic features fit her—coppery skin coloring, short-cropped platinum-blond hair lengthening to a shag that framed an oval face. Penetrating catlike hazel eyes held his gaze. When was the last time his heart stuttered and pounded like a damn kettledrum? He wiped away the cool trickle of sweat from his forehead.

"Thanks."

"Better than nice." Galaxeé tipped her martini glass toward him. "Sheer perfection."

Encouraged, Bryce nodded, smiled. One point for his side.

"This is my partner Rio Saunders."

"Tell us something," she said. "Why aren't you dancing at Silk's?"

Busted. Ears on fire, his face surely flushed five different shades of crimson. "They aren't hiring." God, he hoped not. He'd forgotten to ask his sister. "And Killer Bods is better known, hiring the best of the best."

"Bravo. Smart reply for someone so young."

At least she flashed a brilliant smile. More encouragement, except that degrading "young" crap declared like a long-lost aunt.

Scooting up on her barstool, Galaxeé said, "Grab a seat.

Would you care for a cocktail while we discuss business?" The offer earned a flat-out frown from her partner.

Bryce declined anyway, needing to get back to the office clearheaded. Building and selling desktop computers killed off brain cells the same as man's favorite poison, not to mention the headaches software development induced. If he nailed this gig at Killer's, his work schedule would turn crazier than it already was. After laying his eyes on luscious Rio Saunders, he thought dancing here might be well worth a pounding migraine.

"How long have you been shaking?" the woman of his super-erotic dreams asked.

He dragged a stool across the floor, placed it directly in front of her and said, "Years, but not professionally."

Truthfully, dancing ran a close second to skiing, third to computer work. Dallas had worked with him, claiming he had no rhythm or soul. Lacked funk. He'd laid down the law of the club.

Jam well, if he wanted to get next to Rio. Seductive moves earned the right to get close to her. Above all, he'd better know where to start.

Bryce knew exactly where to begin.

Even now, he imagined her skin felt soft as cotton. Nothing could be finer, except the blond hair framing her face. Would the tuft of hair between her legs feel as silky? He intended to find out one day. Slide his hand up her thigh, part her soft flesh, teasing her relentlessly.

"You do very well for a . . . a baby," she said.

He raked his fingers through his hair, his sensuous thoughts frozen in one brutal second. "I'm pushing twenty-nine. I'm not a damn newborn."

"Ooh, with a temper."

Bryce yanked his head around at Galaxeé's gum-popping explosion.

"Sorry," she said, but the disapproving sideways glare she gave her partner meant otherwise.

She'd sided with him. Add another point for the one-man team.

Sliding down on the stool, he spread his legs wider, nearly made contact with Rio, but she twisted in her seat, crossing a pair of lengthy, stunning limbs. "Am I at least in the running?"

"You most—" Galaxeé began.

"We like to discuss each applicant before we make a final decision," Rio interrupted, which earned another narrow-eyed glare from Galaxeé. She patted the stack of applications. "Everything on your résumé is current? Phone numbers, addresses, etcetera?"

Eyes locked on hers, he nodded. "Email, too." When she didn't deny having Internet access, he mentally ticked off an important item on his agenda.

"Well, Mr. Sullivan." She stuck her hand out. "We'll be in touch one way or the other."

What? The interview was over too damn quick—completely illogical. He'd interviewed potential technician applicants, at minimum, for an hour. And this was what, three minutes? Four? Two-hundred-forty stinking, chitchat seconds? How could she learn anything about him in so little time? Granted, he had abbreviated his account of the duties at his day job for good reason, but hell.

Bryce leaned forward and clasped her delicate hand. Long and slender, nails well manicured, her fingers curled around his with softness enough to caress a man into delirium while she kept him under the spell of her eyes—eyes he could drown in. He really wanted to drown.

He held on longer than he should have, but for a shorter time than he would've liked, without resistance, until Galaxeé cleared her throat.

"Thank you for your time," he said.

When their palms slid slowly apart, Bryce got to his feet. Galaxeé added a sly wink to her handshake. He slung his jacket over his shoulder and started toward the front door, telling himself not to look back, not to appear too eager or too arrogant. Step two now completed.

A blast of bitter-cold air and snow flurries whirlwinded into the club before the heavy door slammed shut.

"He likes you," Galaxeé said. "And he's got a penetrating pair of gray bullets that were fixed on you every second. When he arrived here, I was concerned, ready to boot the boy out. His aura was dark, murky. It glows now. Maybe it was fear, trepidation."

Rio rolled her eyes.

"Did you notice how he opened for you?"

"Stop," she said flatly.

"He did! An open invitation only for you. He's well hung too. Majestically." She grinned, winked. "You couldn't hide your attraction either. Your tits swelled."

"Stop it, Galaxeé." She had to admit, her lacy bra still felt uncomfortably binding.

"I saw your nipples perk up under the silk. Bet Bryce saw them. Stood out like cat's-eye marbles. Bet it made your tattoo spread with bigger, pink ears."

Rio hated the sound of a cackling witch, but she agreed with Galaxeé on one item. Bryce Sullivan was very well endowed.

She'd felt the first signs of pleasurable interest: nipples tightening, quivering between her legs when she'd glanced down at the bulging thickness nestled inside tight jeans. Lots of inches. Lord. What would it look like during an erection, a big oak tree? She shuddered.

Why couldn't he have a tenor or sissy voice instead of an I-can-make-you-come-multiple-times bass? God, she loved hearing a seductive, low-pitched rumbler, whispering, promising a thoroughly carnal interlude. A tenor would've made it so much easier to forget Sullivan and file his application at the back of the folder. Or in the circular file.

Still, at her age, any twenty-eight-year-old was too young, too inexperienced; she would consider it robbing the cradle.

Uh-uh. No way.

Anger crept under her skin for thinking of the sinful images, if a liaison ever happened. It never would, not in this lifetime. She had more important issues on her mind, like Killer Bods and her future. Denver's metro area had plenty of room for another women's club to strip Killer's of its dancers and clientele.

"I bet he's got a hundred young chickies chasing after him. Besides, I don't like men who flaunt their meat and put it on display like a hot item on a smorgasbord. Especially rookies." Temper had crept into her tone.

"He can't help it. It's part of him. What do you want him to do, cut it off? Is that why you like Dallas—Dickless?" Galaxeé laughed hard, mouth wide open, head falling back.

"You drink too much," Rio said. She meant it to sound snappish and snatched up the applications. "I'll make copies for you. When you're sober we'll discuss them."

Rio stomped toward their office above the club. Four-inch stilettos clicked noisily on the wooden stairs as she planted each foot, climbing each riser. She might hide her innermost feelings, but they never slipped by Galaxeé. The woman had an impossible perception, able to see through her, see inside her brain, read her thoughts. Ever since childhood, darn her.

Galaxeé had the nerve to call herself a fortune-teller and worked as one for a year, back in the good old days. She'd changed her first name from Cecilia for that reason alone and legally processed the paperwork. Astrology, palm readings and dreams were her best games. She'd said it was all in the hands and mind.

Two weeks ago, Rio had had a nightmare involving snakes. She should've known better than to tell her partner, who explained any visions about snakes meant a good "fucking" encounter and, if the dream included an anaconda, a big cock.

Rio chastised her for using foul language and laughed off the prediction, even when the dream featured one very large, very stout serpent chasing after her. She'd awakened startled, drenched in a sweat when it wrapped around her body.

Yeah, so she was afraid of too much meat. Too much meant pain and no enjoyment. Good old Devon had cured her.

But she was also aware of how her body had responded seeing Sullivan leisurely sprawled out like a sultan deciding on his daily choice from an ever-ready harem, displaying every thick, tempting inch of his staggering . . . Her mouth had watered and something else had shimmered from within. Something maddeningly metaphysical swept through her on one long wave from pinky toes to the roots of her hair, like the hot flashes she'd begun having recently. A sudden fire searing her flesh.

Even now, heat flooded her insides as she recognized the tingling of erotic sensations. Excitement coursed through her body, though Bryce Sullivan had already left the club with his fine self.

He did it on purpose, damn him. Just like a man. Baby! He's a baby!

She slammed the office door. These thoughts were absurd. Why hadn't she listened to Galaxeé and bought a vibrator for all the cold, lonely nights she spent without companionship in her downtown loft, for any time when horniness riled her libido and fantasies ruled her dreams?

"There're always the personal digits," Galaxeé had hinted.

"Forget that. If I ever decide to have sex again, I want the real thing, not fingers, not toys." She had avoided adult stores for good reason, still unable to defy her staid upbringing with too much change at once. Hopefully, one day she'd have another chance at a sexual encounter before she was too darned old to enjoy it.

By the time she finished work today, all of these flaming thoughts should melt the frost on the skylight, break the glass and fly away. They'd better fly somewhere. She had no insane reason to entertain them or Mr. Too-Young, Mr. Too-Hot Sullivan.

2

They discussed each applicant, but every time they ran through the list, one man surpassed all others in every way.

"Guess that settles it," Galaxeé said. She searched through her purse, found her cell phone. "I'll give him a call."

"Hold your horses," Rio ordered. "Richard Monroe isn't a bad choice. He's cute, he dances well and he's black."

"Shit, he's also rangy. Women want to see muscle on our dancers. They want to fantasize about them as good lovers, not about crushing chicken bones or believing they'd squish him flatter than a damn pancake."

"Okay, fine. David Chambers."

"He's gay, remember? A waste, but gay. He wears a Mickey Mouse watch and wiggles like Minnie. Totally uncool."

Chambers was the best-looking dancer in the remaining group, a fine-looking African American who sported a decent body, but wasted manliness all the same when he paraded his feminine side. He'd risk having his delicate feelings injured if the crowd booed him offstage. And that would even hurt Rio's feelings because Chambers was quietly sensitive.

"Quit trying to eliminate Bryce. He's perfect in every way. Our clientele will love him."

"We might lose clients over this."

"Bet?" Galaxeé snapped one hand to her hip. "Buck says you lose. Put your money where your mouth is." They never wagered more than a dollar.

Rio scratched at an imaginary itch near the corner of her mouth. Why was this niggling sensation tickling her skin, now of all times? Sullivan surpassed good. He had talent. Everything about him was steeped in excellence—like a high-quality Bordeaux worth hanging on to, saving the best for last.

"All right. You call. See if he can start tomorrow night. Call Dallas, too. Let him know his partner in crime will split dance routines."

"He won't be happy, but his bitchy little girlfriend will jump for joy."

"Forget her. Shannon is just a silly, jealous heifer."

Rising from her chair, Galaxeé said, "Actually, I think I saw her mug plastered on a telephone-pole poster that read: Lost dog. Breed: Slut."

Rio closed her eyes at the poster's image forming in her mind, her shoulders rocking.

"Answers to 'Tramp.' Last seen: In bed with any willing mongrel."

Rio burst out laughing. "Stop."

"Shannon ought to be happy Dallas made money here. Good money."

The dancers earned more in tips than salary. Shannon hated seeing her man touched by other women, although Miss Fields had no qualms about caressing any other dancer. She worked her hands better than two washcloths when performers left the stage to give customers a closer look and better feel. Tips came in the form of G-string insertion. Every dancer accepted the code and women paid to do the honors.

"What about the bet? Chic-ken?" Galaxeé asked. Flapping her arms, she squawked.

"The devil with you." Rio laughed again. She swung her soft leather stool around, picked up her favorite gold pen, scribbled her signature on a service document and shoved it into the out-basket with an attached check.

When a loud gum pop filled the room, she murmured, "The bet is off." And she flinched at the next explosion.

"He'd make a good birthday present for you this year. You could thank him for giving."

Every year for the last thirty-five, they'd exchanged gifts on birthdays and Christmas. This year, they had included Killer Bods' sixth-month anniversary.

She spun around again. "Giving what?"

"You a good fucking." Galaxeé imitated a hyena's laughter better than the natural-born creatures.

Rio didn't crack a smile. "Girl, you need to tame your tongue."

"Why? Randy likes me to talk dirty without cussing."

"I'm not Randy. And you cussed."

"Well, it makes him horny. Makes me horny making him horny." Biting her lip, she looked down at her diamond-faced wristwatch. "I'm taking an hour. Got to find my old man. For some reason, I feel a juicy climax coming on. And Randy—"

"Too much information," Rio admonished. The woman was as horny as a bitch in heat and open as a busted fire hydrant. "Criminy."

"Sorry. Forgot you've been doing without." The cheesy grin on her face said it all. "Be back shortly. I'll tell you all about it later."

Rio tsked, tossing the pen onto the secondhand drafting table she used for a desk. She needed earplugs.

No, what she needed was a good man to hold her, a gentle companion to ease the aching deep inside her body, a special guy who looked for the same contentment as she—simple companionship.

Fantasy.

All the decent men in this world were married, dead or gay and most of them were far from Thoroughbred stallions. She held up one hand. Were there even five decent ones in the vicinity?

Doubtful. She went back to her daily duties.

An hour and a half later, Galaxeé hung her new red fox-fur jacket on the coat rack. She flopped down on her desk chair. "I called Bryce."

"And?" Rio asked.

"The man is excited, but he tried to conceal it. Vibes, you see. He's got a powerful energy that travels through the phone lines, even in this raggedy weather." She crossed her legs, tapped the toe of her high-heeled, tan-colored boot against the metal file cabinet. "It's gotten cold, perfect for your birthday."

"What's that supposed to mean?" She kept her gaze glued to the document she held, bracing for Galaxeé's unveiling. Lord. What in the world was filtering through her mind at this particular moment?

"It does fall on Thanksgiving this year. Got any plans? Randy and I decided to go to an island and soak up some heat. Fiji, Caymans, maybe some place called the Seychelles that he wants us to visit. I still have a bunch of air miles to burn. You're welcome to—"

"And do what?" Rio glanced over her shoulder. "Fry in the sun while you and Randy engage in orgies? No, thank you very much."

"You can't sit around by yourself on your birthday. That's illegal."

"In whose eyes?"

Fat grins always grew wider. "Mine, Venus' and God's. Remember, I worked up your chart. Turmoil in your future calls for companionship."

Rio snorted inelegantly. This woman always came up with the most absurd revelations. "Nothing can happen if I'm completely alone at the cabin. No turmoil, no havoc."

She'd purchased the remote bungalow for when she needed time away to tame the funky emotions invading her well-being. Hormones, she'd told herself. The way she'd been feeling lately, an extended leave of absence had moved high on her list. Alone, secluded, a good distance away from Denver's fast pace.

"What if a bear breaks in? You won't have anybody to protect you."

"I don't need protection, and no one's spotted a bear up there in years. Besides, bears hibernate during winter. I don't plan to be outside, either, romping around like a snow bunny in my new snowsuit. It's too cute to get wet. I don't ski, sled, or build snowmen. If a blizzard socks me in, bring it on. I'll have a couple books to read, a roaring fire, soulful music and plenty of food. Best of all, excellent wine."

A robust French Bordeaux and any top-of-the-line cabernet were favored. At the loft, the petite wine cooler was filled to near capacity for intimate gatherings. Those, however, were house parties with friends.

Lifting one eyebrow, Rio asked, "What else could I possibly need?"

"A man—a big, hot body to absorb the chill from your frigid heart."

That statement dragged out another snort. So maybe she had chilled, but she had good reason. An unfaithful husband normally changed the temperature of a woman's heater. It had hers. "The fireplace, thermostat, and blankets provide heat."

Galaxeé glared, her eyes thin slits. "I hate that tacky-assed snorting sound you make."

Another explosion sent shivers racing through Rio's body.

"I hate your gum popping, but my complaints never have stopped you from detonating a bomb." They argued daily.

Planting both feet on the floor, Galaxeé said, "Listen to you—evil, bitchy. No wonder you don't have a honey." She crossed her arms under the pair of 750-milliliter implants she'd purchased last year, against Rio's motherly objections and outright horror, and clamped one leg over the other, swung it like a hypnotic pendulum. "You do need a good dick, just to—"

"E-O-D, Barnett. End of discussion." Good lord. "I've got a ton of bills and payroll."

"Don't change the subject."

"I already did, and you and Luanne have an inventory to complete." She swiveled her stool around, opened the metal file cabinet's top drawer and picked through file folders.

"Guess I'll have to work out . . ."

Rio closed her ears to whatever Galaxeé finished saying. What next, tarot cards? Not again, but she hoped her best friend hadn't gotten into séances, crystal balls and Aladdin's lamp.

Abracadabra, she thought, as her partner left the office, boot heels clicking noisily down the stairs.

There was plenty of work to do before the club opened its doors for tonight's show. She looked up at the octagonal wall clock, a gift from Galaxeé's mother the day they signed their life away on Killer Bods. Mama Barnett had always said, "Time is short. Don't waste it away."

Fours hours until showtime.

The phone rang. Sighing, Rio secured the receiver between her shoulder and ear and grabbed her favorite pen. Another holiday party reservation would be great. "Killer Bods."

"Hey, it's Phillip." His voice sounded scratchy, sickly. "Can't make it tonight. Bad cold. Flu."

'Tis the season. "Don't worry about it, sweetie, just stay in and take care of yourself. We'll manage. Need anything?" She

took good care of the dancers, considered them all close as family members. When they suffered from outside forces, she worried as much about the boys as the mothers who had sheltered them for nine months.

"Jewel's here." His latest conquest was a shy woman, so different from the wild young lady he'd dated three months ago. "She'll make sure I stay alive. Thanks for the offer."

"Call if you need me." Rio hung up. "Well, shoot."

She chewed on her bottom lip, knowing she should call Bryce Sullivan and ask him to work tonight if possible. With Saturdays typically designated as date night, Fridays drew a big crowd. And after the performance she had seen today, he was no doubt ready.

She dialed the bar's extension. Galaxeé answered.

"Got a problem. Phillip's home sick and can't make it."

"Call Bryce."

"You call him."

"I'm busy, Rio."

"So am I." She shuffled a few papers together and rapped them on the desk for emphasis.

"You took the time to call me when you should've contacted him. You're the one bitching about the inventory."

"Galaxeé—" A loud click ended the call. "The nerve of that woman."

She didn't have far to look for his phone number. Sullivan's résumé was sitting in the center of her drafting table. On top of the pile. Gathering much-needed strength, she dragged in a deep, fortifying breath and punched in his work number. She really didn't want to talk to him, didn't want to hear the rumbler.

"Thank you for calling Thorobred Computers. How may I help you?"

So, what kind of work does a muscle-bound, gray-eyed stud do at a computer company requiring him to moonlight? Data entry? Plugging boards? Screwing parts? Working every available woman with that enormous screwdriver hanging between . . .

She gave her name and asked to speak with him.

"He's currently in a meeting. Could I have Mr. Sullivan call you back or would you like to leave a message?" The woman sounded older, formal and middle-aged. The boss's secretary?

Figuring the "exec sec" might add two and two and come up with a few too many, Rio left her private cell number.

All but one of their dancers worked a daytime job. No one had wanted their first-round boss to get wind of their second gig, secretly moonlighting at a playground catering to women. Rio and Galaxeé had been discreet over the months, honoring their employees' wishes.

The male population had every right to enter Killer's, but few took the risk. Invading female stomping grounds meant potential degradation if a sneak peeker refused to hop on stage to flaunt his wares during a frenzied evening. Women went stone rabid when the mood struck them.

As for Bryce Sullivan, they should eat him up. Bit by tasty bit.

Normally, she stayed in the office during the dance routines. Galaxeé ensured all went well, introducing each dancer, motivating the crowd.

Not tonight. I want to see the frenzy take place, if there is one.

Someone had to take Phillip's shift, whether that person was black, white or covered in green polka dots.

"It's filling up fast," Galaxeé said.

"Are all the dancers in?" Rio asked.

From upstairs, she'd heard the chatter. Bryce Sullivan's sexy bass laughter had filtered up the stairs when she'd peeked out of the office.

Earlier, she'd spent little time on the phone with him; she'd offered him the job and asked him to dance tonight, he accepted and she ended the conversation within thirty seconds.

"Yep. Bryce, too." Galaxeé smoothed her slinky, wine-colored dress with both hands, showing a great deal of cleavage as always.

"You've got wrinkled ankles," Rio said.

"Shit. I hate wearing these things. They never fit, and stockings cost a shitload of money." Wiggling, she fought with the hosiery. "Are you coming out to watch the show to see what effect Bryce has on the crowd?"

"Hadn't planned on it."

"Liar." Her partner knew her all too well. "What're you wearing?"

"Exactly what I have on." Spreading her arms, Rio looked down at herself. Today she'd dressed in a cream-colored silk blouse with navy jacket matching a knee-length skirt, business attire for interviewing applicants.

"Wear something sexy."

"Why? This is just fine."

"Too conservative for evening wear at a strip club. Dressed like an administrative officer, you make us look old and crusty." Galaxeé fished through the hanging outfits they both kept at the club for special occasions.

"Here," she said, dragging out a shimmering sheath designed for a sex machine. "Put this on and wear those strappy, fuck-me-silly kicks. Show some leg. You have good ones, unlike my toothpicks—the reason why these damn hose always bag. Flaunt them for the boys. They like seeing your Tina Turners and the chickies hate you for having them."

She'd selected the titillating, red clinger. The tailor-made, backless, thin-strapped dress fit an expensive call girl. Rio had worn it once. That night she'd danced onstage with Dallas. The bump-grind-and-rub sent the crowd into a wild frenzy. Then, Miss Fields barked her way into his life.

"Not tonight. Nope." Dallas's mind was draped around someone else. Rio had nothing else but fantasies and unproductive dreams.

"Put the damn thing on and come on out. Take those stupid hose off, too. You don't need them. Luanne's holding our seats at the bar. Oh," Galaxeé said halfheartedly, "and Frankie's got her big behind propped up next to our chairs."

Frankie Perino, a twenty-nine-year-old Italian beauty with sparkling brown eyes and lazy, blond curls tumbling over her shoulders, had become their friend four months ago. "Don't use that tone. She's a very nice person."

"Was."

"I understand your feelings, Galaxeé. If she'd known you and Randy were an item, she would've apologized then and there. Besides, look how much time she's given us. She set up our computer, taught us the basics, designed a website that's—"

"Incomplete."

Rio sighed. "Some people have regular eight-to-five jobs. She puts in more hours than most. Remember, she's not charging us."

Frankie had offered to build their site. Jobless at the time, she seemed to be looking for a friendly face when she'd ventured inside Killer Bods. She enjoyed the show and struck up a conversation with Rio and Galaxeé. A regular now, Rio had added Frankie's name to the short list of patrons who never paid the cover charge.

Galaxeé dismissed her with a wave of both hands. "Whatever. Get dressed." She went out the door, slamming it shut behind her.

Well, why not? When had she jumped *clean* last? And if Dallas beckoned her onstage again, so be it. Let Shannon whine puppy-dog tears. Who owned this club?

Ya home wrecker.

Rio locked the door. She stripped out of her clothes and

poured herself into the dress, sucking it in. She'd never get it zipped again if she gained one more pound of fat.

Dieting and exercise, she chanted. She'd had little time or inclination for either until recently, when she'd earned a waistline bulge and her clothes seemed to have taken on a sloppy appearance.

"Metabolism slowdown. We'll need detailing," Galaxeé had said. "We're getting old and our bodies are going straight to hell, south for the final countdown."

No way. Not yet.

"Except, my new boobies will always hang tough."

"If they don't burst beforehand."

The ballet bar Rio used helped if she took the time to stretch and practice. Years ago, modern and jazz dancing freed her mind, energized her soul and kept her slim.

She'd splurged and cleared a generous area of the loft for workouts. So into maintaining her weight and staying trim, she charged a stair stepper and stationary bike to the only credit card she carried. The mat, bench and rack of dumbbells had helped a little, but she'd hired an in-home trainer to assist instead of frequenting a gym. It was worth every credit card dime and monthly fee. She hated perspiring in front of other people.

Rio smoothed the slinky dress down her hips, slid her feet into the pair of red shoes, which Galaxeé called "fuck-me-silly kicks," and fastened the ankle straps. Mules were what Rio's grandmother had called open-heeled shoes, but her devout-Christian mother begged to differ. She called them whore-steppers.

In private, Momma was a kick in the pants when her minister husband had spiritual duties. The Rev preached the good word and read the Bible daily. Sort of like cramming for finals, and it was final.

Sure miss Momma and Daddy.

They hadn't stood a chance. Emotionally and spiritually

bankrupt following her parents' tragic car accident, Rio's depression had sealed the end of her marriage to a husband who had cared little for her or her family.

Banishing the devastating thoughts to a dark corner of her psyche, she straightened her body from the slump that always managed to consume her when she thought of her parents. She still had a younger brother and good friends to lean on.

She twirled in front of the full-length mirror, stopped and checked her reflection over her shoulder. Biting her bottom lip, she bent forward to ensure the short-tail thing covered her butt. Barely enough fabric. Lord. She really needed to stop wearing clothes fit for a wealthy teenybopper. At twenty it was fine, thirty was pushing it, forty . . . she should've updated her evening wardrobe last year.

The telephone rang.

"They're about to start," Galaxeé announced.

"Who leads off? You didn't put Bryce first, did you?"

"Nah. Got to incite the crowd. Jason's first, Orlando's second up, then comes our shining newbie and his boogieing self. Get your ass down here. We're packed, and there's a line outside."

Rio set the receiver down. After one last twirl, she bent forward again to ensure her boobs stayed secure, her butt stayed covered.

Satisfied, she muttered, "Showtime."

"How ya feel?" Dallas asked. "Ready?"

"Nervous as a freakin' mouse with a pride of big cats on the prowl," Bryce replied loudly. Killer's DJ spun the latest tunes at maximum decibels.

"Chill out. Keep your mind on the music rather than the crowd. Show a little arrogance. You'll do fine and rock."

Bryce hoped to hell Dallas was right. Standing in the drafty hallway, he peeked through the curtain's opening into the audience. He wanted to shit. A ton of women crawled all over the place, wall to wall. Tall ones, short ones, thick down to lean, superfine and quite a few . . . others. Dallas had said the latter group tipped the best if dancers gave what they wanted.

He didn't recognize any woman other than Galaxeé, luckily. Sure as shit, if a worker at the company showed up, word would spread faster than a computer virus through the office.

Galaxeé had wandered backstage earlier, informed him of the dancers' sequence, offered a few pointers, then wished him luck. She added an interesting request he had no problem fulfilling. In fact, he looked forward to it.

Where was Rio?

Then he saw her. Whoa. She was gliding down the stairs in filmy red, satin skin, and all the dick-enhancing visions of a sex-starved man. She lacked only a hazy fog billowing about her feet.

Fortunately, he hadn't tucked his long black shirt inside his black trousers. The length concealed his sudden arousal. Beneath the slacks, a sparkling ebony G-string put a tight squeeze on him. Bryce shifted the confining garment to accommodate the swelling. He couldn't step onstage iron hard.

He followed Rio's movements as she greeted customers, flashing her brilliant smile, saying a few words. She eclipsed the group like an exquisite ruby among a display of costume jewelry.

Real. And everything she wore, no doubt, was real. Glittery earrings, a single-stone pendant nestled in a set of hooters worth wallowing in, even her dazzling bracelet—most likely diamonds—glistened as she reached for a wine goblet handed to her.

Bet some dumbshit dropped a few paychecks on her, probably one of the fifties guys. Some idiots can be so damned stupid. Be a cold day in hell before I give my money to any broad.

Bryce squinted, zeroed in when she sat next to Galaxeé and

crossed her luscious legs. What did she have on beneath that short dress, anything? He noticed she'd gained other's attention as well. One server damn near broke his neck trying to get an eyeful. The son of a bitch.

"See anything worthwhile?"

Bryce recognized the baritone from a phone conversation he'd had with his sister. Interrupter Jason Simmons, this man. They'd never met face-to-face. "Who's the big dude serving the woman in blue sitting in the center?" He angled his head around, gave Simmons the once-over: same height, slightly leaner, arrogance written all over his brown face and in his slanted brown eyes.

"Cockroach."

"Been here long?"

"Since we opened. Why? You want his job?"

No, I ought to bust his nose, just as I plan to bust yours.

"Thought he looked familiar."

Jason grunted. "Galaxeé's onstage. I'm up, cowboy. Step aside. I'll show you how things are done here."

Deep-seated, unadulterated resentment punctuated Bryce's snarl. Fucker. He shifted to his left, let Simmons pass, and sneaked a peek at Rio before the curtains closed.

He swung his gaze toward the dancer waiting behind the heavy, dark drapes, toward the same punk who had marked his sister's face with a fist.

3

"Encore! Encore!" the crowd roared.

Thunderous applause exploded as Orlando—skimpily dressed in a bush warrior's loincloth, wearing straw ankle wreaths, a leafy headpiece made of sticks, and twirling torches—finished his exotic-dance routine and left the stage. He jammed once per set. On opening night, his arms had tired after back-to-back encores. He'd set the headpiece on fire by accident. Scared the life out of him *and* Killer's owners.

"Boys are hot tonight," Galaxeé said. Bracing one foot on the floor, she sat half on, half off the barstool. "Did you see that little girl up front? I'm thinking she got in on a false ID. The child had her hands all up and down Orlando's pretty legs. Mercy."

"You remember Myrtle Thomas, don't you?" Rio asked. "That's her daughter Afrika. She's well over twenty-one."

"Texas Myrtle? Hell, we are getting old." She bit off the queen olive from the decorative toothpick, then drained the martini and slid the glass across the bar top. "Luanne! I need another drink, honey. Get one for my partner, too."

Rio gave her *the* subtle look and Galaxeé begrudgingly ordered Frankie's standard cocktail, Bacardi and Diet Coke.

Galaxeé had reached the rowdy level already while Rio nursed her wine, the Silver Oak cabernet she'd ordered the bartender to decant and allow to breathe. She took another sip. The subtle hint of wild berries swirled over her tongue, teasing her taste buds.

"Do you want to introduce Bryce?" Galaxeé asked.

"Not a chance. That's your job. And please don't stumble on the stairs," Rio hinted as her friend stood. "Imagine yourself sprawled across the floor, kissing the stage, a two-hundred-dollar dress wrapped around your waist."

"I never stumble." She grabbed the remote microphone, took one step and Rio caught her arm. "These heels—"

"Sure." Sighing, she handed over a napkin. "Spit it out, girlfriend."

"It's my last stick."

"Good. Obviously you can't think, chew and walk at the same time after three martinis." As loud as she popped gum, and with the speakers, everybody in the club would duck for cover, thinking someone had fired a shotgun.

The introduction went well. Galaxeé built up Bryce as an ace performer. She had the audience electrically wired for fire. When the music began, she left the stage and came back to the bar, grinning. The soundman upped the speaker volume. The curtains shivered, signaling Bryce's appearance at any moment.

"They're going to love him," Galaxeé said.

"We'll see."

Another few seconds went by.

"Where the hell is he?"

The curtains fluttered again. Rio knew the signs, fear. Somebody had attempted to push him onstage. That somebody was probably Dallas.

"Wait a minute. Here he comes," Galaxeé said.

When Bryce stepped out, the big open room fell completely silent except for the music's bass beat. Not one person clapped, screamed or yelled.

"Uh-oh," Galaxeé breathed.

Rio held her breath. He just stood there like a block of stone. "Do something!" she said quietly.

"Oh, shit. We're in trouble. Luanne, tell Mikey to crank up the music, maybe Bryce can't hear the lyrics."

"Bull," Rio snapped. "He froze." And the crowd would laugh him off the stage if he didn't move soon.

"You do something, Rio. We can't let him stand up there looking stupid."

"What can I do? Get Dallas up." What a fiasco this mess would make. They'd hear it from their friends.

Where'd you get that dumb white boy? Thought this place had all black dancers. We might as well go to SS. The white boys there will at least perform, offbeat maybe, but they'll attempt to satisfy us.

"Go dance with him, Rio. Get him started."

"No. Absolutely not."

Huffing, Galaxeé stood. "Fine. As drunk as my ass is . . . This dog-and-pony show ought to close us down permanently, damn it."

"I'll go," Frankie slipped in. She was always ready to help, but if glares contained the power to kill, Frankie should've dropped dead before the words left her lips.

Through an oily smile, Galaxeé said, "Honey, you couldn't begin to keep up with him, let alone keep beat."

"Stop it," Rio hissed. Sometimes this woman's mouth overloaded her behind. "Get up there, Galaxeé, these people are restless!"

To her horror, Galaxeé stumbled on the first step, and Rio grabbed her arm. "All right. All right. I'll do it." Lord. She'd blame herself seeing her partner horizontal on the stage or, worse, toothless after a spill on the staircase.

God help them. Sliding off the barstool, she dragged her gaze from Galaxeé's and caught Bryce's a second later, held it while smoothing the clinger down her hips.

She slinked her way around tables, chairs, heading for the stage in long, runway strides. At the base of the stairs, she heard a few whispered murmurs by wary customers. In rhythm with the music's downbeat, Rio climbed each riser, swinging her hips slowly, her heart pounding to the bass rhythm. Dancing with Sullivan was only to save the club, to save face.

Onstage now, settling one hand on her hip and tapping the toe of her shoe, she crooked her finger at Bryce. Without a response, she tried a second time.

Darn him. This impromptu sideshow had better look like part of his routine.

Dragging her feet across the slick wooden floor, Rio glided toward their first statue still cemented to the same spot for the last minute or more. She ran her fingertips across his collarbone, stepped behind him, never losing contact with his body. His flesh felt hot, on fire, and a slight tremor skittered through his hard muscles. She continued circling. Skimming her fingers through the soft hair on his broad chest, up again to his shoulder, she finished with a butterfly's caress down one hardened bicep.

"Bryce," she whispered fiercely. "Dance with me."

When Rio faced him again, a flicker in his gray eyes, a gleam boasting wicked sex and sin snatched her breath away.

Moving closer, he slid his arm around her waist, forced one bulky leg between hers and yanked her forward, hauling her up against his solid chest, pressed so tightly that dragging in the next breath was a haphazard struggle. Behind her, a few stretched "oohs" hummed through the audience.

He threaded his fingers into her shag hair, tugged and leaned her backward, exposing her throat down to the rise of her breasts. White-hot, he licked a long, slow path from cleavage to chin. There, he bit gently.

Electricity fired a high-voltage current through Rio's body. At the same time, the silent crowd noisily sucked in the last few atoms of oxygen.

Oh. My. God.

He held her suspended, hovering intimately over her body, his penetrating eyes boring into hers, his lips a mere inch away—close enough to kiss. But Rio was more aware of *him* near to half-mast. In vibrant contact with her pelvis.

She swallowed. "Let me up." He'd never allow her to fall, not with the coiled strength in his arms. Still, she was helpless in this position, helplessly enjoying his hot, minty breath scorching her face and the dominant pressure from his very hard, very large . . . screwdriver.

"Yank on my shirt. It'll come away easily. Do it now."

Rio conceded and tossed the black fabric aside, which brought the throng of female watchers statically to life with a blaring roar of approval. Up close and personal, she quickly scanned his upper body—powerful, pure brawn.

As if on cue, the soundman swapped the song for a sensuous tune. Bryce drew her upright, bent her back again in three successive movements, swaying from side to side. Each time, tantalizing hardness pressed a delicious slide-and-skim cadence at the juncture between her thighs.

Yelps, hoots and whistles echoed throughout Killer's, but Galaxeé's voice over the microphone rose above the rebel rousers', repeating the phrase, "Go, baby!" She sang along with the lyrics, sounding amazingly like Alicia Keys on her first top-ten hit—"*I Keep On Fallin'*."

Ooh, Bryce was good, and Rio followed his lead. They dipped, spun, grinded, rubbed and gyrated to a beat exclusively meant for their bodies. He kept her firmly against him, a taut mass of male potency, and never allowed air to circulate between them.

Bending her backward again, the bunched muscles of his

chest flexed under her hands. She ran her fingers through the dense mat of hair up to the pair of generous shoulders, caressing his sweat-slicked skin, and spread them along his corded neck, where his pulse throbbed, beating an unruly pace. She glided her hands higher, laced her fingers into his sable hair. The silky waves parted, settled into smooth layers.

This was the closest she would ever get to screwing this gorgeous male and she enjoyed every touch, every caress, every second.

Mercy.

Sliding one hand down her body, he grazed the side of her breast, continued down to her midriff, her hip, and palmed her behind in a gentle squeeze, a caress that lasted seconds too short in her estimation. His hand eased under her thigh, drew her leg around his hip.

Rio sucked in air, a hiss threatening to leave her lips.

She knew better than to let him continue. He was in full-blown erection. She would bust a nut in another second or two if she didn't watch out. The head of that stout tree was there—right there!—at the gateway to her heat, damp already, quivering with need as thick, bulging meat throbbed against her sensitivity.

Staring into his eyes, she made the second serious mistake: circling her hips, wanting to feel every satisfying inch of him inside her if possible. But she failed to corral the sensations striking her infallible senses, one by one.

Her mouth watered, ears rang . . . her brain shut down.

She came.

Climaxed ferociously and unraveled. The tide rushed through her system speedier than a shattering ride under an avalanche down a steep mountain.

Rio gulped in air, stifling the shriek rising in her throat, and gripped Bryce's shoulders, sinking her nails deeply into his skin. She held on for dear life to keep from tumbling completely out of control, to keep her sanity intact.

And he kissed her, savaging her mouth in a mind-blowing assault that spread her toes and curled her hair. He kissed her so thoroughly, the music, screams and yelling seemed miles away, fading until nothing mattered.

Nothing mattered, except the torrent of emotions flooding her mind, the shock waves jolting her body and the sweet taste of the man who sensuously teased every corner inside her mouth with his tongue. Nothing mattered, except Bryce Sullivan's fiery lips, how he held her so tightly in his strong arms, preventing her from coming apart atom by devastated atom, protecting her from a tumultuous landing.

As the fierce tremors tentatively wore off, the kiss ending, Rio lifted her heavy eyelids. She blinked, embarrassed and slightly dizzy, barely controlling her breaths. She stared back into his expressive eyes.

He knew. He knew!

Bryce continued holding her, continued caressing her, his sensuous gaze bearing the power to melt her down to a sheer liquid mess, a puddle at his feet like the creaminess soaking her panties right now. She shuddered under his intense scrutiny.

He never let anyone know but her, and he didn't break a knowing smile. Instead, while one big hand stroked soothingly up and down her body, his gaze shifted downward, focused on her mouth, then up into her eyes again.

Was he seeing the bewilderment she felt inside her body, even now?

He touched her lips with his, light as a snowflake's landing and fleeting meltdown. Her response was a gasp.

As the music died away, Bryce drew her slowly upright and steadied her. Thank God because Rio's legs wilted, nearly crumbled beneath her.

He took her hand into his warm grasp, twirled her in two tight circles, finishing their erotic dance, her back flush to his hard chest, his arms wound tightly around her waist. They faced the roar of the crowd through a standing ovation, a call of the wild loud enough to bring down Killer's roof.

When Bryce lifted her hand and pressed a tender kiss to her wrist, she shivered from the hot contact. But when his warm lips touched the one hypersensitive place behind her ear, Rio thought she would faint.

Certain her legs would indeed hold her, she attempted to step away from a man whose unnatural power ransacked her very being. Bryce held her firmly in place through the second noisy ovation, the room truly vibrating with shrill excitement and unbridled energy.

Finally. Finally, she moved aside. And the ladies went stone berserk.

Rio knew why, but these women would never spoil the exquisite torture she'd experienced minutes ago. An instant later, Bryce released her and strode away. Apparently, they'd ruined it for him.

Slithering down the stairs, she weaved a path through the mass of tables, chairs and women, heading toward the bar, smiling at customers, accepting their lucky-you grins with a yup-I-was smile of her own.

"Ooh, yowza," Galaxeé said excitedly. "Y'all were too hot up there. Hottest dirt dance I've ever seen tear up the stage. You worked it, girl."

No, not her, and incinerated fit the rocket-ride better, Rio thought. She'd burnt up on reentry. As for Bryce Sullivan, he simply lit the match, watched her burst into flames and kept the fire under his strict control.

"You're flushed, sweaty. You never perspire in public."

Rio grabbed a napkin from the bar top. She patted her face, ran it around her neck and over her shoulders. "It's hot under the lights. Luanne, get me a glass of water, please. No ice."

"Didn't seem that hot to me. AC's running full blast."

"You weren't dancing." Sensuously under spotlights with a

hunk. She took the glass from the bartender and gulped down every drop to moisten her dry-as-a-bone throat. Seeing her hand tremble, she set the glass down a little hard.

"None of our boys ever complained."

"It's hot, Cecilia. All right?" She didn't mean to snap the words, but by the look on Galaxeé's face, she'd made the wrong comment. Flustered when her best friend laughed loudly, Rio realized she'd called her by the name she hadn't used in years. "Shut up."

"You busted a nut, didn't you? It's written all over your face." Leaning closer, Galaxeé sniffed. "Oozing from your pores."

Had they not been friends for thirty-odd years, she would have gladly slapped her partner stupid.

"I knew this would work. I knew it."

"What the devil are you talking about? What worked?" She'd saved the night. She'd saved Bryce Sullivan from the crowd booing him off the stage. She'd saved their business! That was all.

Until the very end, until she'd made a complete fool out of herself. How could she face him again knowing what he knew? Rio shook her head. He could've screwed her blind, in public, without her slightest resistance.

"Honey, you were set up," Galaxeé said and snickered.

"What?" Blood pumped through her ears, a deep droning hum.

"I talked with Bryce before the show and told him what to do. Not everything, but enough to get you onstage. I thought I'd have to drag you there myself."

"You what?" Unsteadily, Rio got to her feet, hands riding her hips, breaths shallow and rapid.

"He did a lot more than I expected. A *lot* more," Galaxeé said dramatically. Her smile mutated into the usual cheesy grin.

A setup? What the devil?

"Don't let Cockroach get near you. He just might jump your tail."

"Cockroach?" They were talking about Bryce and some stupid setup. Who cared about the Roach? She wanted to know about this other mess.

"Pheromones. The boy can pick up the scent a mile away. I swear he's got about ten genes of Bloodhound." She sipped her martini. "Uh-oh. I told you."

Rio followed her gaze.

A big, burly devil of a man flaunting a bristly beard, eyes the same shade as pecans, and massive hands and feet, Cockroach thought the word "suave" pertained to him. They'd hired him for his size, mainly as Killer Bods' bouncer. His expertise had come in handy occasionally; he had ejected a couple of jealous boyfriends from the premises.

She knew Cockroach was sweet on her, but no matter what congenial put-down she'd used, he had always managed to return and try, try again. At this particular moment, she had no desire to spend conversational time with the bouncer. She had important issues to discuss with Galaxeé.

"Hey, little momma," Cockroach greeted. He smiled broadly, showing perfect white teeth. "Looking mighty good tonight. Hot."

"How many times have I told you, Cockroach?" Rio snapped. "I am not your little momma, your big momma, or any other momma to you. I am your boss."

"Wuh-oh," Galaxeé whispered as the bouncer's smile wavered.

"I tally your hours, sign your checks and I also have the right to dismiss you for insubordination. Is that clear?"

"Yes. Yes, ma'am."

"Cockroach, there's a woman who needs a drink over there," Galaxeé said, using the martini glass to point behind him.

Rio regretted the outburst the second she closed her mouth, knowing she'd hurt his feelings. Cockroach really was a nice guy and he'd protect her with his life.

Guilt raced through her brain for lashing out. She placed her hand on his arm before the bouncer spun away, gave him a light squeeze. "I'm sorry, Barry. I didn't mean to sound evil and hateful." She looked over at Galaxeé for help. "We wouldn't know what to do without you."

"Rough night, Cockroach," Galaxeé added. "You're our most valuable employee."

He nodded, smiled, but the dull sadness in his eyes crushed Rio's heart. She hugged him, brushed a kiss over his bristly cheek. "I really do need you as my friend."

Eyes narrowed, jealousy ran a long, bumpy course through Bryce's private thoughts.

Were they lovers? Didn't Rio Saunders have any scruples at all? Seeing her with another man riled every wound-up molecule dividing in his body. And just where had that emotional shit come from when he hardly knew her?

He stood beside the stage, peeking out through the curtain's sliver of an opening, trying to get a glimpse of the passionate woman who had trembled, surrendered and dissolved in his arms a few minutes ago. The same woman who now hugged another man with dedicated passion. He'd all but screwed her onstage! Now, she was wrapping herself around somebody else like a snug blanket.

What the fuck?

Didn't he show how well they fit together? Didn't she recognize the passion they'd shared? Didn't she feel his goddamn hard-on?

Well, duh. How could she miss it? And look what happened.

He'd swelled to an enormous size while she sizzled in his arms. Hell, he still had an erection. Had the song not ended, he would've embarrassed himself and her. He was so close, on the damned edge of blowing his load when she'd viciously clamped the tip of his dick with the strength of pliers, her heat scorching hot.

Drowning in the glorious depths of her eyes, he'd almost forfeited what little self-restraint he had left. Kissing her hadn't helped. She had the sweetest lips, pliant, irresistible and she'd matched his passion with as much intensity as he'd given her.

Then the music began to fade away, the scent of her sex filling his nostrils while he caressed her back over ecstasy's threshold. He'd reined in the tempestuous, searing lust charging through his veins, arteries and his throbbing dick.

Drawing her upright, spinning her quickly, he'd tried to hide behind Rio, keep her protectively where she stood. But she eased out of his embrace, stepped aside, exposing his blatant erection—unleashed from his G-string—to a whole goddamn nightclub full of unabashed, uninhibited prowling cats.

And what had the owner of Killer's done? She'd teased the living shit out of him, then moved on to the next unsuspecting "baby" and enticed him.

Some dick-teasers needed to be taught a lesson or two. And knowing—witnessing—Rio's seductive response to him, a plan already in motion . . .

Then turn this freakin' joint inside out.

"Cake," Bryce mumbled darkly.

4

When the music blared to life and the next dancer emerged, Bryce made a beeline to the dressing room. Point-blank, he asked his buddy to assist him.

"Are you crazy?" Dallas asked. "Man, you must be nuts."

"Just watch."

"I don't want to watch," Dallas snapped. "Why are you doing this anyway? Are you thinking you can make her jealous? It won't work, Bryce. She's not like the little mommas. Rio's got style and class, time on her side. You'll ruin every chance you ever had, *if* you had any at all. What the hell's the matter with you?"

"I've got my reasons." He'd banked on their sixteen-year friendship. "Come on, man. Just this once. I'll never ask anything of you again."

Dallas sighed long and hard. "I must be crazy. All right, go ahead, but don't come a-whinin' when it blows up in your damn face, fool."

Bryce stuck his hand out. "Thanks."

"Thank me when it's over. In fact, I will watch this stupid fiasco."

* * *

Galaxeé crossed her legs and glared at Rio. "That was really fuck-nicious, Rio. You want him to quit?"

"Who? Bryce?" Dismissing him, the feel of his hard body against hers, was impossible. Still, this other stuff.

"No, not Bryce. Cockroach. You hurt his feelings. I found him for us. And if he quits, *you'll* have to find a new bouncer."

"Bryce would never—I mean, Cockroach would never quit."

"He might after that stupid mess you pulled." Sometimes, "Indignant" was her middle name. "Shit, if this is how you'll act—snapping at everybody, cussing people out—after a good nut, I hope it doesn't happen."

"I didn't cuss Bryce. I mean," she said, shaking her head. "Cockroach."

"Well, now," Galaxeé said, sitting taller, folding her arms beneath prominent implants. "I see he's put a stamp on your brain. Or your cootie bug."

"Stop it." She fidgeted with the napkin. As if on cue, she and Galaxeé looked down at the tattered mess in her lap. Freaked, Rio flicked the tiny pieces to the floor.

"The boy's got you in a fluster."

"Does not."

"Uh-huh."

Galaxeé knew her well. She was flustered all right. Skin heated, a fine sheen of perspiration dotting her face. Her emotions were in a ball of confusion over Bryce Sullivan and her awareness of him, unconsciously nervous before she saw the napkin torn to tiny shredded beads.

She caught her partner's gaze and pleaded with her eyes. "I can't let anything happen, Galaxeé. I won't." Something had occurred between them, a spark that had turned into a blazing inferno.

"Why not? He hot Tarzan, you horny Jane." She drained the martini.

"He's too young. He's too—"

"Age is nothing but a damn number. We live in the twenty-first century. Get over it. Women have every right to get their jollies with a young hunk, Miss Goody Two-Shoes. Men have been making time with young chickies since forever. Run with it, honey. Work it."

"Oh, sure, you can say that mess since Randy's ten years older than you, and he's black."

"I wouldn't care if Randy was twenty years younger, sported chartreuse plaid or he came in oxblood paisley. Why should you worry?"

"Remember Carson? I can't go through that kind of mess again. I'm done with younger men."

Carson was a thirty-five-year-old, lying slickster. A jailbird now, busted for dealing drugs, selling stolen property, racketeering, running a prostitution ring, etcetera, etcetera, etcetera.

Rio had argued with Galaxeé about his guilt, certain of the innocence he'd adamantly proclaimed. Naïve, she had believed the best of people. She'd graciously accepted Carson's gift, the diamond and citrine ring for her thirty-ninth birthday. But when her attorney, Victoria, had heard the police handcuffed and dragged Carson from the restaurant he owned and read the charges, she jumped on the telephone. Victoria urged her client to turn the jewelry over to the district attorney. Luckily, Rio had never let the convict get into her panties.

"Ancient history," Galaxeé said.

"No, ancient history is listed under Marcus's name." At thirty-seven her younger brother was as set in his ways as their father, who had trained him.

"He'll get over it. And he's not here anyway. What are you afraid of at your age? Bryce isn't asking you to marry him." Galaxeé looked over her shoulder. The current dancer was leaving the stage, his G-string stuffed with dollars. "Yet," she murmured and scooted off the barstool before Rio burst open with outrage. "I have to get onstage."

Chaos reigned three minutes later.

"Holy buckin' bronco! That's what I'm talkin' about." Galaxeé said. "Somebody switched routines on me."

Oh, my God. Rio groaned, turning away. She rested her forehead against her fingertips.

Bryce had parted the curtains and stepped out in a cowboy getup—snakeskin boots, tight blue jeans, plaid shirt opened to his waist. Perched on top of his head sat a big ten-gallon hat. To make matters utterly ridiculous, the theme song from *Rawhide* acoustically reverberated off the walls while he cracked a long whip on cue.

She looked over her shoulder again and shuddered. Oh, my God. What had they done? A cowboy, in a club catering mainly to African American women?

Galaxeé's ear-busting whistles brought the audience to their feet. She had phenomenal talent to start a full-blown riot. "Giddy-up, cowboy," she yelled into the microphone. "Head 'em up, move 'em out!"

Shocked, Rio's mouth dropped open as the wild bunch mutated into charging lunatics, much like startled cattle. And when the cowboy flung his hat into the audience, a mad, clawing stampede resulted for the discarded headpiece. This chaos resembled sworn enemies at their first bridal-bouquet scramble. Plastic drinking cups fell to the floor, hardwood chairs crashed loudly against each other and tables had surely scored the new wax.

What had gotten into these women? Rio searched the arena for her servers, and Cockroach, for backup. Just in case.

All the waiters had retreated to the corner beside the curved bar. She couldn't blame them. The rowdy crowd would likely trample or string them up for blocking a hot-to-trot lady's view. These women meant business.

The melee didn't stop Bryce's routine. He kept with the rhythm of the song. Thank God, he'd tossed the whip aside.

The way his hips gyrated, has he ridden a horse before? Rio tsked. He'd ridden too many women from what she could tell.

"This boy's a stompin' fool," Galaxeé hollered. She blew another shrill whistle. "Didn't I say he'd work out? Wuh-oh, here we go."

Everyone knew when the music mellowed to a sensuous tune the actual show-and-tell had begun. The room buzzed with anticipation, eager beavers waiting to chomp on the next oak tree.

Alone now, just what had he planned? Would his dance routine be as suggestive as when they'd swayed together?

Not a chance. Not as a solitary performer.

When he slid his shirt free, exposing all the glory of his muscular chest, Rio licked her lips and swallowed. He had one magnificent physique, and she'd caressed it. The onlookers didn't know—would never know—how good he felt under her fingertips, plastered against her body.

Bryce unzipped his blue jeans, and she followed the movement of his big hands, watched them slide teasingly down the bulging length hidden behind the denim, remembering its size during arousal, its firmness, its insistence. Pressure. Throbbing heat.

"Breathe, girl," Galaxeé said, laughing. "Don't pass out on me now."

Controlling the air that rushed out took every ounce of strength.

Bryce tossed the plaid and denim aside. The volume in Killer Bods increased twofold as he circled his hips, then dropped to knees, spread them apart, displaying all sorts of virile splendor.

Goodness. Rio felt the beginnings of a brand-new melt-down, sizzling heat filtering through her core, raising a tide of aching between her legs.

"I bet he'd wear you out," Galaxeé hollered.

"Would you stop it?"

"You're glistening again. Or shall I say, sweating profusely?"

Rio patted her face dry with another napkin. "We're packed. With all these people, it's—"

"Not." Galaxeé burst out laughing. She glanced at the stage and her smile faded worse than sun-bleached fabric. "That trashy little ho."

Rio jerked her head around and saw Bryce's extended hand. And who had taken it?

Shannon Fields—Dallas's girlfriend. The hussy hightailed up the stairs and threw herself at the man. Within five seconds, the dance went beyond sensuous to downright lewd and filthy. She was under him. On him. All in him.

Heart hammering against her ribs, Rio wondered if she had appeared the same when she'd danced with Bryce. Had their choreography turned raunchy?

Instantaneously, anger marched under her skin like fire ants on the attack. The she-cat hiss escaped her lips as wrenching knots twisted in her belly, moved to her heart and cut off circulation.

Rio hopped to the floor, stormed toward the stairs. Hearing Galaxeé call out, she ignored the summons, thoroughly disgusted with her own licentious behavior, completely disenchanted with the immature bastard who had not one gram of class, one iota of damn pride or respect for himself. Or her.

She shoved the office door open with gale-wind force. It hit the stopper, rattling the frosted glass as cold fury crackled through her arteries like chipped ice. Rio looked over her shoulder at the vulgar spectacle below.

* * *

Bryce couldn't believe it.

Shannon had gone way too far. No matter what he did or how far he pushed her away, she always came back. How the hell was he supposed to get her offstage, toss her? Where was Dallas for Chrissake? This was his woman.

"Go sit down, Shannon!"

Either she didn't hear him or she chose to ignore him. The music blared, but not loud enough to drown out his voice.

"Shannon, get off the damn stage. Now."

Twining her leg around his thigh, she hooked her arms in a stranglehold worthy of the best professional wrestler, grinding her hips against his pelvis. What the devil was she thinking? That he'd get an instant boner? He'd never shown any interest in Shannon, never had the desire to lay his best friend's woman.

He searched the club for help and saw Rio at the top of the stairs. Oh, shit. The scowl on her face had the power to slice dried leather; the angle of her shoulders signified tension. He had to rid himself of this grappling woman hanging on to him, or risk losing the job too soon.

He looked to his right and his left and caught Cockroach's gaze. When the big man ignored him, Bryce shouted his name over the deafening noise and mouthed, "Get her off."

Cockroach fought his way through the masses. Seconds after clearing the crowd, he climbed onstage and carried a squirming Shannon down the stairs straight to her man. From Dallas's deadly glare, his bulging biceps flexing from the hold he'd put on Shannon, all hell would soon break loose.

Out of breath from wrestling Shannon's steel grip, Bryce abruptly ended his routine, not bothering to venture toward the wild bunch waving bills. After the fiasco with another man's woman, screw the money. He didn't need it.

He pasted a half-assed smile on his face, bowed quickly and

saluted to all yelling for more action. He collected his clothes, jerked the curtains apart and made a fast getaway to the dressing room.

Damn.

Bryce shoved all ten fingers through his damp hair, smoothed it back from his face and collapsed into a chair.

This was the biggest mistake he'd ever made, rooted by anger, saturated in jealousy. Dallas had been right about ruining any chance he'd had with Rio. Forget burning up the sheets. He could only imagine what she thought of him now.

Silly. Immature. A foolish little boy caught up in a grown-up fantasy.

Damn it.

What the hell had he been thinking? He should've thought things through first. Instead, he'd jumped to conclusions and allowed his bruised ego to rule his once-logical brain.

Now what? he wondered, pulling on his shirt. He started fastening buttons, but forgot about it.

He should've never met the woman. He should've kept to his plan, his original plan. He should've called the police on Jason Simmons or beat the hell out of him in a back alley. But, no, he hadn't thought. He hadn't thought at all. What he should've done was kept his nose out of everything and minded his own damned business.

The dressing room door opened swiftly and slammed shut with the force of a category-five hurricane, loud enough to drown out the music for a hot second.

Bryce looked up into the mirror, straight into Dallas's squinted, midnight eyes. "Look, man, I had no idea this would happen," he said and held his breath. From the look in his friend's ferocious glare, he wanted to kill him.

Dragging a chair to his side, Dallas plopped down on it and instantly grabbed a fistful of shirtfront. "I ought to beat you to a bloody damn pulp."

They'd never had a real fight. Bryce sat there, still holding his breath, waiting for a thick fist to connect with his jaw, imagining the pain and the coppery taste of blood. He deserved one good tag for engaging his best bud's woman in degrading theatrics.

"If I hadn't seen it myself, if I didn't consider you a friend, I'd beat the shit out of you, Sullivan. I'd beat you within an inch of your worthless life, punk."

When Dallas let loose of the shirt, Bryce let out the stagnant air burning his lungs. He had every right to be pissed off. Their egos matched; both had fierce tempers. They'd had arguments and shoving matches and tossed out biting words that caused most men to go to blows, except a woman had never come between them. Their friendship had always prevailed. But, this time was different.

Dallas rubbed the back of his neck. He slid down in the chair, propped his feet on the counter. "I sent her home."

"Maybe you should follow her, have a sit-down talk. You can't have this kind of stuff hanging over your heads. The wedding's next month."

"I'm cuttin' her loose, Bryce. We're history."

"What? After one jacked-up incident?"

He couldn't believe it. Dallas had given Shannon a diamond ring, pledged his love and promised to be a good husband. Granted, they'd only been together five months, but Dallas had said he knew love when it slapped him upside the head.

Bryce had never crossed into the same frontier or felt the same type of backhand. However, he was as lust-struck as any manic rabbit his first moment outside a cage surrounded by females.

"It wasn't all her fault, Coop. If I—"

"This wasn't the first time. I caught her at SS. Same shit, different day. My fault. I put the blinders on. Didn't want to see, didn't want to hear, didn't want to accept." He tugged at his ear and let out a snort. "She played me for the fool I am, and I let it happen."

What could he say to a statement put so bluntly? Coop wouldn't show emotion any more than he would, even to a best bud. "You okay?"

"Yeah, I'll live." Pinching the bridge of his nose, Dallas sighed long and hard, then scratched at his clean-shaven head. "Gonna be tough. I really did love her. Still do."

"What now? Walking away won't be easy. I think it'll hurt like hell."

Bryce had walked away from lust. The last infatuation and breakup hadn't fazed him either. Catherine, a good-looking curvy accountant, had sought better-fertilized pastures when he'd flat out admitted having no interest in marriage. Ever.

"Hurts now."

"Go after her, Coop. Talk to her. Get this mess straightened out. You'll stay together if you love each other. If not, at least you tried."

Seventeen years old when he entered college, Bryce had headed down the devil's lane to keep one coed a lover. Pussy-whipped, he'd let her talk him into *streaking* through Stanford's campus on a sultry night. The nineteen-year-old, rich, daddy's little girl was into nearly everything unconventional for Bryce's logical-working mind. They'd engaged in high-powered sex under a temporary platform at an outdoor political rally during her mother's bid for mayor. But Bryce was too selfish for the kinkiness of ménage à trois, too possessive to share his lover's body with either gender. He knew when their relationship had ended, meant to stay buried in the darkest caverns before they reached hell's castle. And he would not go as far as marriage to keep her.

How far would he go for Rio?

They had a relationship now. He knew it as sure as tomorrow's sunrise. Well, maybe. He'd embarked on the subtle chase along a curvy lane. Yet they were veering sideways on an entirely different path. She hadn't responded until the dance and her acute reaction was as overwhelming as drowning in luxury for the first time. Totally seductive, fiercely unsettling.

Funny, they hadn't spent a minute alone together, not one second. But, deep inside, Bryce knew they were a perfect match. They belonged side by side, on each other, wrapped in each other—in bed.

"I've got another set to do," he heard Coop say.

"I'll take it. Tips go to you, my man," Bryce insisted. "Go ahead. Get out of here."

"Sure?"

Damn right, he was sure. "No problem." They bumped knuckles and Dallas was gone for the night.

Galaxeé closed the door to the office. "I'm beat. Drunk."

"Should've thought about that after the third martini," Rio said. She shuffled a few invoices together and stuffed them inside an accordion folder. In the last few hours, she'd completed a good bit of work.

"Think I need a cab." Galaxeé fell into her chair, knees spread apart, dress drooping between them, sitting like a two-bit streetwalker.

"I'll call Randy or I'll take you home myself."

"Nah. Randy'll want more than I can give tonight. Don't wanna hang around to wait for him, either." She had the weirdest-looking smirk on her face, lopsided. "I locked down the place tight. Waiters are gone. There's no sense in you driving to West Hell and back. Call me a cab. I can't read the numbers on the phone."

"Jesus, Galaxeé. You really need to stop drinking. You can't get loaded when I'm not here."

"No problem. I won't. Even when I do get a buzz, which

only happens on Fridays, the peroxide-blond heifer would watch over me if *you* asked her anyway."

"Don't start with me."

"Perino's kissing ass every damn time I look around."

"It's her nature to be kind."

"Well, it gets on my last nerve. She's sneaky, and I refuse to put my hands on her when I know she's hiding a secret. Tonight, her aura was blue-green then jumped blood-red. Hell of a combination."

Rio wished Galaxeé would lighten up. She was taking this fortune-telling too far. *Blue-green and blood-red fits better in an abstract painting.*

Rather than argue, she dialed the usual cab service. They'd called one a few times for a tipsy patron. No one left the club stinking drunk without assistance. She'd take them home herself if necessary. "Couple minutes. I'll walk you down to the curb."

"I do not need help," Galaxeé snapped. "Later." She stood, snatched the red-fox jacket from the hanger, left it clanking its own melody, and marched out of the office, sweeping the floor with her fur.

"Call my cell when you get there."

Rio tried to glare a hole through her back. Her partner hadn't stumbled, tripped or bumped into a wall. Or slurred her words, come to think about it.

She listened to each step on the staircase. Even. Smooth. Steady. What game was this woman playing now?

Galaxeé hadn't mentioned any problems with Randy. Their relationship had seemed stable and secure during the four months of complete and utter bliss they'd shared. She'd say if they'd had a situation, wouldn't she? They were best friends.

Minutes later, Rio looked down at her watch. Quarter to

three. Surely, Galaxeé was safely on her way to her cozy West Denver home.

Then, she heard a noise and looked up. Someone was making his or her way deliberately up the stairs.

"Galaxeé?"

Without an answer, Rio grabbed the phone base and rolled the stool back toward the corner of the room. As the footsteps closed in, grew louder and louder, her heart pounded just as noisily. Galaxeé had said she'd locked down the club. Had she been too drunk to remember? Rio knew she should've checked the doors before her partner left the premises.

Swallowing first, she forced out a whisper. "Who's there?"

The desktop phone unit contained a panic button: five-second notification. Five seconds for an intruder to kill her. Five more seconds and she'd die of a heart attack. The police would find her on the floor, unable to help, unable to bring her back to life. They'd arrive five minutes too darn late.

She should've listened to Galaxeé and bought a pistol for protection when she spent late nights in this big building. She should've had Cockroach stay with her until she'd finished working. She should've left with Galaxeé!

But, darned if she'd go down easily. She owned this club. She'd put everything she had into this place. Killer's was her life!

Silently, Rio replaced the receiver. She stood and snatched up the letter opener, drew it back over her shoulder. Whoever thought they'd get away with her murder may get a dinner, but she'd sure get a sandwich.

*I'll leave a permanent **mark** on their behind.*

As the footsteps drew **closer**, her heart worked to burst out of her chest. She'd bleed on everything—stain the floor, the walls, and even change the color of the expensive red dress she still wore.

She readjusted the weapon in her hand, ready to spring forward, ready to defend herself and her thriving business.

The footsteps halted at the top of the stairs. She heard breathing, heard every sound inside the building and every noise outside.

Why was the person waiting? She was ready, alert, most of all, capable.

And, scared, on the verge of panicking.

Bryce stepped around the corner. "Rio?" The letter opener clanged on the wooden floor. "Are you all right?"

Her eyes were huge, clear and vivid gold with wild fear. "My God."

He crossed the floor of the small office in a few long strides and gathered her into his arms. Holding her rigid body tightly against his, she trembled almost violently while he stroked her satin-smooth hair, bare back and arms. Her breathing sounded as ragged as if she'd run a mile, but her hot breath caressed his neck like a dove's soft feather.

When he climbed the stairs, he'd wanted to ensure she'd heard him coming. He'd stopped to take a calming breath and ebb his heart rate before he faced her, certain she was upset after seeing the silly fiasco with Shannon.

He'd scared the shit out of Rio instead.

Soothing her was easy. Her supple body molded perfectly to his. He could stand here for hours, holding her, caressing, inhaling her intoxicating scent, filling himself with her. But containing the rapacious lust screaming through his veins presented a problem and his pulse rate strummed a new beat.

Now, his cock was at attention. Potent, hard and throbbing, flagrantly pressed against this luscious woman, poised and needy as they come.

Relaxation forced the tension in her body to seep away slowly. Bryce leaned down and brushed a kiss over her earlobe, then to a place behind her ear he remembered was sensitive.

She responded with a shiver, accompanied by an audible gasp. Oh, yes, she liked that. And he pressed a lengthy kiss to the very same place as his hand traveled down her back, splaying his fingers over the tight muscles, kneading. He stopped the forward progress at the base of her spine. He wasn't foolish enough to push her too far or rush too soon after a traumatic episode. He'd simply hold her as long as necessary.

"Don't," Rio whispered, but her arms lifted, fingers curling into his shirtfront. She held him in place, held him immobile.

He'd heard the unsteadiness in her voice, felt the subtle movement of her body. She was fighting him, warring within herself. Cupping her chin, he forced her to meet his gaze. "Tell me to stop and I will. I'd never force you into anything you don't want." Studying the bewilderment in her beautiful eyes, he cupped her chin, ran his thumb over her unpainted, silky lips.

"But I want you, Rio," Bryce said softly. She didn't move out of his embrace. "I want to kiss you everywhere, caress every inch of your body. Chase the fear away."

"I . . . you can't," she stammered, breathless, trembling. "We can't."

"Why?" When she frowned, he smoothed the furrows away with a tender kiss. "Why?"

"You're . . . you're," Her mind raced for words, looking for a satisfying reason. "Too young. Too . . . we're different."

Damn it. "Different how? We're both adults." Sliding his hands farther down, he gripped her behind, pressed her more firmly against his ripened erection. He strained toward her, gritting his teeth from the sweet torture.

Somehow, he had to relieve an unjustified apprehension. An unimportant number separated their ages. Need for one another meant everything. At this moment, he needed her.

And he knew Rio felt a similar need for him. Earlier, she'd

passionately responded to his kiss, allowing herself complete freedom, and she'd dissolved in his arms with free-flowing ease. Alone and secluded, they could chase the stars across the sky and capture the universe together.

She huffed, broke bodily contact and shoved his hands away. She was more upset about age than he thought.

"I'm . . . I'm," Rio stammered. "You're . . . you're . . . Caucasian."

"Son of a bitch."

What the devil did that have to do with anything? The entire club had watched while he'd kissed her. The entire club had watched while they'd dry fucked. The entire club was all black except for him and very few ladies. He still didn't feel like the Lone Ranger.

With one hand, Bryce raked a vicious path through his hair. When he moved closer to Rio, she tried to sidestep, tried to circle around him, but he boxed her into the corner, hands flat against the walls. "What we do is our business. I don't care about our backgrounds. I don't care what other people do or think or say. I live my life the way I want."

"An understatement, Mr. Sullivan. Remember Shannon a few hours ago? Ring a bell?"

He cursed under his breath. He had expected resentment, but not biting sarcasm. The dagger went deep. Still, Bryce was determined to win her over.

Catching her hands with his own, he squeezed lightly. "It meant nothing. She meant nothing to me. Never did. I just handled the situation way stupid and imma . . . silly. From anger."

He stepped closer. As her breasts brushed against his chest, nipples peaked and hardened, he remembered the first time today she'd reacted to his nearness. He'd seen the telltale signs.

"And jealousy," he added. A streak of uncertainty crossed her face. "It's true. Seeing you hug Cockroach, right after we'd finished dancing, I lost my cool." He wound her hands behind her back, pinned them in a bracelet hold without her slightest resistance.

Confessing inner turmoil or discontent to a woman had been the furthest admission from his mind, but Rio was like no other woman he'd ever met. Kissing her now would certainly prove how much he wanted her. He'd make sure she would never regret a moment of their joining if she'd allow him to pleasure her.

Bryce leaned toward her, but he left the last inch separating their lips up to Rio.

5

She knew better and still refused to listen to the staccato voice inside her head demanding she walk away from this madness.

Rio kissed him, long and hard, thrusting her tongue into his mouth, fencing with his, as searing liquid heat spread smoothly as slick oil through her belly. Meltdown.

She knew this was wrong, knew it, but he tasted so good and felt so strong squeezing her tightly. Who would know? The building was empty and, according to sneaky Miss Galaxeé, locked down.

Released from his grip, Rio wrapped her arms around Bryce's neck, pressing closer, wanting to feel his muscled body surrounding hers, pleased when his arousal swelled with fortified boldness. A blaze of electric fire sailed through her nerves, scorched her inside out.

One of his hands found its way into her hair and tugged her head back. The kiss was savage and primitive, breathtaking and devouring, brutal and possessive. A powerful heady combination that, quite frankly, sparked fresh scalding steam.

Rio rubbed her body against his, her nipples tight and hard, breasts heavy and tender. Needing his touch, she dragged his hand up to one and it swelled. He had big hands, strong, but the caress was a stroke of tenderness as he squeezed the fullness and strummed her nipple.

Gliding his hand down her back, he unzipped her dress, slipped his fingers under one strap and lifted it off her shoulder. The other thin strap came free. When he released possession of her lips and body, the slinky fabric slithered to the floor, leaving her all but nude in lacy white bikinis and red stilettos.

Bryce lifted her effortlessly into his arms. She clamped her legs around his waist as he swung her around. The tall cabinet's cool metal sent an icy chill up her spine, punctuating the flames burning deeply within her soul.

She wanted him inside her, every hot, thick filling inch of him. When his lips cruised down her throat and chest, found her waiting nipple, her head fell back against the cabinet. He worked his teeth, swirled his tongue, and laved a blistering path of starburst heat through every molecule.

Merciful God.

He wrenched her panties free.

Oh, Lord. She knew she was wet again, soaking, but ready and waiting for his molten touch. The sweet torment of his fingers smoothed over her slick folds, teasing her senses, tantalizing her sensitive nub, stirring the fire already consuming her.

He inserted one finger and retreated, then two slowly inside her passage. Her hips bucked from the building pressure, stretched. She remembered his large hands, bulky fingers, but there was no pain. Only pleasure, sins of pleasure as he retreated and repeated the torturous movements. Deeper. Much deeper. Over and over, enticing her to the next devastating level.

Rio groaned, bearing down.

Lifting his dark head, he claimed her mouth again, sank his teeth into her bottom lip and sucked, then plowed his tongue into her mouth, withdrew and plowed again in a seductive ritual matching his gifted fingers.

Rio tore her lips away from his on a gasp and spread her legs wider. The first tremor had begun, shimmering—a fiery glow from the burning embers he'd fanned. She opened her mouth to say any coherent sentence, hoping to halt the eruption seeking freedom. What, she didn't know. She couldn't form a decent thought while the tornadic climax steadily approached.

"Now, Rio. Now," Bryce whispered against her lips, a soothing sensual order—the bass rumbler.

He nipped at the tendon down her neck and she squirmed, fighting back, denying the torrent of emotions sending her toward mindless desperation.

His lips sailed downward and over the swell of her breast. She arched forward in offering. And when Bryce latched onto her nipple with his teeth, sheer static shock waves coursed through each hungry atom of her system.

She came.

So suddenly, so intensely, Rio screamed. And shook. And writhed, blinded by a climax so fierce, her hips pistoned forward and clenched around his fingers with every starving muscle she owned. She rocked, bucked, panted and shamelessly rode the numbing orgasm with reckless abandon.

She clung to his hair and neck, his shoulders, anything to keep from melting to a liquefied pool at his feet. In the end, she burrowed her face against the curve of his shoulder and thick neck, whimpering, "Damn you. Damn you. Damn you."

Opening for Bryce, she'd given him more than she'd ever cared to give again, and he took it all, left her with nothing in reserve.

Weak, barely able to lift her heavy eyelids, Rio vaguely felt his arm tighten around her, felt him shift and move. Seconds later, she became very much aware of the bulging, hot-blooded tip of his erection at the perimeter of her damp heat. She quivered at the searing contact, shivered from the renewed excitement feeding her infallible senses.

Looking up, a hint of green and hazel flashed brightly in his smoldering gray eyes, pupils dilated. Need, passion and an urgency she couldn't quite define etched his starkly handsome face, a masterpiece worthy of an artist's fine brushes. His face so young, so arresting, she traced his features with her fingertips—smooth skin, supple lips, perfectly shaped eyebrows any woman would kill to have for herself.

Restless as they caressed her, Rio realized his hands vibrated against her flesh. She'd given her body to him, but he'd yet to give to her. Holding back with seasoned strength, he was asking for permission, the strain evident on his face.

He'd maintained self-control while she'd swan dived over ecstasy's cliff, and he'd brought her safely back to sanity. But still he'd waited for approval to invade her body more intimately.

Where had this man come from? Where had this rare gem been hiding all of her adult life? Why wasn't he fifteen years older? The thought fluttered through her mind, a quick fleeting flurry that faded, disappeared.

"Yes," she whispered, running her fingers through his hair, knowing they would both surrender to the same exquisite delights. "Yes."

Rio closed her eyes as Bryce lowered his head. He kissed her in a gentle but demanding assault while he penetrated her slowly, carefully, with excruciating tame finesse. She unfolded like petals of a morning glory.

He helped her rise, shoved her down his length inch by mere inch in forceful yet subtle pressure.

Again and again, a possessive, feral growl slipped from his lips. The sound penetrated her befuddled mind, heightened her awareness of him and skittered over her hot flesh. Shivering, she dug her nails deep into his skin and responded with a feline purr of acceptance.

His breathing became as ragged and uneven as her own, hissing each time she tightened around his swollen erection. Still, he persevered.

Fully embedded, Bryce flexed his fingers against her velvet-smooth skin. He'd nearly reached the limit of his endurance. Sweat trickled down his temples, over his cheeks and continued dripping down to his chest. He gritted his teeth and worked hard at holding back, fearing he'd hurt her. She had enticed him toward a wild state, teasing the primal nature known to all mankind.

Swinging her around, he deposited Rio on the drafting table. With one swift movement of his arm, he cleared its top, scattering papers and pens, sent them careening to the floor. The light suddenly came on, silhouetting a goddess at sunrise; an angel he had never expected to come into his life, an exotic woman who held power to dominate his dreams and rule his thoughts.

She was beautiful, satiny skin moist with perspiration, and he trailed his hands up her body, stopping at the small tattoo on her left breast, an elephant, gray, large pink ears. It fit her—cute, not risqué or kinky, a tattoo that she'd kept hidden from view even beneath the skimpiest of clothing, hidden as well as she'd masked her life.

He leaned over her body, still intimately joined, still throbbing inside her, and hovered, barely touching her lips with his own, and ran his tongue over the smooth texture of them. She tasted honey-sweet, intoxicating as the essence of her scent drifting up his nostrils.

When her tongue stroked his, he covered her lips and drew it inside his mouth, drank deeply, as deeply as he would if he'd sipped from the sweet nectar a woman's body possessed. He would taste her, drive her to the brink of rapture again, and together they'd soar to a universe all their own.

Straightening, he stared down at their connected bodies, knowing he was slipping out of control, shaking from restraint. Withdrawing slowly, he watched his glistening cock, veins pulsing with hot blood beneath the condom, watched it disappear as he penetrated, endlessly penetrated her tightness. With Rio's legs wrapped loosely around his waist, hips undulating seductively, she was wringing the shit out of him.

Far too soon.

Touching the tip of her swollen nub, he massaged, added pressure, made vibrant contact with his cock. She shuddered in response, spreading her legs wider, giving unrestricted access, and moaned incoherently, egging him on.

"Yes," she whispered, eyes closed. "Right there."

He withdrew from her snug cocoon, suddenly, deliberately, which only inflamed the woman controlling him.

"No!" She wrapped her slender fingers around his hardness and tried to guide him back inside her.

Bryce stopped her, gently peeled her trembling hand away and clamped one of his around both her wrists.

"I want to taste you, every bit of your body," he said, his voice ragged with need. He'd climax before she reached the same level of intense arousal if he stayed inside her delectable body too much longer.

"I want you back . . . back again. Don't . . . Don't make me wait. I . . . I . . . want . . ."

She was there, desperate. In need. Wanting. Bryce held his cock in one hand and squeezed, forcing back the threat of release. He pressed the bulging head to her slippery heat, sliding gently, swirling, teasing, drawing a gasp from them both when he pierced her again in slow, languid thrusts, retreating at the same tempo. Catlike, she arched her back, then lifted her hips to meet him, to greet him, and purred with feline aggression.

He accepted the invitation.

And Bryce surged forward with one powerful stroke, lifted
Rio high, held her impaled, withdrew and speared her again in
the same rhythm of a predatory beast. He accelerated the speed
and she matched his thrusts with equal animal ferocity, drawing
him back deep inside her.

Rabid now, he shoved his arms beneath her legs, lifting her
hips from the table, spreading her wider and pounded, smacking against her at a ferocious pace with hard, almost violent
thrusts stimulated by unbridled lust and the scent of her.

He wanted all of this woman, everything, and with each driving blow he begged with his eyes and his body, straining to
control his release, and asked for more.

"I want it, Rio. I want it now."

She unequivocally answered with controlling hotness, took
siege of his body, constricting around his cock in an uncompromising, tight grip.

Bryce opened his mouth. "Oh, sh—"

Shuddering, he dragged in a lung full of air, gnashed his teeth
together and hissed out the breath between them, fighting to
contain the volcanic spasms threatening to erupt.

She gripped him tighter.

His resolve fractured. On a mighty roar, triggered by the be-
witching angel holding him captive, the floodgate opened.

He came and came and came more.

"Goddamn it!"

He couldn't stop the rampant flow, couldn't stop the raging
tremors, and he couldn't see past the glaze of dizzying sensations.

But she reared up and clamped her body around his. Together, they lifted and he shoved her down, determined to take
her to the same magical summit. Gripping his hands beneath
her thighs, Bryce raised her, forced her down while he plowed
upward deliriously with pillaging strokes.

He never let up.

She wouldn't let him.

Through the blinding, brilliant flames, he heard Rio's strangled scream and he caught it on his next breath, smothering her mouth with a barrage of passionate kisses as her clawing nails raked over his back, vicious as freshly sharpened talons. She'd joined him now, clenching and pulling, taking him deeper, sucking out every drop of desire.

Unable to remain upright, cradling her with one weak arm, Bryce pitched forward onto the drafting table. Her climax took them both past the pinnacle, hurtling into a new dimension on a blazing journey—a furious trek along the greedy edge of insanity.

And, there, they caught a racing comet.

Long minutes passed before he found the power to move, before he was capable of movement, still working to catch the breath he'd left somewhere behind, still paralyzed by the intensity of sex with Rio Saunders.

Where had they gone? When had they returned?

As the powerful sensations receded by degrees, a soul-deep satisfaction claimed him. Not once in his life had he experienced such contentment and completion, whether on a soft mattress or here on the hard surface of a drafting table.

Thoroughly sated, he smiled at that. Always a first time for everything.

The woman beneath him was exceptionally refined and passionately sophisticated, yet she had allowed him to make love to her, here, in an office, at a nightclub that was packed, quite recently, with wildness. Tame, though, compared to the torrid celebration he and Rio had just shared.

They had chemistry, a prescription made for loving. They were meant for each other—a matched pair with strong desires, fevered passion and tempestuous climaxes. Neither could object to that.

Then, he'd dump her when the timing was right, when he'd finished with her.

Quiet calm settled over both and their breathing slowed to a tolerable rhythm.

Rio moved ever so slightly. She swallowed as the last tremor faded, licked her lips and swallowed again. Her throat was as dry as parched earth. She knew why. The remnants of a high-pitched shriek echoed loudly in her brain, alongside a lion's conquering roar.

And here she was sprawled on a slanted table, her legs wrapped around a little boy a dozen years her junior. A Caucasian little boy.

Had she lost her mind? Had she lost all sense of propriety? *Apparently.*

Okay. This was it. She had to get out from under him and close the door on this foolishness. She had no right to allow this encounter to happen. No right whatsoever.

She planted her heels on the table, shifted, twisted and attempted to scoot away when he withdrew. Until she felt penetration again, something hot and pulsing. Inside. It swelled, gained length and thickened. Rio sucked in air.

When Bryce lifted his head, a wicked gleam glowed in his gray eyes. He'd asked before, but a new glint smoldered there now. Insistence? "No," she said, shaking her head. "No. I can't. We can't."

She couldn't do this again. He'd drained her. She had nothing left to give him. She could not, would not give him any more.

"Yes," he replied, his voice low, rumbly, and unyielding as he withdrew slowly and glided smoothly inside her, sparking infinite pleasure.

Drugged with erotic delight, Rio closed her eyes and caved. She lost sight of refusal when the world as she knew it tumbled into oblivion.

* * *

At six fifteen, Rio stepped into the red clinger, wiggled getting it over hips, her breasts swaying with the movement. How had she managed to keep her shoes on?

Bryce tried to zip her dress.

"I can do it myself," she declared and moved away. Every time he came too close, the heat from his body penetrated hers, setting her on fire.

"I'm just trying to help."

She didn't need his help. Nor did she want it. They had to get out of Killer's before the janitors arrived, before someone caught them together.

She picked up her tattered panties from the floor. Her favorite ones. Fifteen-dollar drawers ripped apart. She held them by a shredded piece of lace, glaring at Bryce.

"They were in the way," he said, shrugging, buttoning his shirt. He'd finally undressed near the end of the night, rather, morning.

She rolled and stuffed the lingerie inside her purse. What else did she need to hide? She snatched the matching bra off a coat hanger. At least he hadn't gotten the chance to tear it apart, wasting another thirty-five bucks.

And the drafting table? Well, that would certainly cost a few extra dollars. They'd cracked the hard plastic. Would the light still work? Probably not.

"Guess I was a little rough."

Rough? He'd screwed her cross-eyed, wore her out into the wee hours of the morning. She gathered pencils, pens and papers from the floor, put them on Galaxeé's desk in an ordered fashion.

"How about breakfast?" Bryce asked. "At my place. I've got eggs and bacon and—"

"No."

"No? Why not?"

"I'm going home." Far, far away from him and the growing attraction she had for Bryce Sullivan. No, not attraction. Forbidden horniness, nothing more.

"So you're cooking." It was not a question. "Great. What's on our menu?"

"No, Mr. Sullivan, I am not cooking breakfast, lunch or even a snack." She found her key ring inside her purse and lifted her black swing coat from the rack.

"Fine, I'll fix it for you there. I'm starved," he said and helped her with the coat.

Rio looped the strap to her leather handbag over her shoulder. "Bryce, you are not coming to my place." She turned on her heels, opened the door, started out of the room and sniffed. Good lord. "Leave the door open."

He grabbed her arm and dragged her back inside. "What do you think happened here?"

What happened? Besides wild, hot, volatile . . . the best she'd ever had. "Sex."

"It was way more than just sex."

"Okay. We had a one-night stand, period." An excellent night, one she'd never forget. "An encounter that never—"

"But it did, Rio, and I want to see you again. Outside the club."

Had he lost his mind? No way, not a rematch. Never. "Look. Um." How difficult was it to tell him they had nothing in common, that she couldn't possibly have a relationship with him, anything outside work, just a professional alliance? "We don't . . . we can't . . . we have nothing—"

"Yes, we do. You know it and so do I."

He backed her against the wall, pressed his muscled body against hers. Rio's bones rattled all the way down to her knees. He was hard again, and her lower belly quivered in response. "We have nothing in common. Nothing. No reason to even think—" The kiss was a sensuous attack melting her thoughts.

Breathless, she forced herself out of his embrace before his magnetism and finesse caused her to lose all reason again.

"Rio—"

"We have to get out of here." She hurried down the stairs, running from what his nearness did to her mind and body. Outside the building, she locked Killer's down tight. Snow was ankle-deep. Why hadn't she changed shoes? Wiggling her toes, she took a tentative step. Even with the remote to unlock the doors, the Mercedes was a good twenty yards away. She pulled the coat's lapels together to block the chilling breeze.

Bryce scooped her up into his arms. Why fight him, ruining her shoes and freezing her toes? Holding her securely, he managed to open the Benz's door and set her inside.

"Thank you," Rio said and stuck her key in the ignition. The engine turned over, purred.

"Let me follow you. I can carry you to the door."

My, he was persistent. "I have a garage. Go home, Bryce." She closed the car door, locked it.

Galaxeé tossed her clutch purse onto her desk, smirking. "I got a hangover that's kicking my behind."

"Really?" Rio said. She knew better now. The sneaky partner had pretended drunkenness last night.

"I do. Don't you feel sorry for me?"

"Sure." She went back to writing figures into the ledger. The journal contained as much information as Killer's computer. Backup, just in case the system decided to crash and burn, or get sick. She didn't trust its mathematical computations anyway, even if they were right so far.

"You don't sound sorry."

Rio dropped the pen and looked over at her friend. "I know all about it, Galaxeé."

"Yeah? Well, you don't have a pimple on your forehead anymore."

Her laughter sounded worse than a snickering hyena. Rio resented the noise and the insinuation. The woman knew too much, guessed too much. She was always right, darn her, with her know-it-all self.

"So how was it?"

"E-O-D, Barnett. End of discussion."

Galaxeé's jaw went slack. "You're not going to tell me if he was good or bad? He's got the biggest—"

"E," Rio admonished, "O-D."

"Ah, hah! Stand up so I can see if your legs are bowed. Was it good? I know it was."

Rio groaned. Sex with Bryce surpassed good. Unimaginable. Sinfully wicked. Deliciously powerful. And painful. But who cared about pain? The lingering reminders started her juices flowing and she outright shivered. For someone so young, someone else had trained him well. "Jesus, Galaxeé. The subject is none of your business. Did you and Luanne finish the inventory?"

"I'll ask Bryce."

"Don't you dare. Don't. Don't say a word. Please."

Last night was a mistake. She never should've let him seduce her, even with a condom's protection. After a long, celibate period, she was needy. Horny. He looked so good, his body felt even better, but any continued relationship with him was impossible. She'd said as much to him. Sort of.

"You didn't sleep last night, did you?" Galaxeé asked.

Mirrors spared no one mercy. Rio had seen the puffiness around her eyes. Slices of cucumber hadn't helped and she never wore makeup, except mascara and eyeliner on occasion, and, of course, lipstick. She'd grown up under strict religious rules. Sure enough, Momma was wearing a permanent scowl on her heavenly face because of her daughter's improper behavior. Rio grimaced.

No, she didn't sleep at all. She'd tossed and turned for hours, finally climbed out of bed and dressed in workout sweats. She'd stair-stepped until her quads, hamstrings and calves burned, thinking the exercise would tire her and she'd fall into a deep slumber for a few hours, devoid of her mother's reprimanding glower. Fat chance. After Bryce, exhaustion racked her at the time, but she still hadn't caught any Zs.

"I slept some."

"Liar. Why are you so freaked out?"

"I'm not."

"Are, too. Don't try to hide it from me. Your aura is shimmering as much as your hands are trembling. He didn't hurt you, did he? I hope he didn't force you into lewd sex, vulgar or undignified. I'll kill him if he did."

The sneer stretching across Galaxeé's face suggested she'd castrate him. Or maybe she thought to cast a hypnotic spell, have him going stark raving mad.

But Bryce had not used force. He'd conquered her with tantalizing temptation, coerced her with a gentleman's caressing touch and voracious sexual appetite. "No. He's not like that at all. He's gentle. Caring and mature. Teasing and playful. Lo . . . Affectionate." All the attributes she'd looked for in an older companion.

Rio shook her head. He was more mature, in mind as well, than she'd realized. Still, twelve years, their backgrounds . . .

She grimaced again, wondering what people would think if Bryce and she were an item. How might a relationship with him affect Killer Bods' growing success? She'd put everything she owned on the line. Quit the job she'd held for three years and convinced Devon to cosign for an equity loan. Well, her attorney had convinced him.

She had a lot at stake to risk on a most-likely-useless encounter that had no chance whatsoever of blooming. One bizarre night of hot, rough sex had spread her toes and sent wave after tidal wave of thrilling shudders up her spine.

"Lots of good-sounding adjectives, especially that 'loving' part you slipped on."

Rio huffed out a sigh. Darn her. "It won't work, Galaxeé. Bryce and I . . . We made a huge mistake. I'm thinking we should dismiss him from the revue and find a replacement."

She wouldn't have to see his handsome face three days a week if they let him go. She could free herself of the temptation and easily forget him. Couldn't she? She had to banish Bryce Sullivan from her thoughts.

"Fire him? You must be out of your ever-loving mind. He did fuck your brains out. You don't have any left," Galaxeé said, stomping her boot heel on the floor. "Rio, give him a chance. You can't blow him off like you'd flick away a chinchy-bug. He likes you a lot, and you like him."

"I don't. No, I don't like him. I hate him." Temper had crept into her tone. She knew darn well she'd told a bald-faced lie, sounding like a silly, teenaged girl.

But she hated Bryce for making her feelings come alive. She hated him for his gentle tenderness. She hated him because she hated the sinful thoughts of her ancient self with a vibrant teenybopper who was able to light her fuse and rocket them both to an unspecified destination at blinding speed.

"Give me one good reason why you think you hate him." Galaxeé, wearing jeans for a change, crossed her legs into a yoga position and clasped her hands demurely together. All she needed was a genie getup, a belly-dancing outfit, a turban with a large, spectacular jewel attached to the pleated front or a veil covering half her face.

"I'll give you three," Rio snapped. "Age."

"That's one."

"It's two, his and mine."

"Both smack of bullshit," Galaxeé crudely fired back. "What's the third? Too chicken to admit you already have feelings for him?"

Our backgrounds, she wanted to blurt out. They were far too different. Rio knew she worried much too much about other people's thoughts, how they reacted and what opinions they had of her. Growing up had not been easy in Denver. She was a mere child when racially charged violence broke out across America and flower people and gay rights headlined newspapers.

Attending Howard University in Washington, D.C., and, not much later, marrying a prominent attorney twelve years *her* senior, had satisfied her parents' hopes and prayers.

Following her mother's example, subservience and proper decorum had kept Rio's marriage together for nine of the eleven years. But her dangerously debonair husband had strayed to more fertile grounds during his midlife crisis. The union had ended in a less-than-congenial divorce. Exactly how Galaxeé had said it would before Devon proposed, yet she'd still stood by Rio's side at the church altar.

Starting a new life and a new job she detested after years of quiet domestication, Rio took orders from a lazy, tyrannical manager without so much as a whine, even when his supervisory methods bordered on harassment.

Finally fed up with the cards she'd dealt herself, she quit the job, put her entire life on the line and took a spontaneous flying leap with Galaxeé. They opened Killer Bods.

She'd pleased everyone all of her life. It was time to please Rio Saunders. Unconsciously, though, she'd continued satisfying the outside world without a second thought.

On the other hand, Galaxeé was free and open, and she hadn't cared what people believed or said. Anyone resenting Ms. Barnett's outspoken opinions, they were, in her words, S-O-L. Society didn't pay her bills. Society didn't buy her groceries and society sure as the devil didn't own the lien to her mortgage. E-O-D.

The partner had more than one ball in her court.

"Look into your crystal globe and see if you can dredge up a vision since you know so darn much." Frustrated, Rio swiveled the seat around and clamped her hands over her ears. Galaxeé wouldn't let that one pass easily.

She didn't let it pass at all. She pulled Rio's hands free and whispered, "I already have."

Great. His techs were good, but sometimes they needed handholding, sometimes too much guidance when his days were filled with odd hells aplenty. The new marketing director wouldn't come on board for another week. Oscar Berman, lead technician, had been harping, needing another worker. Personnel was weeding out applicants since Bryce only had time to interview the top three candidates.

"How soon can you ship?" Bryce asked. They needed printer paper. *Pronto.* Berkowitz Paper Company, located in Tennessee, had given his secretary too much grief this morning.

Just then, the office opened. What now?

He recognized the mail cart, but not the nice ass backing into the room. But then, his secretary had said they'd filled the position.

"I need it sooner than that, Thurmon ... One day late and we're no longer—" The blonde turned in his direction, and Bryce wanted to shit. "One day." He dropped the receiver into its cradle.

"Hello, Bryce. It's been a long time."

"Over ten years." He was seventeen, a freshman, when he met her. He'd fallen into deep lust with the college sophomore.

Bryce stood when she approached his desk. Same smile, silky hair shifting about her shoulders as it had way back when. He'd once loved crushing it between his fingers while he thrust his tongue into her rosy, heart-shaped mouth—while they'd screwed like horny rabbits. The years had been good to her.

"How are you, Frankie? What are you doing here?"

She gestured toward the cart. "Delivering mail, obviously, and working for you."

They'd studied at the same university. After their breakup, he'd lost contact with her. Most Stanford grads found top-paying jobs, not the menial position of a mail clerk.

"I suppose you're wondering why. Remember, my father lives in Parker. And, well—"

"This is the first time I've ever seen you blush." Embarrassment was not her trademark, although the tinge of red highlighted her radiant skin. She wore it well.

"I dropped out of Stanford not long after . . . I wasn't exactly the best student in school."

He hadn't known. At the time, when he was a juvenile, only three factors consumed his brain: his dick, Frankie Perino and fucking her. Four, allowing his hair to grow simply to annoy his mother. As for grades, cake. He'd graduated magna cum laude.

"That's all history anyway. I have to get this mail delivered before your secretary starts in on me again. How about we get together for drinks somewhere?" She propped her hip against his brand-new wood desk and folded her arms beneath a pair of hefty hooters he'd wallowed in once upon a time. "Maybe melt the wax off a few dance floors like we used to do."

They'd never stayed at a nightclub long enough to boogie. One beer, if he wasn't carded, then off to anywhere available for blistering carnality. They'd shared compatible horniness. And Bryce recognized the sultry look in the eyes of a huntress. Frankie hadn't changed. He had, to some degree, and he'd planned on milking Rio's juices after tonight's show.

"Can't."

She stood again, the recognizable pout firmly in place. Frankie had played him well so long ago. Seventeen, studly, and stupidly horny, he'd fallen hard for all of her mature (hah!) behavior. She'd dominated his young life for months: told him what to do, when to do it and how.

He was an adult now, smarter.

"That's too bad. I was thinking we'd check out a club I passed by." She sauntered toward the cart, hips swaying seductively, and opened the door. "In LoDo. A place called Killer Bods that looked pretty hot. Oh. Hi, Maureen."

Bryce half expected every ounce of his blood to squirt through his pores.

6

She had ignored him all evening. Why, after the hot-blooded sex they'd discovered?

Did she really believe they'd simply had a one-night stand? A chance fling, a quickie, well, a longie, that meant nothing?

Bryce knew he should steer clear of this woman if he had any damn sense. But ever since he'd met her, wisdom had deserted him. She'd unknowingly stripped him of judgment and peeled away the protective barrier he'd concealed his ego with for years.

And now she'd tossed him aside like roadkill. What the hell was up with this shit?

He tipped the beer bottle back, draining the last few ounces of cool ale. Standing beside the drafty stage, he watched Rio glide across the room in a sexy Caribbean wave of blue, swaying a set of delectable hips he knew fit perfectly in his hands.

Somebody tapped his shoulder and Bryce spun around. "What the hell are you doing here, Frankie?" He did not need this shit.

"Hello to you, too, and like the rest of these women," she

said, gesturing toward the audience, "I'm here to watch Killer's new showstopper."

Agitation twisted the tight knot overloading his gut.

"I met the owners."

Crap.

"Nice ladies." She stepped close. "In fact, I'm building their website. Actually, that's what I wanted to talk to you about, Bryce. I like working at Thorobred. The people are nice. We all get along pretty well. You know, like a big family. Gossip spreads quickly."

Some grins reflected personalities so well. Hers was shitty.

"I wonder how the *family* would react if—"

"Loyalty supersedes bullshit, Frankie, and this conversation is now over." Bryce stalked off.

"Not yet. We have a lot more to discuss. How's Claudine doing these days?" That brought him to a dead stop.

"Hey, my man," Dallas said and jabbed a fist at Bryce's chest. " 'Sup?"

"Nothing." Nothing but bullshit. Jason passed by, skinnin' and grinnin', followed by Orlando, whose tongue dripped worse than a panting hound dog.

Dallas puckered his lips, staring at Frankie, then back at Bryce as he turned. "Orlando was ready to spring on this one," he whispered. "Thought she was on the prowl. Didn't know you were a-sniffin' behind a new trail."

"I'm not."

"Then, how does she know Claudine?"

"Leave it alone, Coop."

"We're old friends," Frankie said, and Bryce mapped his face into a deadly scowl. "You're the Panther Man. Too bad the club is losing you."

Coop's jaw went slack. "Well, guess I'd better see what Rio wants." He hightailed down the hall in her direction.

Bryce's shoulder bunched when he saw her. Since when had

he turned into the Invisible Man? Great. "Look, Frankie, I have to get ready for my set."

"Fine. We'll talk later about Claudine, Thorobred and a get-together we really should have." She sauntered away.

Rio continued ignoring him. She mingled with the last of the crowd gathering their belongings. After a minute, she said a few words to the servers wiping down tables and spent time with dancers who lounged nearby.

Not once had she spared Bryce a glance or even said boo. She'd stayed in her office when he danced, but she'd spent a fair amount of quality time with Cockroach while others performed. Yeah, he had watched her every possible chance while dodging Frankie.

Now, Jason inched his way into her circle. Bryce chugged the last of his ale, watching.

The filthy son of a bitch wrapped his arm around Rio's shoulders. When he leaned down, said something into her ear and kissed her cheek, cold fury froze Bryce's blood into dry ice. He hurled the beer bottle into a nearby trash bin. The scream of breaking glass brought the heads around of two servers.

Why should he care? Balling his fists tightly, his mood suddenly bursting hot with the temper of a territorial beast facing an invading opponent, he cursed savagely under his breath. The anger broke free and he slapped the wall with his open hand.

"Hey," a voice said from behind him.

Bryce spun around. So caught up in the moment, he had no idea someone had sneaked up, witnessing his tirade.

"Chill out, baby. It's not all that bad."

Under the dim overhead lighting, Galaxeé glided toward him, high heels tapping on the tile floor with the movement, long braids swaying gently. In comparison to Rio, she wasn't very tall. The top of her head fell short of reaching his shoulders. She did have a hefty set of hooters drawing attention away from her height, and she was damn pretty. Sexy, even.

Galaxeé had a type of spunk different from any other woman he'd known. Independent, open-minded, but pushy in a mysterious sort of way, hell, she was just plain bossy. He didn't particularly care for a stubborn woman who seemed to have an uncanny perception, who seemed to know his thoughts and vulnerabilities. Big tits or not. Until now.

"You're making progress," she said.

Her fingers hovered above his arm. He sensed a warming sensation as she moved them up to his shoulder and over his chest. Little by little, he relaxed from the tingle circulating over his skin, invasive but quieting his thumping heartbeat, transforming hostility into guilt-ridden embarrassment that caused his ears to burn.

Bryce settled down, dragged in a cleansing breath.

He looked sharply into Galaxeé's eyes. How the hell did she do that? Damn it, at this moment he'd rather percolate in anger. Somehow, she'd snatched it all away.

"Better?" she asked. Her voice was soothing, her face bright, serene, smiling.

He chewed on the inside of his cheek. Just how the hell had she done it? Inside, he felt relaxed, calm. Bryce grabbed her wrist, looked down at the palm of her hand. Empty. He thought she'd used some sort of instrument, a device discharging electrical currents through his system.

"What are you looking for?"

"I thought—I have no idea," he replied, but a strangely warm sensation flowed through his hand and up his arm. Bryce squinted. "How do you do that?"

"Do what?"

He must be crazy. Or she was some kind of witch. A good witch, if there was such a thing. She'd helped him get close to Rio. "She hasn't said a word to me tonight and wouldn't answer or return my calls today."

"Guess that means you need to do . . . whatever," Galaxeé replied, fluttering her lashes. "Tonight."

"Like what?"

She tsked. "Use your imagination, Tarzan. Think spontaneity, not that computer-nerd logic."

Computer nerd? Bullshit! "She won't let me near her." Every time he'd tried to approach Rio, she took off in a different direction. In a mad dash.

"Oh, yes, she will."

"How do you know?"

Galaxeé grinned. "I just do. In the meantime, keep your attentions focused on her." She circled around him, hips swaying gently from side to side. "I'll deal with Cockroach. Jason, too." She closed the curtains behind her.

Stunned into silence, Bryce's blood chilled to an arctic low. What did she know? How the devil did she find out about . . . How the *devil* did she know about his damned inherent logic? He snatched the curtain back.

Where the hell was she?

"Put me down!" Rio squirmed, pounding his back.

Galaxeé had said spontaneity. Bryce figured he was an impulsive sort of guy, logically speaking.

When most everyone had left the club, he sneaked up behind Rio, scooped her into his arms and tossed her over his shoulder caveman style. She kicked and bitched until he gave her a good, solid smack across the ass, drawing an indignant yip. Bryce yanked the blue fabric away from his face and beelined to the front door.

Light snow fell on a really cold night. A thin layer covered the iced ground. Most had melted during daylight hours.

He marched over to his customized Cadillac Escalade, unlocked the door and dumped Rio inside. She tried to bolt, but the seat buckle automatically snapped into place. He locked the door. Escape was impossible without his help. The special locking mechanism he had installed matched a police cruiser's system.

Satisfied with his clever techniques, he strode around the front of the vehicle, but he slipped on the ice. Flailing wildly, Bryce went down like a drunken horse. He managed to get his feet under himself and, with the help of the Cadillac's running board and door, climbed into the driver's seat.

Rio would have to laugh at his clumsiness. Women. They bruised a man's ego without thought or care.

Sobering quickly, she said, "Served you right."

From the look on her face, he was in for some real hell. Big time.

"Unlock this door."

Bryce started the engine.

"Did you hear what I said? Unlock this damn door. I'm not going anywhere with you."

"You're shivering. Here, take my coat." He struggled out of the leather, handed it over. "Couple more seconds and the heat'll blast us out of here. You can adjust your own temp right there." He pointed to the controls.

Half an hour earlier, he'd warmed up the Cadillac. The temperature outside had dipped well below the freezing level and frost had covered the windshield.

"Forget the coat and the blower. Unlock the door, Bryce. I don't have my keys, my purse, my—"

"You won't need them." He put the SUV in gear, coasted toward the street. At this time of night, traffic was all but nil. He maneuvered the oversize vehicle onto the main drag.

"This is kidnapping. When you get out of jail, *you are fired*. You're fired now."

"I didn't need the job anyway." He stopped at the red light.

Beside them, a carload of rowdy young people hooted, howled and sang along with the blaring rap music. When the light changed, they sped off into the snowy night.

"Where are you taking me?"

"My place."

"Why?"

"Why?" He had his reasons. Bryce knew she would've refused if he'd asked her to come willingly. Kidnapping was his only recourse. Mr. Spontaneity.

"Why!"

He flinched. "You don't have to yell," he said civilly. "It's very simple. I wanted to spend time with you. The club is shut down for the next four days and neither of us has to work." He did have to call his office Monday morning. The joy of top brass, the boss wasn't required to show his face.

"Four days?"

He pressed the switch to illuminate his watch. "Three and three quarters, give or take."

"You're insane."

Yeah, he was nuts all right, insane over her delectable body. "Would you rather we went to your place? I could go back and get your keys." Ignored, he grinned and veered onto the freeway, continued driving in the direction of his home.

After Rio had left him standing in the parking lot, he'd skipped food for once and catnapped. At work, he'd made more mistakes in one day than he'd made since Thorobred Computers opened four years ago. He tried to blame it on lack of rest. Bryce knew better.

The worst of his errors, he'd signed Rio's name instead of his own on a big contract he'd won. His secretary, the motherly type, had informed him of the mistake. She liked working half days on weekends. A nosy woman, Maureen Jamison had remembered talking to Rio and wondered if she was a prospective client.

Client, no. Lover and companion, he wished, but he kept his mouth shut on that one. Anyway, he needed to find out if all they had in common was rapacious lust.

Bryce glanced over at Rio. She stared down at her hands, fidgeting. "Are you warm?"

"Frigid," she snapped. "I will remain so unless—"

"Don't say that." Shit. This idea had the possibility to turn into a chilly fiasco instead of a three-day, explore-our-options sex fest.

"Then take me back to the club."

"No." Not yet. Not until she proved she had no feelings for him, not until he knew he had none for her. "Is spending a little time with me so awful?" The question was loaded, putting everything on the line.

Up ahead, a snow truck shoveled the highway, blue lights flashing brightly. A mile beyond was an exit he could easily take and drive Rio back to the club. Bryce slowed the SUV, pressing delicately on the brake, gripping the steering wheel tighter. Damn, he really hated having to take her back.

Thinking clearly for a change, he'd put her in a difficult position, one he might regret. Rio didn't know him, even after one night of mind-blowing, explosive sex that jarred his brain and stunned his dick. For all she knew, he might be someone who would hurt her. Maybe this spontaneous crap wasn't such a good idea. Illogical, and way different from his norm.

Waiting for an answer, he quickly shot her a glance.

Rio avoided his gaze as anger simmered beneath her skin, steaming through every pore.

This stunt reeked of immaturity, recklessness, stupidity and, God help her since she, at the moment, had none, courage. Alone with Bryce for three days scared her more than anything on Planet Earth right now. He could've easily done something terrible last night if his intentions had been to hurt her. He hadn't. What he had done to her was far from terrible and registered off the Richter scale.

Yet, she feared him. Her body reacted so unnaturally to his nearness. Panic consumed her now. His image had branded itself in her mind ever since he'd touched her and, from the look in his eyes at the club tonight, he wanted to rip her panties off again. Terror threatened her emotionally. Given time, she just might lose herself to him. And that should never, ever happen.

Spending time with Bryce had been the furthest thought from her mind, sort of, but as the words penetrated her brain cells, she swallowed, her breaths coming in short pants. It wasn't an awful notion. Just nerve-racking. Nail-biting nerves. Pick-the-polish-off-the-fresh-manicure kind of nerves. She stilled her trembling hands.

But a three-day marathon enjoying the best sex in her life with a young hunk, in seclusion of course? What woman could possibly turn down a proposition so inviting? Even the silliest, the frigid and the virginal would jump at the opportunity.

Me, I'd probably lose my ability to walk.

"What's so funny?" Bryce asked.

Thank the Lord for darkness. She could see herself melting under his smoky gaze. Rio bit her lip to contain the flow of hot juice soaking her panties. "Do you happen to have a spare toothbrush at home?" She gripped the armrest. He'd jerked the wheel. "I think it's easier to pass this truck on the left. It's against the law to use the shoulder."

She had trouble freeing herself.

"How do I get this seat belt off?" Rio asked as the garage door lowered.

Dim overhead lighting illuminated the three-car area. Bryce had cut the headlights on his SUV. "Let me."

When his hot hands grazed her thigh and hip, Rio jumped. When he looked into her eyes and held her gaze, she broke out in a sweat. And, God, she hated perspiring. When his hand lifted to her face and touched her cheek, she almost came. She kissed him.

And climaxed. A quick orgasm wrung a tiny squeal from her throat, the vibrations jolting the smallest molecules through her system.

Growling into her mouth, Bryce's arms went around her body, dragged her from the bucket seat and onto his lap. She shifted, straddled him. The driver's seat moved in reverse, the back support lowering.

Heat from his sexuality nearly burnt a hole through her panties. Not for long. He wrenched them free.

Breathless, Rio said, "Bryce—" Mercy, he was quick on the draw, already shoving inside her.

He growled again, sent a flood of shivers up her spine. To accommodate his size, his hardness, the massiveness, she spread her legs wider and gradually, if not thoroughly, engulfed him. For a few hot seconds, she held steady, cocooning, enjoying the feel of him.

Then she began to move, up and down, circling, slowly at first, then picking up speed. Straightening, she arched, pressed her hands to the ceiling, forced her body down his length and lifted again. His big hands covered her breasts, squeezed a painful caress, strumming her nipples in a delicious rhythm.

She almost cried out when they left there, but he soothed her, hands slipping beneath the hem of her dress, thumbs toying with her sensitive nub. He knew exactly where to touch, how much pressure she needed and how long to tease. And she rocked against his gifted fingers, hips undulating, and tightened around his thickness.

"Ooh," she purred. "Yes."

Caught in the euphoric haze, Rio closed her eyes, leaned back and braced her hands on his thighs, giving him unrestricted access.

Bryce took full advantage.

He pressed the heel of one hand firmly against her mound, thumb drawing half circles between his cock and the lips of her opening, giving both pleasure.

Flicking the switch, he raised the seat's back support. Another moved the seat forward and thrust him deeper, wedging

Rio between the steering wheel and himself, immobilized, unless he moved.

On the brink of a powerful orgasm, nothing could stop him from moving. She'd taken him that far, that close, that soon. Bracing his feet solidly on the floorboard, he lifted, shoved forward and retreated.

He held his breath, trying to hold on, wanting Rio to join him. When she opened her slumberous eyes, the battle he fought hung by a thread.

Her lips curved into a seductive smile. She shoved forward, tightened, panting. Lifting a mere inch, she glided smoothly down his cock, wriggled her lush ass, took more of him inside and rocked against him. Rocked again. He sucked in more air and released it. Shaking now, Bryce squeezed her small waist and pressed her down the last possible millimeter. His hand moved over her belly, his fingers grazed the bulging head of his cock, then shifted down to toy with her clit, pressing firmly to make contact, sensitive flesh to wet sensitive flesh. He smoothed her juices over the lips to her opening. When she lifted again, he delved his fingers toward the place he planned to pierce one day soon.

Drawing his fingers away when she lowered, he rubbed her nub against his cock.

"More. Much more." She purred a sensuous sound, a timbre like music to his ears, and he obliged with a delicate pinch and soothing caress.

"Do you know how long I've waited for this moment?"

"Christ." Surrender, a combustible release, struck the same second. "Come with me, Rio. Now, goddamn it!"

Clutching the steering wheel, he leaned forward and caught her lips in a possessive kiss. The horn went off. It quieted, but sounded each time his hips jackhammered. The blaring noise hardly stopped him, or Rio. She'd wrapped her arms around his neck, rocking hard and fast through the tumultuous climax, moaning, whimpering, constricting tighter than a vise around his cock. She squeezed out every drop of pleasure and still wanted more. He gave and she took—until he had none left to give, drained.

They had three days: three solid sex-filled days at their disposal.

Shuddering from the fierce orgasm, Bryce sort of laughed and said, "Woman, you're gonna kill me. Or we'll kill each other in these conditions." He found the power-seat button and moved the chair back.

She giggled, her breath hot against his ear. "Wonder what the neighbors are thinking? Burglar alarm?"

A thief could steal everything he owned at this point. Bryce didn't care as long as she was with him. In his arms. In his bed.

If they ever got there.

The overhead garage light went out, casting them into total darkness. Only their harsh breathing and the sound of their beating hearts broke the Escalade's eerie quiet. Yep, he could hear hers, thumping loudly, as he heard his own racing at breakneck speed.

He ran his hands up her back, massaging, soothing. She felt so good in his embrace and he kissed her earlobe, nibbled. He had yet to taste her honeyed nectar, but he knew he'd get the chance. Soon. But she wriggled, and his dick stirred to life. Hard. Again? She'd all but sucked him dry of life-giving . . . His jaw went slack.

Oh shit.

"We really have to get out of this car," Bryce said. She circled her hips. "Ah, hell, Rio. Don't do that."

"Do what?"

"That," he said and buried his face against her neck, hands sliding down her back, cupping her sweet ass.

He spread her cheeks apart, dipped his fingers toward the juncture where their bodies joined. Wetness. Slickness. She lifted and slid down slowly, bringing forth acute pleasure.

"Rio," he croaked.

"Hmm." She shifted again, angled differently, drove forward instead.

"I-I don't have a c-condom on."

Her body stilled for a mere second. She jerked away from his erection, left him in suspended torture and crawled back into the passenger seat, the musky scent of sex filling the air.

Rio clenched her teeth together. "This is just great. Just great. Do you always do this?" What if he was poking that serpent into every woman without protection?

"Do what?" he snapped. "You started it."

"Screw every woman that comes along without a condom. That's what."

"I always use a condom, and I don't screw every woman in sight."

He flicked the map light on. Aroused, the head of that bulging serpent was a beautiful, glistening masterpiece under any lighting, poised like a striking cobra. Unable to tuck it away, Bryce zipped his trousers partway and pulled his shirt free. The fabric did little more than shield his sex from view.

"Except, I don't know why I didn't with you, why it slipped my mind," he said quietly. He yanked the keys from the ignition and opened the car door. "You make me forget my own damn name."

Fault lay in her lap as well as his for allowing an unprotected encounter. "You owe me thirty bucks."

Bryce looked over his shoulder, frowning. "For what, a pregnancy test?"

Let's not even go there. "You've torn up two pair of my most expensive panties." Grinning, she caressed his cheek. "We're both at fault, but you still owe me."

"Tomorrow, I'll take you shopping at your favorite boutique, pick up enough lace to last a while."

She snatched her hand away. Shopping, as in public? As in together? "No big deal. Got plenty at home. I don't need them."

"You sure won't need any while you're here," he replied. His eyes twinkled like stars on a moonless night.

Here, hidden inside his house from prying eyes and tattlers spreading juicy gossip. For now, they had the cover of darkness. When time came to go home . . . No need to worry for the moment. The next seventy-two hours, give or take a few, were exclusively set behind locked doors and thick walls.

She followed Bryce into his house. Correction, his mansion. Three bedrooms, three and a half bathrooms, big office and all other essentials, he said, showing her around the first level. It had once contained a fourth bedroom and bath. Renovations.

"You have a basement, too?" Rio asked, incredulous. "Why so big? Who else lives here?"

"Lots of new and used computer equipment stored down there," Bryce replied proudly. "I live alone, needed the space."

"So you turned your home into a warehouse? Who cleans this place? When do they clean it?"

He looked crestfallen. "I clean."

She huffed under her breath. "Don't get me wrong. I'm not saying the house is filthy. It just needs—" Whatever she said now, she'd hurt his feelings more than she already had.

"What, a woman's touch?"

"A cleaning service. Janitorial. Male or female," she said and laughed, easing the sudden tension.

An embarrassed-looking smile curved his lips and his face changed shades.

"And somebody to get you organized." She glanced around the kitchen, stared into the dining room. "Sugar, do you eat out every day?" Papers, boxes, paraphernalia—all sorts of junk covered tables, chairs and the floor.

She wondered about his sleeping quarters, since they'd yet to go upstairs. She'd call a cab if it resembled the main level's disarray. Mice slept among papers and, so far, Bryce Sullivan represented the pack rats' sovereign leader. She cringed. What about the bathrooms?

"My work stays outside the master suite."

Lord, he'd read the pained expression on her face. She smiled brightly. However, his bedroom might be free of papers and equipment, but what about . . .

"Where's your laundry room? You do have a washer and dryer, yes?"

"The sheets are brand new, Rio," he said, hooking his thumbs into the belt loops of his trousers. "I bought a new bedroom set, delivered two days ago, and no one else has slept on the mattress. Only me."

Well, that was a relief. "How long have you lived here?"

He leaned back against the arched doorway dividing the kitchen from the dining room, rather, another collection area. "About six months."

King of pack rats. The Hoarder. Had the bathrooms ever been cleaned in all this time? Could he even find them?

She stepped over a stack of loose-leaf papers, braced her hand against the wall, sort of bent over and peered into what she thought was closet space. Powder room. She sniffed cautiously. The lingering aroma of disinfectant filled the air. Faucet shiny, mirror crystal clear, and the sink didn't have a smudge or stain.

"The upstairs looks nothing like this."

She jumped when his arms encircled her waist. He moved fast as a predatory cat, silently.

"Don't bend over like that if you know what's good for you," Bryce whispered in her ear.

She felt his hardness pressing insistently against her derriere and her next breath lodged in her throat. Mercy. Only fifteen minutes had gone by.

"You left me hanging. Remember?"

Oh, yes. Well hung—majestically. She rubbed her behind against him, felt the glorious swell as his arms tightened around her, lifting her from the floor.

Devon had confined their lovemaking to the usual man-above-woman-supine boring sex, the missionary mount. Pound until he came, ask if it was good, she always said yes and he slept. Nothing new; same old, same old once a week. Afterward, she'd shower to wash him off her body. No cuddling, no loving . . . zip for eleven long years. Then, he found someone else to bore.

No wonder women wanted a younger, more virile man, someone to make lovemaking exciting, enjoyable and worthwhile. Devon did provide her with one eye-opener she'd never regretted. She had a decent figure, and she'd gotten over the embarrassment of exposing her nakedness.

For some reason, just thinking of her ex-husband made her feel used and dirty. Rio wriggled and Bryce set her down. Turning in his arms, she laced her fingers through his sable hair, loving the silkiness, and said, "I want to shower first. Do you mind?"

"You'll like the master suite. Remodeled. Just don't take too long. Turn right at the top of the stairs. Straight ahead," Bryce said. A mischievous glimmer brightened his gray eyes. "Better run while you still can."

7

Rio passed between two huge closets dividing the bedroom from the bathroom. Both contained built-in mahogany dressers and ample shelving.

She unsnapped and kicked off her heels, then hung her dress on one of three dark brown, wooden hooks beside the door, amazed.

The entire area was spotlessly clean. Various shades of subtle blues, grays, camel and rich mahogany adorned this place, same as his cavernous bedroom. This room had the feel of a furnished, elegant spa. Towels and knickknacks filled an armoire. Raised, the Jacuzzi—flanked by an imposing etched-glass window surrounded with the same dark wood—was large enough to seat two people comfortably. The snail shower had space to waltz or jitterbug. Lovely carved sconces combined with recessed lighting brought two freestanding glass basins and slate-stone counter and floors to life.

While running her fingers over velvety towels, Rio wiggled her toes. Even the floor emitted the same warmth.

The glass-enclosed corner sported what must be a steam

room with generous seating. For his size, Bryce needed the space.

She stuck her finger into a pot brimming with ferns. Damp. Good. A variety of thriving, potted vegetation made for a tropical atmosphere.

Rio turned the dimmer switch, lowering the lights to an exotic feel. Paradise.

She, too, had radiant-floor heating, but it ran throughout her loft. Sure would be nice to have *all* the latest technology, but the old building, built in 1911, lacked good floor support for heavy-duty wares. She enjoyed its openness, the extravagance of a private elevator and the fact no one occupied the warehouse below.

Devon hadn't worked hard to rent the open space since renovations were costly. At least, that's what he'd said. She figured he hadn't wanted to share the investment profits with her. Fine, he'd continue losing cash, too.

She stepped inside the sunken shower, slate-tiled top to bottom, except for the thick Italian glass at the wide entrance. Nine stationary sprayer heads were attached to the walls, plus a coiled handheld device. Overhead hung a huge, round rain nozzle.

Bryce had hired an excellent luxury designer for renovations. A woman, probably, and he'd spared no expense. Where had his money come from, inheritance?

Rio turned on each sprayer to a comfortable setting at 100 degrees. The overhead nozzle showered her with the tingling warmth of a summer rainfall. She turned her face toward the ceiling. The refreshing downpour streamed down her body.

Closing her eyes, she knew Bryce had joined her. His hands glided over her skin, caressing, skimming the contours of her shoulders, her neck, into her hair. She inhaled the sweet fragrance of shampoo and bent her head forward while he massaged, working the liquid into a thick, foamy lather. He possessed better hands than the gay hairdresser who tended to her tresses weekly.

Leaning back against his hard chest, Rio moaned.

"You were taking too long," he whispered. His hands slid down her throat, to her breasts, cupping, lingering.

She purred, feeling the familiar swell against her backside. "I'm glad I did."

"You have nice—"

"Are you saying you're a breast man?"

"Nope. I like your hips. Like the way they move."

"Like this?" She rubbed sensuously against him, felt the memorable bulge thicken and realized her own juices had begun to steep.

"Just like that. But I like it better when I'm inside you."

"What are you waiting for?"

She started to turn, but he held her still. "Not yet."

On his knees now, while she leaned back against the cool slate, he lifted one foot, ran the washcloth over it and up her ankle. He kissed her toes, swirling his tongue over each one, and Rio squirmed with delight.

Continuing up her leg, he teased the juncture where it met the triangle of dark curls. He lowered her foot, then lifted the other and enacted another worshipful service that lasted too short a time. He dropped the washcloth and his fingers delved between her legs in a tormenting dance.

Rio closed her eyes and gave him better access. She tipped her head back to the shower water drenching her face and body. She wanted to feel him deep inside her, wanted the full thrust of his clever, talented fingers. But when his warm, rough tongue touched her most private possession, she tried to snap her legs together.

"Bryce, don't. I've never—"

He forced her leg over his shoulder and clamped her hips with both hands.

"Stop. Don't, please."

He devoured her. And she responded, hips undulating to his rhythmic thrusts. Her mind adamantly denied what she felt, but her body needed what he gave.

Dizzy, faint, the first shimmering sensation began way down deep. Bryce held her erect, held her in place when her leg gave way. He continued the sweet assault, driving her to the brink of delirium.

Rio latched onto his hair with all ten fingers, guiding him to that one special place needing his skilled tongue. "There," she murmured. "Right there."

Through the shadowy haze of ecstasy, she heard his command, the sexy, rumbling tone. "Now, Rio."

He bit gently at the little nub, licked his tongue inside her passage and teased her sensitivity again with a rougher nip. In a frenzied swell, the approaching climax broke free. Her hips bucked, shot forward. She nearly scalped him as wave after wave savagely washed through her senses. She couldn't speak, she couldn't scream, she couldn't force a sound from her throat.

She knew she'd died. Thought she'd died.

Weak and trembling as the fierce tremors receded, Rio lost her balance. Bryce drew her down the slippery slate, straddled her across his thighs and caressed her body with magical hands.

Rio managed to wrap her arms around his neck, pressing her cheek to his shoulder and sighed, sated. Relaxed and content.

He held her for what seemed a good long while, stroking her, whispering soothing words that eased her mind and soul. She'd lost her thoughts while he seduced her with his scandalous caresses. Under his onslaught and against her better judgment, she'd given him a little more of herself. Temporary insanity. That's it. That's all it was. She refused from this point on to give more.

"I'm taking you to bed," she heard him say.

So depleted, so worn out, she barely nodded and snuggled closer when he pressed a gentle kiss to her forehead.

Bed. Sleep. Exhausted, Rio closed her eyes.

* * *

As the arrival of dawn broke through the quiet of night, Bryce shifted in the new bed and pulled the sheet up their bodies. He'd let Rio sleep the last four hours while he snoozed off and on. And he'd failed to keep his libido in check, rock-hard during every waking moment.

Soft and smooth, her coppery skin was as flawless as a sunrise. He'd kept her close to his body, her sweet ass cuddling his cock, until he could sleep no longer. Each time she moved he ached a little more, ached to be inside her.

Toying with the blond curls at her neck, he traced the delicate curve of her ear and continued smoothing his hand down her lithe body. She'd slept through most of his ministrations, but twice she swatted his hand away when he touched the dark curls between her legs, seeking out the little protrusion he'd finally teased and tasted. He'd milked her of a woman's sweet nectar. He would taste her again and again, never getting enough of Rio Saunders.

Growing harder by the minute, he leaned over her, lazily rubbed his lips across her cheek, leaving a damp trail to her earlobe, where he nipped. When she smiled, his heart skipped two beats. The next ones pounded in rapid succession. She set him ablaze with a simple smile, a tender caress, a wanton look in her beautiful, bedroom eyes.

"Did I wake you?"

"You know darn well you did," she replied, yawning, stretching long and pampered-kitten sleek.

Kitten. He'd found the perfect nickname. His cuddly kitten.

Bryce drew her body closer to his, pressed his erection between the cleft of her buttocks. "I need you, kitten." When she purred, a lightning bolt charged through his loins.

Rolling Rio onto her back, he quickly covered her body with his own.

* * *

"Coffee?" Bryce asked.

She slept like the dead.

"Rio?"

He put the tray on the bedside table and sat beside her. She still didn't open her eyes, still soundless.

After making passionate love at dawn, Rio had curled up and passed out. At seven thirty, needing little sleep, he'd climbed out of the sack, put together a breakfast snack and brought it back to the bedroom. For her.

She still slept on her stomach, arms hugging a pillow.

"Wake up, kitten. You're missing the best part of the day." Was that a growl? "Rio?"

Definitely a menacing snarl this time. Kittens didn't make perilous sounds. Kittens purred and cuddled. This noise replicated a wounded panther threatening to strike with ten sharp talons, all at the same time.

"I brought coffee and—"

"Leave me alone."

Well, now. Guess the morning hours weren't her favorite any more than Angelina's.

Unsure if he should risk getting his eyes scratched from their sockets, Bryce smoothed her hair. She sneered and pulled the pillow over her head. With that wordless answer, he knew better than to take another chance. He took the tray back downstairs.

Glancing at the microwave's clock, Bryce clucked his tongue. Maureen should be at her desk working by now and he gave her a call.

"I'm not coming into the office today. Tomorrow, either, and probably not until sometime Wednesday," he said.

"I'll postpone your scheduled meetings. Anything I should know about?"

She was a nosy woman, but a great secretary. "Nope. Call if any problems crop up. And, Maureen, make sure you notify me about major issues only."

She ran down the list of impending crises. Minor headaches that could hold for a few more days, he told her. The only major migraine was the load of paper due for delivery sometime soon. They disconnected.

Bryce went from room to room. So, Rio thought he lived in a pigsty. He had to admit he owned and had a lot of possessions from the company. A lot of unnecessary material overloaded his house in every corner, everywhere.

Hell. He'd never find anything if he let someone else in here to help organize.

But Rio was right. He did need a warehouse or some sort of giant storage unit. The office floor space he rented for Thorobred was overflowing with equipment, boxes, catalogs and documentation as well. During the past year, employees had grumbled about the lack of space and he'd ignored their complaints. Square footage came at premium prices. He'd kept company overhead as low as possible.

Bryce scratched at a vague itch down the base of his neck, frowning, and went to his office.

Maybe it was time to expand. The latest five-year contract would cover excess storage expense, if he found the right location at the right price, and still would leave plenty of funds for Christmas bonuses, promotions, new hires, and the reinvestment his financial advisors suggested, which included Catherine's advice. Of course, he'd lose the tax write-off for storing goods at his home.

Catherine had claimed he was a tightwad, never squandering a dime on anything or anyone outside his business.

He'd scoffed at the insinuation. To prove it, he traded his beat-up Chevy for the Cadillac. Hurt like hell to drop seventy-five grand for simple transportation to and from work. However, he'd told Catherine that traveling up and down Colorado's mountain highways in ski weather would be safer, hauling equipment easier, and he'd thanked her for the insight.

She was unimpressed since he'd spent money on a SUV rather than on her. She'd hinted at a diamond. He invited her to his new house for a home-cooked meal instead. Thirty-two-year-old Catherine broke off their relationship after three winters of compatible lust. Unfazed, Bryce poured spaghetti sauce on everything he ate for the next week. His mother sent another batch of homemade sauce the following month.

The cell phone rang at the same moment the hand-me-down grandfather clock chimed. Never fails. As usual, it was time for the Sunday-morning conversation. Sighing, Bryce picked up the telephone.

"Good morning, Mother," he said dryly.

"Don't use that tone with me, young man. I gave you life."

"Good morning, Mother," he said more jubilantly. "How's the weather in New York?"

He did love her no matter how often Claudine Berardi actively attempted to run his and his sister's life—a two-thousand-mile-away determined woman who worked her damndest to outshine her close friends.

Let one club member send their child to a nursery, Claudine found a better one. Angelina had gone to four different nurseries before she entered kindergarten. When an ally enrolled their son or daughter in a college, Claudine found its rival. Bryce had attended Stanford. His sister had spent a year overseas. But when Angelina flunked out of school, Claudine faked a heart attack so friends believed her devoted daughter had left the university to nurse her ailing mother back to good health. No one could top that.

"Snow. Cold, ugly weather. My arthritis has started bothering me again."

"I'm sorry to hear that."

"No, you're not."

"Mother—"

"If you were sorry or worried, you'd be married already."

Claudine Berardi wanted a litter of grandchildren, since her partners had several to brag about at each social gathering.

"How's Pops?" What better time to change the subject?

"He's fine, the arrogant man. He left already to have lunch with his friends. Have you at least found a nice Italian girl?"

Bryce groaned. Persistent . . . "Mother, I refuse to—"

"Can she cook Italian? I can always give her my recipes or teach her how. She is single, isn't she? No children? Goodness, young women today jump in and out of marriage without concern for their families."

He couldn't get a word in.

"Maybe I should make arrangements to visit," she said quickly. Claudine never knew when to quit. "So I can meet her. What does Angelina think about your girlfriend? What is her name?"

"No, Mother, I am not seeing a good little Italian girl and I'm not marrying—"

"Okay, so she's not Italian. Have you and Catherine gotten back together? Can't cook at all, but she'll do. Don't wait too long, though. She's not getting any younger. Neither am I, Bryce. I want grandchildren and your sister doesn't seem to be in any hurry, either."

She'll do? He couldn't quite get past the statement. Bryce looked down at the cell phone. *She'll do?* He should hang up for that lousy comment. Except she'd call right back and start bitching. He put the phone back to his ear.

". . . the last I heard," Claudine had continued. "Have you met him?"

"Met who?" He lifted a pencil from the desk and tapped the eraser like a hammer smacking a nail head.

"Jason. Bryce Sullivan, aren't you listening to me?"

His hackles rose hearing the name. The pencil snapped in half. "What about him?"

"I've tried to get Angelina to bring him to New York."

Not a chance. "She's breaking it off."

"Since when? Last week she said she loved him. I was hoping they'd set a wedding date. I need good news for the women's club."

Bryce quietly snarled. "She doesn't know what she wants, but it's not him. She won't be marrying Jason Simmons, Mother."

Not if he had anything to do with it. Not in a thousand years. Angelina was Simmons's meal ticket. He worked nowhere else but at Killer Bods. Good tips or not, dancing couldn't possibly cover his living expenses or the cost of his new BMW. Bryce had the feeling that Angelina had paid for it, but she wouldn't admit to the atrocity.

"Maybe I should call her right now."

"Don't call this early, Mother. The club stays open late on weekends. Give her a chance to get some rest. You know, it's only a little after eight here." He should've shown Rio a little consideration instead of waking her so early.

"I'll give her another hour."

Sixty lousy minutes, but longer than he expected. He hoped Angelina had remembered to turn off her phone. Of course, she had. He'd quit trying to call her before noon long ago. "Tell Pops hello for me."

"All right, dear. I was serious about coming to visit. Right after Thanksgiving? The club is planning a dinner party to bring in the holiday."

A long pause passed while Bryce looked around his office. He'd better get this place in shape before she arrived, before she decided to tidy up. "Yeah, fine."

"What school did you attend?"

"Yes, Mother." She hated slang, and he hated hearing her complain. "Call me with the details."

"Good-bye, dear."

Bryce clicked off his cell phone and set it down. Short but not sweet. "Hell."

How the devil was he going to get this place in order before her arrival? By shovel and dump truck? Hire a crew? What a waste of money. But after walking through the main level again and checking the basement, seeing the mountains of stuff, he needed help.

Bryce scrubbed his face with both hands. First, he had to find a place to dump it. Maybe Rio had a few ideas. He'd put the question to her once she surfaced from dreamland. And what the hell time would that be? Noon?

This cleanup was necessary. He hated physical labor, except for working out at the gym, or hot-blooded sex. His dick stirred at the tantalizing thought of making love to Rio again.

He climbed the stairs two at a time, then stood in front of his closed bedroom door and listened. She was definitely in there. Naked. The urge was too much and he reached for the doorknob, but stopped himself. They still had plenty of time together. Only a few hours had gone by since he'd touched her last.

Man, get a grip on yourself. Get a grip on your dick.

He inhaled through his nostrils and let it out between his teeth, did it again.

Using the guest-room shower, Bryce took a cold one to tamp down the lust overpowering his brains.

He hustled downstairs to answer his cell's noisy summons. Probably Angelina calling to raise hell about their mother. He caught it before the system redirected it to voice mail.

"Hey, Boo."

"Wasn't that Angelina's nickname?"

Anger stormed through his body at lightning speed. "How did you get this number, Frankie?" Damn her.

"I do believe each and every one of your employees has it, just in case of—"

"Is this an emergency?"

"Well—"

"Good-bye, Frankie."

"You don't want to hang up on me, Bryce."

Like hell if he didn't, but the voice roaring in his head ordered him to listen. Or maybe to beware.

Physical labor increased his already-heightened agitation.

Minutes before noon, Bryce taped the seventeenth box. He scribbled a short list of contents on its outside and kicked the container toward the corner, where he'd stacked the others into rectangular mountains. Pissed, he kicked it again, put a hole in the side.

The last hour he had expected Rio to come downstairs. The last two hours he'd thought to go up there. The last three hours he'd gotten hornier than hell, thanks to Frankie and her erotic demands.

He'd told her absolutely not, no matter what she'd planned.

. . . *Remember how much we were into each other, fully and unconditionally? How we touched each other so delicately at first, before the frenzy? I used to love running my tongue up and down each and every throbbing vein of your cock, from base to pulsing tip . . . taking you into my mouth, sucking until you gushed all over me. Sometimes you'd fuck me so hard that I can still feel you inside me, wished you were shoving inside me even now. But what I loved most of all was that big cock gliding smoothly into my . . . The way your breathing pattern sounds, I might be able to change your mind-set, given the chance.*

He'd hung up on her and wiped away the sweat pouring down his face.

To keep her mouth shut, Frankie had expected him to dedicate one night each week to pleasure her as if he was her seventeen-year-old, private boy toy. Fat chance.

What the devil was Rio doing still asleep, wasting the day

away when he'd worked his ass off, worked his frame of mind into a sexual frenzy? Damn near six hours had gone by and he hadn't touched her.

She still slept upstairs in his bed, unaware, unthinking of his rampant erection. Each one of these boxes felt lighter than the massive entity hanging between his legs. Did she care? Hell, no. She still slept.

He kicked the box again, put a bigger hole in the side.

"I guess that helps. Next kick should put it through the window for a field goal."

He swung around. Rio stood barefoot in the doorway, dressed in one of his striped shirts. He knew she wore nothing beneath it. The lacy panties were history. From this distance, he imagined the smell of her sex and his nostrils flared.

"Problems?" she asked.

Hell, yeah. He'd had one huge problem for the last three 367 damned minutes while she'd slept nude in his bed without him, without considering his state of mind or the condition of his body.

"No."

Staring at her now caused his dick to thicken. Luckily, he'd dressed in a pair of sweatpants. If he'd worn trousers or jeans, by now they would've pinched the life out of him or scraped him raw.

"Really?" she said, stepping into the room. The French doors were pinned behind boxes, covered so no one could see her. "Looks like it to me. Lot of boxes here. No papers on the floor."

"Just been busy packing material."

"In that case, I'll get coffee. Want some?"

Coffee was the furthest thought from his mind. The way his hands shook, he'd spill it. Besides, he wanted to get his hands on her. "I'll pass."

Inhaling deeply, he realized she'd showered, smelled clean, inviting. Edible.

She looked over her shoulder and said, "I thought you didn't want any."

"I don't."

"Then why are you following me?"

"To show you where it is."

"Tell me. I don't want to keep you from working."

"Fridge."

When she stepped over a stack of papers by the arched doorway, the shirt rose nearly high enough to see where her legs met at the crack of her ass. Bryce snarled. She didn't care about his hard-on. She only cared about the damn coffee.

Rio opened the refrigerator door and when she started to bend over, Bryce spun her around. The coffee can slipped from her hands, clattered noisily to the floor, making a mess at their feet. He snatched her up, slammed the refrigerator's stainless-steel door shut, pressed her against its cool surface, and claimed her lips with a needy kiss.

"You do have a problem." Rio rubbed against his hardness, cuddling the length with both legs. Changing positions, she wrapped her luscious limbs around his waist.

She knew exactly what she'd done. Teasing wench. In his current condition—a frenzy he'd lost control of now—Bryce hated teasing as much as he hated physical labor, and the fight with his sweatpants redoubled his drive.

"Easy, baby. I'm not going anywhere," she said, cupping his face with both hands. "Go—"

Blinded by need, shoving inside her tight passage on one demanding thrust, he claimed her mouth before the scream left her throat.

Fully embedded, he bent his knees and came up hard again. She pulled his hair and wrenched her lips away from his. Nothing could stop him from surging a third time.

"Condom," she panted. "Condom."

Oh shit. God, he didn't want to leave her cocoon. Not yet. "Okay, okay. Condom."

He swung her around, still rooted inside her body like a steel post while she clung to him.

She climaxed before they reached the first landing midway up the stairs, whimpering and tightening her arms around his neck. He knew she would. She always had multiple orgasms.

He made his way up the final steps on shaky legs, wondering why he'd bought a damn two-story house. Bryce all but collapsed onto the bed with Rio sprawled across his hips. He searched through the bedside table, finally found a foil package. The last one. Jesus, he needed to make a trip to the drugstore. Later.

"French tickler?" Rio asked incredulously.

Heat raced from his chest to the top of his head. Catherine had bought several styles during one of her freaky moments. He'd packed it with everything else from his old apartment. "Does it matter? It's the last one."

"It just might." Climbing off his rock-hard dick, she left it bouncing against his belly and crawled to the opposite side of the bed.

"What difference does it make? It's a condom." Christ, he really needed to get back inside her. Bryce reached for her leg. He missed.

"Who bought it? You?"

Ah, hell.

"Truthfully. Do you buy ticklers?"

Crap. One day the truth might bite him in the ass for lying. Then again, Rio might not let him touch her, knowing the truth. The damn condom was unsealed, untouched and had sat inside the drawer with the ones he'd used earlier this morning. She didn't ask any questions at the time. Didn't seem to care, either, or she didn't see them in the dark.

"No," Bryce said.

Rio stared back, hazel eyes as sharp as a cat's.

"They've been here for months." He reached for her leg, but she scooted farther away.

Rio stayed mute, jaw clenched, eyes glittering jewels.

"I haven't slept with anyone other than you since moving into this house. Six months." That should ease her mind, knowing he hadn't slept around. He'd kept his zipper up, his cock confined, his libido in a state of ill discontent. Because of Thorobred.

"I don't believe you."

Shit. He'd spilled his guts, told the truth and she didn't believe a blessed word of it. All right, Bryce thought, scratching at his brow. "When's the last time you slept with somebody other than me?"

"That's irrelevant." She slid off the bed, got to her feet.

"Bullshit," he snapped and his cock deflated like a punctured tire.

Raging jealousy quickly replaced agitation. He should've known better than to ask, but he had expected an honest answer.

Bryce shot off the bed like a missile, sweatpants looped round his ankles. He kicked them off his feet and started around the furniture. For what, he had no idea, except to get the truth. Had she been sleeping around? With Cockroach, other dancers, her fifties man?

She attempted to walk on water across the bed, but not in time. He dove, caught her and dragged her across the mattress' satin sheets. Damned if he'd let her dodge this question, not when he'd opened the gates to his celibate life.

She slapped him, tagged him good and hard. He hadn't been slapped in . . . Hell, no woman had ever slapped him. It stung like a son of bitch.

Bryce caught her wrists and yanked her arms over her head, but she fought harder than he thought any woman could, squirming and kicking. Nestled between her legs, each struggling movement dragged the shirt higher, to her waist, to her naked breasts, until their bodies pressed intimately together. Skin against skin, slick with hot sweat.

His cock jumped bone-hard.

8

Rio's eyes closed the moment he took siege of her body. Slowly, smoothly insistent, he retreated, only to fill her again, lifting her from the bed.

"Bastard," she muttered as her legs clamped around his waist, drawing him deeper inside her body.

Feeling her first tremor, Bryce released her wrists. A quick jolt and he smiled. She always had multiple orgasms. Multiple teasing ones, but the last took them for a long, hard ride.

This time he planned a different journey, one he hoped she would enjoy as much as he would. As he witdrew from her soaking heat, she protested, but he rolled Rio to her stomach, dragged her hips up, balancing her on hands and knees. He stretched her thighs apart with his bulky legs.

Without preamble, he thrust slowly, carefully, but full length into her cocoon again in one, long surge.

She gasped, arms crumpling.

He held her up, cupping her breast with one hand, her hip with his free one, and maintained her balance, steadied her. Spread like this, he had full control over her, all control, and he massaged her sweet ass.

"Rio?" He drew back, watched her liquid fire leave a damp trail on his thick cock, watched the bulging head become visible, and shoved forward again.

A second gasp.

"Talk to me."

She whimpered.

Sliding one hand around her body, he fondled her protrusion, knowing the sensitivity she now felt. As her head lifted, an agonizing groan tore from her throat.

Bryce cupped her behind with both hands, spread her wider and withdrew completely. He wanted more and rubbed his engorged length along her back, over her ass, touched the tip to the opening forbidden to some.

"I want to make love to you everywhere. Will you let me?"

"I want you back inside me," she said on a ragged pant.

"Where?" He teased her sensitive nub with his fingers while holding himself in one hand, squeezing, stroking, and pressed the swollen head against her damp flesh. "Where, Rio?"

Only her heavy breathing filled the room's quiet as he guided his cock to the place he wanted to penetrate.

"Answer me."

"Not there," she whispered. "No."

He could easily surge forward with a languid thrust. Take what he wanted, and give her pleasure as well. "One day?" he asked, disappointed. "Will you let me one day?"

"I—" He heard an audible swallow. "I don't know."

He touched her with his fingers, spread her slick opening apart and bent down to lick his tongue over her sweetness, tasting her dripping nectar.

"No. I want you inside. All of you." Desperation threaded her tone.

Straightening, he wrapped his hand around his cock again, stroked, stroked again, watched the bulging head inflate, veins pulsing, and guided himself to her opening. He probed, tested, gave a little and took away. Teasing retaliation.

"Now, damn you." Impatience. Need. Urgency.

"Not yet." And revenge for denying him the savage pleasure he'd wanted them both to share, but he was on the verge of bursting.

Bryce pushed inside her a mere inch and when he began to withdraw, Rio thrust backward, engulfing him, tightening, stripped his last bit of willpower.

Arms wrapped around her waist, he dragged her from the bed and onto his thighs, back flush against his chest. He tormented her nub with his fingers, squeezing, pressing, and skimming his own hot, wet length, adding pleasure to his already whetted appetite.

She went up on her knees and sank, plunged, and lifted again.

Bryce cupped her breasts and found the cumbersome shirt prevented full access. He wrenched the fabric between his fingers. The buttons scattered in every direction.

Panting, still rising and falling, Rio asked, "Do you own stock in a clothing store?"

"Damn the clothes. You wore one thread too many."

He kneaded her breasts, worked her nipples while she rode him, rode hard, taking the lead, blurring his vision and driving him to the greedy brink of insanity with every sleek sensation. Like a predatory king, he growled a conqueror's victory and clamped teeth into the tendon between her shoulder and neck.

Arching her back, she reached around with one hand and threaded her fingers into his hair, purring acceptance, moaning, and bearing down. Harder. Faster. Bludgeoning speed with scorching electric friction stimulated each nerve ending of his body as he thrust upward, lifting her from the bed reaching for . . .

Reaching. And together they caught their comet.

He roared, truly roared, and his body shook with the violence of a major earthquake with every passing moment while she viciously clamped around him. And he poured into her, draining the very best of his soul. For the first time, Bryce gave it all. Gave Rio everything he had and more.

When the last tremor ceased, she slumped against him, arms dangling to her sides, still perched and suspended on his throbbing length, panting.

He nuzzled her ear, tightened his arms around her body, and lowered unsteadily back onto his heels.

Rio finally came to her senses. "Darn it, Bryce."

"W-What?" He kissed a path down her neck to her shoulder. "I didn't do this intentionally."

"Do what?"

"This," he said and kissed a spot he knew would be tender. She shied away. "Bite mark."

"Ah, for God's— You bit me?"

"Didn't you feel it?" He forced a laugh. "I almost took a big chunk. Could be worse, but no giant hickey and I didn't break the skin."

"You didn't use your French tickler in the meantime, darn you." If she'd had a foul mouth like Galaxeé, she'd curse a string of filth. "You have to go to the drugstore. Now. I need douche." She looked over her shoulder. "Or do you already have a supply?" How else could she mask jealousy?

"That's enough, Rio. I've told you the truth. You, however, have yet to come clean with me."

"There's no time for explanations. You have to—"

"Not until you answer the question."

She tried to crawl off his body, but he held her in place, fingers flexing into skin. Had she tripped another spasm from him? Seemed like it. His hands vibrated against her skin.

"Answer me."

"You'll go to the store first."

"You'll answer me first."

What could she do? Douche wasn't essential, but he wanted answers. She had no car, no keys, no purse. No money.

"Fine," she snapped.

She hated admitting how much time had passed since she'd had sex. Some men would claim frigidity kept her legs locked together. She just hadn't found any man worth . . . She wasn't desperate. Until now. Until Bryce had touched her.

"Three years. Satisfied? Will you go to the drugstore, please?"

Lifting her, he gently set Rio on the bed and turned her to face him. "Did I hurt you?" he asked quietly, cupping her chin. "Did I, even before? I never meant to hurt you."

Surprised at his concern, she clasped his hand and drew it down to her heart, held it there, watching his Adam's apple bob up and down as much as his hand trembled.

"No, I'm fine."

"Sure?"

She smiled. "Once you go to the store."

He looked so relieved after a shaky breath. "Anything else you need while I'm there? You'll have to write it down. I've never bought that kind of stuff before. Jesus." His face looked truly pained, colored a pretty crimson.

"Buy a supply and you won't have do it again for a while. At least," she added, "not for me."

He pinched her butt.

While he ran through the shower, then dressed, Rio sat on the edge of the bed and wrote a short list, including groceries they'd need. She planned to cook for him.

"How does lasagna sound to you?"

"Love it, but I thought we'd go out for dinner," Bryce said, pulling up his jeans. Naked beneath the denim, he left the low-riders unbuttoned, displaying perfect abs pronounced by dark hair.

She liked watching him dress, loved seeing his lean muscles flex, relax. When he turned toward the closet, she realized just how broad his shoulders and back were in comparison to Devon's physique. Bryce strode back out, tucking in a tan knit pullover that clung to his big arms. Clung tightly, as much as his jeans clung to the serpent. Rio swallowed before she drooled.

"Let's go to a classy restaurant tonight."

Dragging her gaze back to his face, she shook her head. "I don't have clothes, remember?"

"Then I'll take you shopping, buy whatever you need."

"Just buy the food, Bryce. It's easier. I don't mind cooking," she replied and screwed up her face. "Well, do you have pots and pans?"

"Of course," he said and laughed a rich, deep sound. "But I want to take you out. Call me selfish. I'd rather you spend all your time with me than in the kitchen cooking."

"It's no big deal to bake in an oven."

"Tomorrow, then?"

"We'll see."

He leaned down and kissed her, harder when her arms went around his neck, fingers latching into his hair as she arched toward him. Bryce growled into her mouth, pushed her back onto the bed and climbed aboard, straddling her naked hips. He thrust against her pelvis in a delicious motion, moved in a sensual rhythm like he danced onstage, like he danced sensuously inside her.

But Rio recognized the intent of his second deep rumble and tore her mouth free of his on a chuckle. "Well, that sure was easy. Store. Remember?"

At her practical demand, he didn't look happy. His breathing sounded ragged. "I won't be long."

When he tried to kiss her again, she shoved at his hard chest. "Go. Now."

"In a—"

"Now."

He hurried out of the room.

Good Lord. He kept a perpetual hard-on, and if she got

pregnant . . . she couldn't. Impossible. Her periods were too erratic, and all those years with Devon were unproductive.

Besides, I'm too old for this kind of worry, and much too old to be seen in public hanging on a little boy's arm. Wouldn't be in this predicament if Galaxeé had kept her mouth shut.

Rio huffed. *Yeah, blame it on someone else, silly. Who forced you into having sex with him?*

Biting her lip, she climbed off the bed and hobbled into the bathroom. She hurt again, ached. The best ache ever, too. For a guy so young, he knew exactly how to turn her out, have her losing control, have her screaming for more. Lord, she really needed to stop screeching louder than a siren during climaxes or the poor baby'd go deaf. She wiggled the tip of her finger in her ear, wondering if she'd already lost partial hearing from the man's blaring roars.

Funny, making love to . . . correction . . . screwing Devon had always been a quiet session. After one year of boring sex, she couldn't bust one. She'd faked it to make him happy, faked it to get him off her body.

Making love with Bryce made her want him even more.

Sighing and leaning toward the mirror, Rio tilted her head to one side and squinted. He did bite. Left his mark on her like a punch card.

"What took you so long?" Rio asked, sounding irritable. She peeked inside the grocery bags. "I thought you were buying from the list. What is all this stuff? Why did you buy these giant cans and jars? Jalapenos? Mayonnaise? Mustard? Bryce, are you planning a picnic for an army? It's wintertime. Why buy five loaves of bread?"

He had to hide that feminine crap somehow. Two guys from the gym had showed up when he was guiding the pushcart down the bread aisle on his way to the cashier. They'd followed him, chatting. He couldn't continue wandering the store, thinking he'd lose them, when they'd stuck with him like glue.

At the cashier stations, the bodybuilders had opted to take the express line and waited for him at the automatic doors. Bryce couldn't decide which would embarrass him more, a male or female cashier. He finally ran the groceries through the self-service checkout, loading it all in brown paper bags. So nervous, his ears burned when he'd dropped Rio's *stuff* on the floor.

"Sale," he said. "Everything was marked down. Thought I might need it. Party sounds good."

"Bread goes stale in a couple days and you have nowhere to hold a party here. Where's my douche?"

"It's somewhere."

She looked up at him and grinned. "Your face is red."

"Cold outside."

"Bull." Rio burst out laughing. "I should've had you buy a big box of Kotex."

Appalled, Bryce said, "Like hell. I gotta get the rest out of the car."

"There's more?"

He heard her laughter from the garage. Women.

The grocery bill had mounted to a whopping $163 and change. He'd cursed a nasty streak when he left the supermarket's parking lot, cursed more when he had to double back to the drugstore to buy condoms. Plain ones, every one they had on hand. He'd need them.

After dragging the last four sacks from the backseat, he shoved the SUV's door shut with his hip.

"Your cell's ringing," Rio said from the doorway, waving the unit in her hand.

How in the hell did he miss seeing her stunning legs, wearing another of his shirts? Naked underneath. "Answer it," he replied, mesmerized. Shit, he was horny again.

"Not a chance, buster." The cell rang again. "I'd rather carry groceries."

Bryce blinked. Did he just tell her to answer his phone? Sure as hell, Maureen was calling about some minor incident she thought was a major blowup. But he did not want the Gossip Queen hearing Rio's voice. "All right. All right, I'll get it." Or it was Frankie, damn it.

He hurried inside, set the bags on the counter and answered the fifth ring in his usual business tone.

"Hi, stranger."

Oh, shit. Automatically, Bryce looked over at Rio. She unloaded groceries, shaking her head, setting food on the counter. "What's up?" Balancing the phone between his shoulder and ear, he picked up the big can of jalapenos, spun it in his hands while he walked toward the pantry.

"Haven't talked to you in awhile," Catherine replied. A long, breathy sigh came through the phone.

The Drama Princess. What now, a broken fingernail and her manicurist played hooky for the day? Or her puffball poodle had a temperature and too-dry nose? Someone scuff her new Kenneth Cole spike heels? She had a fetish about brand-name anything, wasting her money, not his, but she'd tried hard to dip into his bank account—unsuccessfully.

He really didn't want to hear whatever was going on in Catherine's life and looked over his shoulder. Not with Rio half-naked in his kitchen, on tiptoe, reaching toward an upper cabinet, shirttail sliding up those long, long legs.

"I miss you, Bryce. I miss being with you."

Stunned into silence, he fumbled the can.

"Can I come by this evening? Maybe have a few drinks while we reminisce?"

The can hit the floor, which brought Rio's head around.

While she was distracted, Bryce said, "No can do. I'm busy."

"Tomorrow?"

"Busy then, too."

"When?"

He looked right into Rio's glittering cat eyes. "Look, um, I'm tied up right now. I'll touch base with you later."

"When?"

Hell, she was as persistent as her poodle. "Later," he emphasized and clicked off the phone.

Trouble. Much trouble. Catherine, a *ten* brunette, had a body worth killing for and a bizarre sexual nature most men had wet dreams about. He sure as hell had. For three long years, they'd burnt up sheets. Sex with Catherine was unique, kinky as hell. She was into it all—bondage, domination, spankings, you name it. He had obliged, to a degree.

Sex with her, or anybody, just wasn't enough to tie a freakin' knot. Not a woman out there could force him into the ball-and-chain action. Bed partners. Lovers even. He might get pussy-whipped, but there'd be no gold ring dangling from his nose, and nobody's diamond engagement carats would ever debit his checking account.

"I won't ask what that was about," Rio said, breaking into his thoughts. "Where do these go?" She held up the giant container of whole dill pickles.

How weird was that? If Catherine had been in the same position, she would've started a fight, wondering who was on the phone, while he was *on* the phone. "I'll put the rest away."

"Fine. I have some business of my own to take care of."

Bryce watched her hightail up the stairs, a little shell-shocked by Rio's couldn't-care-less attitude. For some reason, he'd wanted her to show concern, a taste of jealousy, if only just a little bit.

All afternoon Rio had refused to have sex with him. She'd made him work, hard physical labor, and she'd worked him half to death.

The living and dining rooms looked like . . . a living and dining room. Not only had he boxed the papers, catalogs and
equipment, Bryce had taken it all to the garage, stacked neat
piles in the third stall.

"You have to vacuum," Rio said. She wiped her hands on a
dish towel.

"I'm not vacuuming right now," he said, irritably. "Need a
shower."

"Whatever. Dinner will be ready when you're done with the
carpeting." She started back into the kitchen.

Bryce yanked the closet door open, grumbling.

"What was that? Did you say something?"

"I said I'd do the goddamn vacuuming, but I'm not doing
any more fucking work tonight."

"Ooh, temper."

Yeah, he had a damn temper. A hot one.

She'd pranced around the house in a goddamn thin T-shirt,
showing every curve of her breasts and perky nipples right
down to the snatch between her legs, teasing the shit out of
him. She wouldn't let him touch her. Hell, yes, he had a temper.
With an unbelievable hard-on.

He should call Catherine. She'd take care of him in a split
second. Take him a half hour to get to her apartment and back,
wouldn't even have to take his clothes off. She had a delectable
mouth that worked wonders in a pinch.

Bryce plugged in the vacuum cleaner. This labor took twenty
more minutes of his valuable time while his temper raged on.
When he finished, he shoved the cleaner back into the closet
and slammed the door.

"Is there any furniture left?" Rio asked. "Or is it in sham-
bles?"

Ignoring the sarcasm, he took the stairs two at a time,
straight to the shower. He stripped out of his clothes, left them
on the floor and turned every showerhead on full blast, pip-
ing hot.

Damn her. I'm kicking her ass out, calling Catherine.

He poured shampoo into his hand, scrubbed his scalp viciously, then stood under the rain head while the suds streamed down his body and swirled into the drain.

Frigging games. I don't need it. Besides, I've already conquered and fucked her. It's time to initiate step four, move in for the kill. It's so freakin' easy to leave 'em.

He soaped his face and body to wash the scent of that teasing bitch away and rinsed.

Damn it, he could still smell her, still smelled her intoxicating scent and his nostrils flared wide open. Bryce turned up the cold tap and shut down the hot.

Maybe she had pushed a little too far. He deserved it after talking to some tramp while she stood there listening to the one-sided conversation. She knew darn well it was a woman, just by the look on his face.

"I'll touch base with you later," Rio mimicked.

She slapped the towel onto the counter and marched around the center island to the staircase, prepared to tell him off, tell him to take her back to her car.

Flustered, she went back to the kitchen. First, she didn't want to come here, now she didn't want to leave. Make up your mind.

Rio bit her lip. From the look on his face, an angry sneer, he was going to make her leave, rudely call her a taxi as soon as he finished doing whatever he was doing upstairs. Showering probably. Dressing. He planned to go to his waiting hussy.

What could she do to make him stay home, to let her stay the planned three days? There had to be a way.

Bryce strode down the stairs, fully dressed, feeling a little more composed. His cock was still running at half-mast, but that was to be expected. Rio's natural, sweet-smelling scent was everywhere.

He went into the kitchen and the sight brought him up short. She sat on the counter without a stitch on, legs crossed, arms braced behind her, breasts thrust forward in all her beautiful glory.

"Close your mouth. You're not going anywhere. Not out of this house and definitely not to see some heifer while I'm here."

Heifer? He swaggered toward her, eyes traveling up and down her body, fighting the urge to strip off his clothes.

They locked gazes. While he held hers, he skimmed his fingers over the top of her foot, up her leg to her knee. When they reached so very close to the juncture of her thighs, she uncrossed her legs, parted them a mere inch or two, enough to entice him. His peripheral vision was as excellent as holding her gaze in a stare down.

Bryce ignored the invitation, though it was damned difficult. Unnerving. Unsteadily, he traced the curve of her hip and she shifted. She wrapped her fingers around the granite countertop's beveled edge. Her hands were just as unsteady.

Circling to the back of the small island behind her, he leaned against the counter, laced his fingers into a single white-knuckled fist. She'd teased him today, tortured him. Sitting so provocatively on his kitchen counter, she tormented him now.

"What are you doing?" Rio asked.

"Contemplating."

Her back straightened. "Contemplating what?"

He let the question hang and tapped his fingers on the counter, watching the muscles in her shapely back tighten.

Silently, catlike, Bryce stepped around the island. She sounded testy, almost angry. Almost as angry as he had been earlier in his hours of need.

Rio darted a quick look over her shoulder, then shifted again. "Well?"

She was anxious. Impatient.

When he licked a long hot path from the cleft between her butt cheeks up her spine, Rio squirmed and started to turn, wanting Bryce to hold her before she lost the battle fighting inside her body.

"Don't move," he ordered in that deep, deep rumbling voice.

God, she climaxed and gripped the edge of the counter, squeezing her eyes shut, trying to contain it and the whimper threatening to leave her throat. But she could not, would not let him get the best of her. Shuddering, she lifted her chin and opened her eyes, stared straight into a pair of piercing grays.

"Again," he said in the same deep tone that caressed her inside out.

He knew. Darn him. "I . . . no . . . I can't," she replied, still panting. "Not without you."

His gaze dropped to her breasts, slowly lifted to her eyes again. She felt the same caressing, the same burning sensation inside from his hot gaze.

"You will."

The simple statement marched a litany of tremors from nerve to skittish nerve.

"Or you'll sit there until you do. You're not allowed to touch me until you bust another one."

"What?" she snapped.

"If you put one finger on me, Rio, you won't get this big dick you need so badly. Simple as that." With a smile on his face, he'd said the words so pleasantly. Then, the grin slowly faded. "I'll leave you hanging."

He brushed his fingertips lightly over her nipple, drew a tiny circle, and she felt her breasts swell, felt a renewed quivering at the center of her core.

"This is not funny. It's imma—"

"Now, Rio."

"No."

When he stepped back, she grabbed his shirtfront. "We're done here," Bryce said and pulled her hands free.

He planned to walk away, leave her hanging in worse condition than she'd left him. "Don't. Don't do this," Rio said, desperate now. How could he leave her and walk away so easily?

"You'll keep your hands to yourself and follow my instructions?" He released her wrists. "If not—"

"And if I don't? I can outlast you." A standoff. She could do this. Couldn't she?

She looked down at his pants. Bulging, straining against his trousers. Of course, she could beat him at his own silly game. He wanted her as much as she wanted him. She could hold him at bay longer than he could outlast her.

"I can easily walk out the door, get into my ride and get all I need in—"

"Forget you," she snapped as venomously as a spitting cobra. "Bastard. What's good for the gander is even better for the goose. Go find your little tramp. I'll find a grown-up man—"

He pinned her flat on the counter, moved so fast she didn't get the chance to bat an eyelash, catch her breath or snap her legs closed.

9

Apparently, she'd made the wrong comment, suggesting Bryce had a few years yet to adulthood.

From the savage glittering in his eyes and the hard set of his jaw, Rio thought he would strangle her. Or snap her neck in two. His face was so close to hers she smelled the breath mint, the heat from his harsh pant scorching.

Raw fear skated across her nerves.

She didn't really know Bryce, or know what he was capable of doing. He was strong, more powerful than anyone she knew. But she had strength, too, just not enough to win when she chose to fight back. She would not go down easily, wrists clamped above her head or not.

However, spending one day alone with him, seeing his concern this morning, surely he wouldn't hurt her. Would he?

"Do it. Just once," he said through clenched teeth. His tone had slipped an octave if that were possible for a bass. "I'll take a leather strap and burn your ass but good. We'll see if you'll want to look at another man."

A loud chorus of warning bells went off in her head. Had

she heard him correctly? A strap? Her parents had never spanked her. "Excuse me?"

Here she thought he was angry because she'd all but called him a child and, to her surprise, he was jealous, because she'd threatened to sleep with another man. He didn't own her.

"Try it. See if I don't."

After he'd almost walked out, straight to his waiting hussy? "You've got your damn nerve, buster." She wrenched her left hand free, drew it back, ready to slap him silly. "You were leaving."

He caught her wrist in mid-swing. Then he kissed her, his tongue thrusting down her throat.

Startled, Rio didn't know whether to close her eyes and enjoy his savage thrusts or snatch him bald.

She closed her eyes, gave in to the matching movements of his hips, his erection grinding against her. Scratchy, the trousers heightened the acute sensation shooting from the tip of her throbbing nub, spiraling all the way up to the roots of her hair, teasing every atom in the process.

Oh my God.

She felt the first climax rising from deep within. Her legs automatically bent at the knees, feet planted firmly on the counter, and she lifted, straining toward him.

He broke away from the kiss, looked down into her eyes, a knowing smile on his darkly handsome face.

She squeaked out a groan. "No. I won't." Not before him. Absolutely not.

He used fail-proof encouragement, fingers slipping inside her tightness, thrusting gently, teasing and tormenting her sensitivity. And, oh, so very deep, taking her to the next ravaging level.

She fought back the urge to climax, nearly bit through her bottom lip, but she endured the devastating pressure building with blinding speed.

The sound of his zipper shook her to the core. The intense heat of his arousal sent a surge of electric currents racing through her body. The penetrating pleasure all but took her breath away. Her legs spread bonelessly wider and her eyes rolled back. Acceptance, but not complete surrender.

"Long before me," he said quietly in a tone she had trouble ignoring now.

He moved so slowly, excruciatingly slow and easy, saturating her senses with long, languorous strokes. Rio whimpered and laced her fingers in his hair. Lifting her hips, she met him, tightened around his hard length. Lowering her body, *she* set a rhythm he would follow.

He shoved harder, held her in place, retreated, each plunge more powerful, his growl, deep, rumbling. Oh, yes, Rio recognized the sound, and she kept her wits together, knowing he balanced on the edge of no return.

Lift.

Tighten.

Lower. Release.

Concentrate. He will lose.

Another growl, more feral this time. She picked up the pace, concentrating.

Do not feel. Lift.

He shoved his arms under her thighs.

Tighten. Tighten. Oh, no. She panted, fought against the rising pressure on the brink of erupting.

"No," Bryce whispered fiercely, pistoning now. His hands shook and branding fingers sank into her waist.

"No," he reconfirmed. And he withdrew completely, only to plow back inside her with breathtaking force that nearly ripped her in two.

Rio squeezed her eyes shut, dug her fingers into his arms, but she would not scream, would not make a sound.

He stiffened, then jerked violently, and toppled forward,

burying his face against her throat, muffling a bellow as his arms went around her. Bryce convulsed hugely, breathing harsh and uneven.

Rio embraced him, held him tightly and stroked his back while he climaxed with the pressure of a rampant hose released of stress. She felt every heated drop, every milligram he'd held in check all day, shamed knowing how much he'd wanted to make love to her when she'd contemptuously denied him one simple caress.

She'd beaten him at his own game, won righteously, but she didn't feel at all like celebrating when the man in her arms continued trembling violently.

"This is really good," Bryce said.

They were the first words he'd spoken since, but he couldn't force himself to look into her eyes. For two hours, while she put together a tantalizing meal—the aroma had his mouth watering—he'd worked on the basement mess to avoid the inevitable.

"I didn't think anybody made lasagna as well as my mother's."

"Glad you like it. *My* mother's recipe," Rio replied. "You selected an excellent complementing wine."

He saw her fingers curve around the stem of her wineglass, watched it rise to her lips. Her eyes were closed as she rolled the Cabernet over her tongue, swallowed, licked away the residue left behind.

Bryce looked away. He shoveled a heaping amount of food onto his fork. He'd devoured the mixed-green salad when Rio declined a second helping and was working on the hot, garlic bread and lasagna.

She'd set the table, covered it with an old lace tablecloth his grandmother had crocheted long ago. Two fat, red candles flickered brilliantly on saucers. Adding atmosphere, she'd replaced a silk plant in a worn-out plant basket and draped a red-checkered towel that held hot bread. The simple setting had the flair of Italian appeal. His mother would approve.

"More lasagna?" she asked.

Bryce looked down at his plate. Empty. When had he swallowed the last bite? Hell, yes, he wanted more and nodded. She cut another huge square and levered it onto his plate. Until now, good home-cooked meals happened only when he flew to New York or his mother visited Denver. Thinking of . . .

He finally met Rio's satisfied gaze. "I guess I'm in need of a storage place to rent. Got any ideas? Not huge, just one floor. Somewhere downtown would work best."

Rio coughed into her napkin, cleared her throat. "I have no idea."

"You haven't noticed any rental signs near Killer's or anywhere in the surrounding area?"

She had the biggest hazel eyes Bryce had ever seen, the kind a man could drown in, forget to come up for air. He really wanted to submerge in their magnificent depths, but after his stupid antics, touching her again would take a genuine stroke of luck.

He'd hurt her today, saw it on her face when he'd plunged into oblivion and lost sight of reality. He'd heard the whimper she'd tried to conceal, felt her body jerk in his arms, her nails raking down his back. He'd hurt her badly after saying he never would.

He looked down at his plate, hiding the shame and embarrassment, praying his face lacked a blush fit for a fire engine. And he had yet to apologize. He planned to, once he found the nerve, knowing Rio waited to hear it while she hid behind a congenial façade, waiting for the right moment to tell him to kiss off and take her home—that she never wanted to see his silly mug again. Immature brutes, animals and uncouth youngsters had no place in her life.

"Not a one," Rio said. "Why not try a storage locker?"

"Size. I need more space than a locker has to offer, and a place close to work."

She sipped on the wine. "Did my cooking give you heartburn?"

"No," Bryce said and frowned, lowering his hand to his lap.

Did losing a lover cause an aching pain? A sharp one had sliced through his chest as the grim thoughts penetrated his mind. Why hadn't he gotten this twinge when Catherine walked out of their relationship? He hadn't felt anything so brutal, and damn, this pain hurt like hell.

Watching Rio's tongue glide across her smiling lips, he really wanted to reach out and feel the smoothness, touch her one more time before she tossed him away like trash. "It'll never happen. I mean, you're an excellent cook."

When he fell silent, she smiled and got up from the table. "Thank you."

Bryce picked at the remains of his food. He watched Rio clear away her dinnerware, moving about his kitchen as if she belonged in his household. A short-lived stay. Within the hour, she was sure to exact revenge and call a cab.

Gathering his nerve, he swallowed and said, "I'm . . . um—"

The nagging pain stretched its gangly neck again, noose tight and secure. Jesus. This had to be worse than a damn heart attack.

Rio spun around, wiping her hands with kitchen towel. "Did you say something?"

He swallowed a half dozen times, but the pain twisted tighter than drying rope. "I'm sorry about what happened earlier. I never meant to hurt you, physically or mentally."

He stared down at his lap, waiting for her to blister his ego, waiting for his heart to splinter into a gazillion pieces and bleed a fresh coat of red all over her wiggling toes.

Toes?

She stood beside his chair. She straddled his lap. God, she

was kissing him, really kissing him, and Bryce kissed her back, wrapping his arms around her body, pulling her closer to his chest, caressing, memorizing every curve, every nuance, and the sweet taste of her. The pain in his chest disappeared as quickly as it had arrived.

"Take me to bed," Rio said, panting against his mouth. "Take me to bed and make love to me." She kissed his lips, his cheeks, his eyes, licked her tongue over the curves of his ear and nipped the lobe. She kept her hips in perpetual motion, pressing insistently against his cock, which was straining toward her under his jeans.

Out of the question. Rock hard from the instant she'd put her hands on him, Bryce gritted his teeth solidly. He'd shown an animal nature too often, remembering the teeth marks scoring her once-flawless skin.

Sliding the T-shirt off her shoulder, he touched his lips to the spot, fighting back the swell of rapacious need for her alone. He was addicted to Rio Saunders and the more time he spent with her, the deeper he slipped under her spell. But making love to her now with an erection more like a club, he would cause more pain than she could bear.

On the fringe of drowning in ecstasy, Bryce shoved aside the few items left on the table and eased her back against the wood. He slipped his hands under the T-shirt, lifted the fabric and found one waiting dark nipple at peak with his mouth, the other with his hand. He worked both, alternating, laving, kneading, all but sinking his teeth into her satin skin.

Above him, Rio sighed, purred. The sexy sounds invaded his mind and went straight to the core of his soul. He clamped his hands around her narrow waist, lifted her onto the table and nibbled a path down her ribs to her belly button.

As he spread her legs, the scent of her essence set his teeth on edge and his cock went on full alert at the feast presented, a banquet fit for a starving king. One who undoubtedly would keep his zipper closed.

Bryce parted the soft folds of her flesh.

He toyed with her, inserting one finger, added the second after a moment, testing her resilience. She flinched and he withdrew them. She'd suffer rather than enjoy his rampant erection.

Penetrating her with one finger again, gliding smoothly, and using the pressure of his thumb on her nub, teasing strokes gave way to panting, gasping.

"Bryce."

She put the squeeze on him as he pressed against that special place. He heard the suffocating breath she inhaled. The first signs of delicate creaminess appeared as he withdrew.

He looked up into her delirium-filled eyes and licked the sweet nectar from his finger. His nostrils flared.

"Lie back," Bryce said, "and hold on to something solid. You forgot to feed me dessert."

Three orgasms later, Rio begged him to stop.

He wasn't finished with her, far from it.

She had yet to submit to the ultimate orgasm, a catapulting climax Rio would unlikely ever forget. A roller-coaster ride so tumultuous and fierce, Bryce knew he'd match one just watching each quake rumble through her luscious body.

He lapped, licked, nipped, sucked, and thrust his tongue, but still she held back, pleading to have him pierce her with his solid length. He refused, would continue to decline, but he hoped one day Rio would allow them both to enjoy the carnal pleasure he had in store for her now.

Bryce worked on her relentlessly, pushing every button, cashing in on every technique he knew.

She was so close, on the threshold of losing the battle raging inside. He could see it, felt her muscles contract, snap suddenly, and shoved her knees over his shoulders. And worked her harder when her thighs vise-clamped over his ears. He lifted her hips off the table, balanced her weight in one hand, waiting for the right moment.

He sucked harder, then thrust his tongue deeper and gnawed at her swollen flesh. When she bore down, groaning, the distinctive snap occurred and he pierced her. With two fingers, Bryce breached the berth she had forbidden him to pleasure.

That single move freed her fierce rising. Bryce came out of the chair, leaned over her body, pressing the bulging head of his jean-shrouded cock to the opening where his fingers had once claimed. He held her tightly in his arms, and she wrapped her long legs high around his ribs, shrieking high-pitched tones capable of shattering fine crystal. She splintered, a savage eruption so powerful that, on a mighty roar, he climaxed with her, rocking, his body straining against hers.

They'd knocked over his wineglass, staining the beautiful tablecloth. The red candle had melted and caked in the shag of her hair.

Rio scrubbed furiously at the wine color under cold tap water while Bryce peeled away the wax stuck to her tresses.

"Ouch, that hurts," she complained, ducking her head.

"Hold still, kitten. Just a little bit left."

She felt the heat from his big self. When the length of his sleeping serpent skimmed over her derriere, Rio shivered from the reminder of what had happened. And her response to a primitive sexual act.

"Cold?" Bryce asked. He wrapped his arms around her waist, kissed the side of her neck and nuzzled her ear.

"A little chilled. Did you get it all out?" She eased out of his embrace and ran her hand through the back of her hair.

"Um-hmm. Want me to wash it for you?"

"I'll do it myself," she said quickly.

She'd begged off showering with him, said she'd clean the kitchen first. After Bryce had finished upstairs, Rio quickly showered while he took out the trash and put the large containers on the curb for pickup.

The navy sweatshirt hardly stayed on her shoulders, the bottom reaching as low as her knees. His oversize sweatpants hung on her like a thick quilted skirt, but the baggy socks supported the pant legs, kept them from dragging on the floor. Mainly, she felt somewhat protected. From him.

It wasn't fear of him, but trepidation knowing how easily he'd bent her to his will. How he'd made her feel combined with her un-protesting reaction still grated on her nerves.

As any open-minded woman with strong desires, she had sexual fantasies, just not about *that*. A little voice in the back of her mind passionately objected to the carnality. Another said . . . not so, she chided.

"What's wrong?" Bryce asked.

"What makes you think there's anything wrong?"

"You're picking at your nail polish again."

Darn it. Rio shoved her hands behind her back. "I pick at them when they've been painted the same color too long. Bad habit."

"Bull. In the car. Remember?"

Double darn. Did this man see everything? "It was old then, too. Older now."

"Rio." He stepped toward her and she matched his stride in reverse. Bryce frowned. When she turned her back, he snatched her off the floor and held her against his chest before she blinked. "What's gotten into you?"

Nothing yet, and she feared it just might try again. Held in this position, she tried to wriggle free and felt a familiar stirring on her backside. "Put me down."

"Not until you tell me what the problem is. You haven't wanted me to touch you since . . . Aaah."

"Ah, what?"

He set her down, forced her around to face him. Leaning closer to her face, tipping her chin up with one finger, he said, "I told you before that I'd never force you into anything you don't want, and I meant it."

A mountain of palpable tension lifted off her shoulders. She sighed in shuddering relief.

"But you do respond to me, Rio, giving yourself wholly, completely, and that—"

His cell phone rang.

That what? Rio wondered frantically while Bryce answered the noisy summons.

"Hold on," he said into the phone. Concerned etched his face as he handed the cell to Rio. "It's Galaxeé. She's frantic, and I didn't understand a word she said other than your name."

Rio listened to her partner's hysterical chatter. "Calm down, Galaxeé, calm down. Are you there now? . . . I will be there as soon as possible." She hung up. "You have to take me to Killer's."

Three cop cars had converged on the scene. The front door to Killer Bods was wide open and every light inside brightened the interior.

Galaxeé had planted herself in Randy's arms, wrapped inside his cashmere coat with him.

An elegant-looking gentleman, Randy Maxwell had short-cropped, jet hair teased by silver at the temples. His pencil-thin mustache and perfectly trimmed goatee came together in a classy Fu Manchu, emphasizing the deep dimples on both cheeks and flawless buckskin complexion. Kind, midnight eyes crinkled at the corners when he smiled.

Rio introduced him to Bryce. They shook hands.

"She's a mess," Randy said, his voice a seductive baritone. "All evening long she's had a mixture of feelings, good and bad.

She was worried about you, Rio, for some reason. I kept telling her you were fine and that you'd call if there was a problem or if you needed her. When the phone rang, she came unglued." He placed a chaste kiss on the top of Galaxeé's head. "See, baby girl? She's unhurt and unruffled."

Rio wasn't quite so sure and she shot a quick glance at Bryce. "Galaxeé?" She stroked a hand down a length of braids. "Honey, are you okay?"

She turned in Randy's arms, sighing dramatically. "I'll live. Are you?"

Rio held her arms out, grimacing. Dressed in the same flamboyant evening attire from the night before when Bryce wore jogging shoes and a sweatsuit, everyone knew what she'd done and it wasn't staying home knitting. At least he'd given her a heavy ski jacket for warmth.

Typical of Colorado's climate, snow had melted under clear skies today, but without a blanketing of clouds during evening hours, the temperature had dipped below freezing.

"Just fine. What happened?"

"Brinks called when the alarm went off. They tried to call you, notified me. We both called the police. When Randy and I got here, they were checking the premises and doors. Somebody used some sort of pry at the rear entrance."

"Did they get inside?"

"Broke the lock . . . left the door ajar. The police have checked everywhere. Evidently the person or persons were scared off because nothing is missing from what I can tell, nothing broken, either, except the lock."

"That's a relief. We'll have to get someone out here tonight to replace it. Take her home, Randy. I'll stay." It hit her. "Are my purse and keys still here? Darn it, Galaxeé."

"I've got them in Randy's car," she replied. "Took them home with me last night. You didn't need them." She had another cheesy grin on her face.

Rio provided her a dirty look.

"I'll stay here with you," Bryce said. When he started to put his arm around Rio, she backed away, drawing a frown. "You should have an additional lock put on, maybe to both entrances. I don't want anything to happen to you."

"I need to talk to the police," Rio broke in. She hurried away.

Galaxeé spun around. Cupping Randy's face with both hands, she asked, "Baby, could you warm up the car?"

"Anything for you, snookums." He bid good night to Bryce and went out the door.

"Snookums?" Bryce asked.

"One of many pet names."

His face took on a serious texture. "I don't want Rio to stay here by herself anymore. Not after this," he said, waving his arm. "She's pretending this doesn't bother her, but I know it does."

"How? She looks calm to me."

"The other night I scared the living shit out of her, that's how!" Anger had seeped into his tone. "You know she didn't realize I was still in the building. By the time I got upstairs, she'd worked herself into a goddamn frenzy."

"I had no idea. She didn't tell me." She should've felt Rio's distress, just as she had tonight. Intuition. They'd shared a tangible bond since childhood.

"I'll stay with her every night if I have to from now on."

"No, you will not," Rio snapped.

Galaxeé and Bryce swung around.

"I don't need a bodyguard."

"Kitten—"

Rio stamped her foot. "Nor do I want one, Bryce."

"Sweetie," Galaxeé said, stepping toward her best friend, "we're only thinking about your safety. I don't think it's wise for you to be alone after-hours, either. What if—"

"Forget the bear crap, Galaxeé. They hibernate in winter. With new locks, Killer's will be secure. No one can get in and I'll be fine."

Thick fists at his waist, Bryce was in her face in two strides, had Rio backing up. "I won't have it, so don't try to be difficult with me. Call it what you want, bodyguard, phantom, shadow, hell, Batman. I will be right here any night that you are."

Galaxeé loved it. "Well, guess that clears that up. Randy's waiting for me."

Rio peeked around Bryce's broad physique. "Purse. Keys." She looked back into his eyes. "And Galaxeé, where is my car?"

She hissed. "I moved it to Safety Depot. It's safe—"

"Thank you."

"—there."

Galaxeé thanked the police officers as they filed out and when she took Rio's belongings back inside the club she found the lovers still rooted to the wooden floor, still glaring bullets at each other. Except now, Rio had her hands riding to her hips in a cute stalemate that tickled Galaxeé.

"Good night," Rio said to her.

Dismissed. Damn, she hated to miss the fireworks currently set for blastoff and she slammed the heavy front door.

Galaxeé grinned. Love. Things were moving along just fine and dandy.

"You haven't called the locksmith, have you? You couldn't have," Bryce said. "You were too busy listening to the conversation I was having with Galaxeé."

Rio folded her arms under her breasts. "A conversation you had no business starting."

Agitated, he crinkled his nose. This whole thing was a matter of protection. Her safety. "When do you plan on calling one, tomorrow?"

"When you leave."

Christ. "Not a goddamn chance. As long as you're staying, so am I. When the hell do you plan on locking the front door?"

"Like I said, when you leave. Don't try to bully me, Bryce. I'm a grown woman, can take care of myself."

"Like you did the other night?" He'd snapped out the words before he had the sense to stop them.

Sense, what was that? He'd lost the function the moment he'd met her and, from the look in her narrowed eyes, he should've vanished into the zone ten seconds ago. Okay. She didn't care to budge from the issue and neither did he. The bottom line, he was bigger. No way could she toss him from the premises.

Reining in the spark of temper, Bryce said, "Kitten, all I'm trying to do is—"

"I didn't ask for your help."

She had enough talent to tap dance on the last assailable nerve he had left. It was better than a computer software error, which usually sent him on a ballistic journey accompanied by a skull-splitting migraine. Not tonight. Short and sweet with one conclusion, one finishing touch to end the standoff, sidestep a headache and regain calm composure.

"When I turn my back, when I start toward that door," he said in a deadly voice, advancing on her, following her backward strides. "When you close it behind me, lock it, and I climb into my car, start the engine, put it in gear and drive away, leaving you here, all alone because you don't need me or my help." She bumped into the bar and Bryce boxed her in. "How do you plan to keep the back door secure until the locksmith, the one you have *yet* to contact, arrives?"

Checkmate. Who said dinner plates were big? Rio's golden eyes had expanded well beyond saucer size.

Blinking rapidly, she risked a quick glance toward the dark

hallway leading to the rear entrance and, damn it, she still didn't back down. Meaning, she didn't give a damn about him.

Straightening, Bryce said, "Keep the coat. Dressed as you are, it'll give you at least one layer of protection."

She took off the jacket and laid it across a barstool.

Stubborn . . . Turning his back on her was the hardest thing he'd ever done. Bryce committed a portrait of Rio to memory since this was the last time he would ever see the stubborn-ass woman.

"Cold, sugar?" Randy asked.

Galaxeé snuggled closer and his arms tightened around her. "Not anymore."

They'd taken their pets for a quick potty walk in the crisp night air. Sampson and Delilah hated snow and cold as much as Galaxeé. They were now curled up together on their blue satin pillow, eyes wide open, focused on their owners.

"I've been thinking about the break-in," Randy said. "It worries me that you could've been inside the building at the time. Rio, too."

"We would've beat the shit out—"

"Cecilia." He hated hearing her curse. Randy managed to curb her tongue with the slightest intonation.

"It'd take more than one person to take us out."

"What if they were armed, babycakes? What if they sneaked up and cornered you in the office?"

She'd thought many times about the same situation. Rio had objected to having a gun in the building. "We wouldn't lie down and roll over like Sampson and Delilah."

Randy sighed. "You're not big as a minute and neither you nor Rio can beat up everybody, no matter how tough you think you are. I will not allow anyone to hurt you. So," he said, tipping her face up toward his, "tomorrow morning early, I'll put my security people on duty. They'll mount video cameras in strategic locations. Just inside for now. Later we'll take care of the outside. We'll catch whoever is responsible."

Galaxeé smiled. She loved him like crazy.

"My people will be in and out before Rio says 'boo.' " He knew Rio would object.

10

Men. What made them think of women as damsels in distress? How many nights had she spent here at Killer's without his hulking presence, without anyone protecting her?

Folding her arms, Rio watched Bryce's long, forceful strides as he headed toward the front door. He did exactly as he'd said he would, except she refused to follow his declarations. She had a stubborn streak, too. She would not lock up right behind him, would not give him the satisfaction of hearing the latch thrown.

As the heavy door slammed behind him, she flinched. Well, that's that. All alone, safe and secure.

Thieves never returned a second time, not on the same night. Rarely, according to the police, rarely.

When the air conditioning came on, she nearly jumped out of her skin and chastised herself.

I will not be afraid. I will not be afraid. I am not afraid. I will not let anything scare me.

But when a thumping sound started behind her, her heart downshifted and sped up. Rio turned her head very slowly and looked over her shoulder. She hopped backward, seeing her own reflection in the mirrors.

The main system's motor—the refrigerated cooler—a used appliance holding beer and soft drinks and mixers, had whirred to life. They needed a new one. Why hadn't she noticed the knocking noise before now?

The sound echoed throughout the club like heavy shoes crossing the hardwood stage. Could she hear someone coming through the back door with all this racket? Would she recognize the sound? What if she was upstairs in the office?

Short of breath, she thought about the back door. Unlocked and down that long, long, dark hallway. An ice-cold sweat trickled down between her breasts. The hair at the base of her neck sprang to life.

Oh, Lord. Why did it have to be so far away? She leaned sideways, holding her breath, squinting, trying to see if the door had opened, to see if anyone had gotten inside.

The curtains shivered.

"Bryce!"

Rio bolted. At the entrance door, she shoved as hard as she could. *God, please don't let him be gone. Please.*

The door flew open too easily and she smacked into a solid entity. She screamed at the top of lungs, clawed and flailed wildly. "Let me go!"

It had her now, pulled at her body, wrapped around her and pushed her against the cold brick wall. The icy chill pumped her blood faster. She was going to die because she was too damned stubborn. Too proud to ask for help, too proud to admit she cared for Bryce Sullivan.

"Stop fighting me."

She heard the gruff words, a male's voice, but couldn't quite comprehend. His breath fogged in her face and she couldn't see his. Stop? So he could kill her?

She bit him, hard, sank her teeth into his flesh. They'd find him one day, marked for life.

"Ow, stop it."

Bryce. She recognized the bass voice. Rio released the vicious hold she had on him.

"Son of a bitch." He stepped back, rubbing a spot high on his chest, frowning. "I just left my coat. I was coming back to get the goddamn coat."

Rio had trouble finding her breath.

"What the devil are you doing out here without one, half naked? You'll freeze to death."

He wrapped his warm hand around her bare arm, guided her back inside and slammed the door. Suddenly she was freezing, shook all over, shivering uncontrollably.

"Hey," Bryce said and dragged her into his arms.

Rio clung to him, squeezing her eyes shut, teeth chattering. She was so happy he was here, holding her, warming the chill from her bones better than a built-in furnace. The soft, downy fur inside his jacket caressed her back, and she sighed a shuddered breath. Comfortable and safe in the arms of the only man who made her feel secure.

"Better?" Bryce asked.

She nodded.

"You really should put on decent clothes, layering for protection. Long pants, no skirts, a pullover sweater or similar type of clothing. I'm thinking warmth here since the AC's on."

She nodded again, but she didn't move out of his embrace.

"I need to get home and get some sleep. What time did the locksmith say he'd be here?"

Bryce felt her tense in arms, then she shrugged, damn her. Stubborn . . . He should've called one himself. But if she wanted to be Miss Wear-The-Armor-Nothing-Scares-Me, fine.

He had other things to do in his life than put up with a soft, beautiful woman clinging to him who wanted nothing to do with Bryce Sullivan or any other male except for teasing; he had a business to run, a sister to protect, his overbearing mother to calm. Important issues rather than this gorgeous female, who gave him a hard-on each time he looked at her, melted his heart each time he touched her and, yes, goddamn it, made him fall deeper into lust with her.

No more, once he got her out of his arms. He just couldn't seem to let her go just yet. In a minute. After she warmed, after she stopped shivering, he would walk away for sure, finish his planned business and put Rio Saunders behind him, completely out of his life and out of his mind.

"Have you called a locksmith yet?"

She shook her head.

"Why the hell not?"

She swallowed audibly. "B-Busy."

"Doing what?" Bryce snapped, stepping back, holding her at arm's length, staring down into her face, into unblinking golden eyes.

A few seconds went by and Rio swallowed again. "Looking for you."

Damn her. She knew how to twist the knife so freakin' deep, but a tiny starburst of hope streaked through his heart. "Why? Why were you looking for me?"

She wrung her hands, picked at her nail polish and stared down at the floor.

"Why, Rio?" he persisted, giving her a little shake, forcing her to look back into his eyes. He needed her to admit something—anything—and stilled her busy hands with one of his own. "Answer me."

"Because," she said breathlessly. "Because I need you."

"Why? Is it fear? You want me here because you're afraid?"

"Yes." He let loose of her and started to turn. "No. I-I want you, Bryce. I want—"

He yanked her into his arms, crushing her against his chest.

"Damn you," he whispered fiercely, shoving his fingers into her hair, fisting, tugging. "Was it that hard to say?"

He smothered her answer with a hard kiss and lifted her from the floor, gentling only after she touched his cheek as lightly as a snowflake's caress.

"Where's the phone book? You're calling some goddamn body to come and fix these frigging locks so we can go *home*. You still don't have panties on, do you?"

She shook her head.

He heard his own raspy growl as horniness settled in. "Lock the front door and call the locksmith before I take your clothes off right here. I'll stay at the back entrance until he comes. Damn it, Rio," he said, kissing her face, nipping at her chin. "I want to make love to you. Maybe you'd better go upstairs. Lock yourself inside the office."

"Why?" she asked, frowning.

"To keep me out." He slid her body down his. "Go."

She started to move and stopped. "Bryce?"

"What?" he said impatiently.

"Let go of my dress."

He realized the fabric was bunched in his hands. He was horny and frantic.

Fists clenched, several seconds went by before he released her. "Go," Bryce ordered, flexing his fingers. "Lock the office door. I mean it. Don't come out until I tell you. I'll take care of the locksmith."

When she hurried up the stairs, he damn near gave chase.

At ten thirty, Bryce banged on the office door. He tried to coax her out, but Rio refused him entrance. She said the locksmith had called. The man was running late and Bryce threatened to break the frosted glass.

"What's gotten into you?"

"You. Let me in."

"No."

At midnight, he cursed the locksmith for taking so damn long to get there. He followed the man, helping with installation, hurrying the work. He tipped him a hundred bucks to get him the hell out of the building. The old codger was lucky to pack his gear before Bryce shoved him out the door.

Racing up the stairs two at a time, he stopped at the landing, inhaled through his nostrils and let the air rush out of his mouth. He could smell her unique scent, had smelled her every moment since he'd reentered this building. Blood, hot as boiling water, pumped through his veins. Horniness had claimed his senses for three hours now and his cock was engorged—stone solid—and needing relief. With Rio.

"He's gone. Open up."

"No way, José."

"Why not?" he snapped.

"Because of the way you're acting. I don't like it, don't like the way you sound, either."

He cleared his throat, tried not to sound so gruff and needy. "Kitten—"

"Go home. We'll talk tomorrow."

Snarling, he grabbed the knob, shook even the frame around the door, tried to force his way inside. "Unlock this damn thing."

"No, Bryce. Go. Home."

"Why can't I come to your place?"

She hesitated. "Because."

Temper simmering he raked both hands through his hair. He could easily shoulder the thing to the floor, rip it from the hinges, and take what was rightfully . . . He blinked, and then blinked again. His befuddled brain finally broke through the sex-driven haze, cleared a cloudy path back to reality.

What the hell was wrong with him? Had he lost his mind? Pussy-whipped. He knew it and his dick knew it. Jesus.

Dragging in a stabilizing breath, Bryce slowly said, "All right, I'm cool. I'll take you to your car."

"You expect me to trust you after this?"

Aw, shit. "I won't touch you."

"Promise? I'm sore, Bryce."

Still? For how long? But, she sounded forlorn. He scratched at a vague itch on his neck, then tried to ease his raging meat with a couple of hard pinches, harder thumps. Painful, they didn't improve his condition. "Promise."

The door opened a crack. One beautiful hazel eye peeked out.

"Come on out. I won't touch you." She opened it farther, and Bryce burst out laughing. "How many outfits do you have on?" She'd dressed in more clothes than a bundled-up kindergartner on a snowy day.

"Three."

"Can you make it down the stairs?"

She looked down at the bulge attempting to stand at attention inside his sweatpants. "Can you? Or is that third leg for balance? Pole vaulting?"

Cheeky . . . "Here're the keys for the new locks. I had him make an extra set for Galaxeé."

"How much do I owe you?" Rio asked as they made their way down the stairs.

"Skip it."

"No, I won't skip it. Give me the bill and I'll write you a check."

"Hell. He forgot to give me one." If he had a bill, and he didn't, and she saw the invoice, no telling what she might do. Oh, he knew all right. She'd have all the locks rekeyed. "There're two locks on each door. New ones at the bottoms and the busted one, color-coded to the keys. Already tested. Everything's locked up tight."

"How much?"

"Forty-seven bucks. Discounted," he said before she could protest, "because he was late and I helped install." A tenth of the actual cost with tip and Bryce's wild frenzy. At this rate, he'd spend a small fortune on her.

"I don't believe you."

"Why would I lie? What would I gain?"

"A set of keys," she said and showed teeth. She stuck her hand out. "Nice try, buster, but I wasn't born yesterday."

Shit. He fished through his inside coat pocket and found them. "It was just in case—"

"I lost mine? Never have before." She kept her hand out, beckoned him with wiggling fingers.

Swearing under his breath, he found another set. "There. Christ, Rio, it was just for safety's sake."

"Thank you for your concern." Standing on tiptoe, she kissed his cheek.

Rio set the alarm and, although Bryce turned sideways, he saw the code she punched in. Peripheral vision worked every time. She really should use digits different from her cell phone's last four digits. He fingered the third set of keys in his pocket and smiled while she secured both locks.

Safety Depot was right around the corner. They sat in his SUV while the Mercedes warmed and melted ice off the windshield.

"How about I stay at your place tonight," Bryce said.

"No." No hesitation whatsoever.

"No? Why not?" He flicked the overhead light on.

"Because I have things to do."

"Like what, when I can't be there?"

"Feminine things." Lord, she needed to pluck the stray hairs in her eyebrows, soak in a warm tub while a facial mask worked its magic, deep hair conditioning, pay bills and contact Galaxeé for a heart-to-heart tomorrow morning, or, rather, in a few hours. She really needed to discuss personals with her.

"I'll watch TV while you do feminine stuff."

"It's late and I need sleep. So do you. Don't you have to work tomorrow?"

Leaning toward her, nuzzling her cheek, Bryce said, "My original plan was to spend the next two days with you." He grabbed her hand and ran it down his hard length.

Shivering from the erotic sensation, she forced her hand out of his. "No."

"Come on, Rio." He nipped at her ear, exhaled a hot tickling breath.

She drew away. "Are you always this horny? God."

"When I get near you. Breathe you. Touch you."

She opened the SUV's door and rolled out. "I'll call you tomorrow." She heard him curse ferally as the door slammed shut. Once inside the Mercedes, Rio hit the power switch and locked up tight.

Thirty minutes later, the garage door closed behind her. The loft was only six blocks from Killer's, but she drove in circles, stopped at a convenience store and filled the gas tank, unwilling to risk having Bryce follow and find out where she lived.

Lifting the old-fashioned elevator gate, she stepped out and secured it. No one could get into her loft unless she buzzed open the front door or sent the elevator.

She went from phone to phone, turning each off, for a few hours of uninterrupted slumber.

Mercy. She missed sleeping with Bryce and his heat.

Rio peeled herself out from under a sheet, two blankets and a white goose-down comforter at ten forty and stood, still tired, still sleepy and, cringing, still sore. She crossed the loft's wooden floor hobbling like a ninety-year-old woman in labor and cranked up the thermostat for both floor and gas-forced heat. Back to big utility bills.

She needed coffee and started the maker, then found a quart

of grapefruit juice in the refrigerator. The usual morning feast came with a slice of raisin toast swathed in butter and cream cheese. Lifting breakfast toward her mouth, she remembered the day—weigh-in.

Groaning, she realized today she had to stair step and Troy, her physical trainer, would stop by shortly to work the devil out of her tired body if she'd gained one pound.

In all this pain?

The buzzer sounded louder than a school bell.

Whimpering like a child, Rio fed the garbage pail her morning sustenance and grabbed a protein drink from the fridge.

Bryce slammed the receiver down for the umpteenth time without leaving a message. He'd tried to call Rio after arriving home last night to make sure she'd gotten there safely and let it ring until voice mail answered. Okay, so she went to bed, needed sleep.

He'd awakened at dawn, but snoozed lightly for a while longer.

At seven on the nose, he'd called her. He called again as he drove to the office, again at eight, eight thirty, and every fifteen minutes thereafter. What if she'd had an accident? Damn it, he should've run the stoplight.

A knock came at his door and Bryce looked up.

Maureen Jamison's bifocals balanced on the bridge of her long nose. A flurry of brown curls threaded with gray surrounded her thin face. Two bright powder-puff dots of pale red tinged her cheeks.

Did this woman ever change her conservative, old-fashioned dresses for ones more up to date? Dye her hair? He peered over his desk at her shoes. Wear stilts instead of granny shoes? Jesus. The woman was older, more mature. The female population couldn't all match Rio Saunders' sleekness.

"You have a meeting with Systems in ten minutes," she reminded him.

Hell.

"Here's the agenda," Maureen said, handing over the typed two-pager. Her glasses slipped down. She pushed them up her nose and cleared her throat, holding the small appointment book like the Bible. "At noon, you have a lunch meeting with a Mr. Galestone of Mercury Resonance. Two thirty, the high school tour."

Shit.

"Four, the meeting I postponed from this morning, rescheduled since you came in, and sometime today, payroll."

Christ. When would he find time to call Rio? Why hadn't she called him as she'd promised? He needed an admin assistant to whom he could delegate duties and get some of this crap off his shoulders.

"Sir?"

"What?" Bryce snapped, glaring.

"Is there anything wrong?"

Every damn thing. "No."

"All right. There's also the reception dinner party at seven sharp that requires your attendance. I've typed the topics for your speech as requested."

Bryce groaned.

"Our Mr. Berman is retiring, remember? The award plaque came in a little bit ago. Would you like to see it?"

"No. I. Don't. Want—" And realized he'd pounded his fist with every word. Bryce clamped his teeth together. "Sorry. Yes, bring it in, Maureen." His day was shot, totally jacked. Evening, too.

He scrubbed his face with both hands after Maureen left his office, then picked up the phone receiver and punched in Rio's cell number.

It rang one, twice, a third and fourth time. While he counted silently, using the gold pen for a gavel on his desk, Bryce snarled.

"Here it is," Maureen said, smiling down at the plaque. "It's a beauty, just like—"

Bryce slapped the receiver into the cradle. "Maureen, come back in here," he said loudly.

She stopped dead in the doorway and slowly turned around. "Yes, sir."

"I want you to reschedule—"

"You cannot."

"What the hell does that mean?" Shit, he could take off work when he damn well pleased. Who ran this place anyway?

"The Systems people have some sort of problem with their sister board or father's board."

For God's sake. "Motherboard?"

"Yes, yes. That's it. The problem has already set them back and Broderick Corporation is expecting their new computers next week."

"I know. I know. Cancel—"

"Mr. Galestone leaves for Norway tonight. He wants the new software to take with him. He said, and I quote, 'It had better be ready.' "

He was beginning to hate this woman's New England accent. "Fine. Postpone—"

"The high school tour group is visiting several installations. There's no way for us to contact them."

Hell's bells.

"And, if you don't finish payroll, since it was due Friday, our data-entry people plan to call in sick tomorrow. From what I heard." She smiled brightly. "So you see—Oh, the postponed meeting? There's some sort of roach."

"Roach?"

"Evidently, some sort of creepy-crawly thing got into one their programs."

"A bug?"

"Yes, yes. That's it. By the way, the roach has something to do with Mr. Galestone's request."

For the love of God.

"One other thing. Your dear mother called."

What now?

"Such a lovely sounding woman. She's made her plane reservations for the visit here."

At least that was nothing new. No problem.

"She's bringing two of her dear friends with her."

Fucking A.

Bryce flopped facedown onto his desk.

Rio hurt from head to toe, every square inch.

Troy had jumped all over her for gaining two lousy, stinking pounds and by the time he'd finished thrashing her muscles, sweat rolled off her body in rivers. Not perspiration, sweat. She hated sweating. Sure enough, wringing water out of her navy-blue leotards would fill the bathroom sink.

Oh, and let's not forget the towel draped around my neck.

"I'll be back day after tomorrow," Troy said. He stepped through the doorway.

"Come on—"

"Weigh-in again."

Whining never helped worth a darn.

"Take a hot shower. Drink plenty of water today and stretch again tonight. Or you'll be crying tomorrow. Hurt worse when I come back."

"Can't we put it off until later?"

"If you don't want to do this, Rio, fine. Keep eating cheese and butter and all the carbs that migrate to your hips. The holiday season makes it much harder."

She was required to keep a daily record of food intake and amounts.

"Go ahead, get fat and sassy. I've got potential clients waiting in line for an opening."

"All right." She stamped her foot and closed the heavy metal door. "Darn his fine, black hide."

He banged on the door.

"What now," she muttered and opened it again.

"Bicycling when I come back. Ten miles."

Rio slammed the door in his superfine face and snapped the lock into place.

A hot shower felt better than having sex today. She wrapped herself in a thick, fluffy white robe while padding barefoot toward the kitchen. Lunchtime. She needed solid food, but she would not gain another pound after this, not with a low-calorie salad: two hard-boiled eggs, sliced cucumber, half a tomato cut into wedges, four thinly sliced celery sticks displayed neatly on a bed of baby lettuces. She added a scoop of low-fat cottage cheese to the plate, no dressing.

With a big glass of water to wash it all down, she sat at the breakfast counter. From there, Rio watched light snow falling, although the clouds were broken and allowed sunshine to filter through the loft.

She needed to clean the golden hardwood floors. Footprints marred the dust. Maybe Galaxeé would help.

Rio tsked.

Galaxeé hadn't lifted a finger since Randy had walked into her life. He made sure her manicure stayed perfect. House, too. Whatever Miss Galaxeé wanted, Miss Galaxeé got without question, and it only took a hint. What had she done to Randy to make him give so freely?

Well, she needed to talk to her partner about a few things anyway. She dialed her home number, put the call on speaker, and started in on the boring salad. A week of fruit, greens and protein drinks should trim a few pounds from her hips and thighs. She should practice dancing again.

Galaxeé answered before the first ring ended. "Hey, sweetie. I was sitting by the phone, waiting for it to ring."

"Bologna."

"You called, didn't you?"

"You happened to walk by the phone when it rang and saw the caller ID."

"Did not. Don't need it," Galaxeé replied. "Anyway, don't forget Momma wants us to show up at her honey's party tonight."

"That's tonight?"

"Yep. Sevenish, I think. Check the invite. Dressy. Want to ride with Randy and me? We can pick you up. In fact, why don't you invite Bryce?"

"No."

"Why?"

She scooped a helping of cottage cheese into her mouth, chewed and swallowed. "Because I'm not ready for that step."

"I don't know why not," Galaxeé replied, her tone an octave higher. "You slept with him. Sounds like a logical next phase to me, even if it is out of order."

She stuck her tongue out. "I'm just not ready." Not ready to flaunt their relationship publicly, if ever.

"Have you talked to him today?"

She hadn't, and knew she'd promised. "Not yet."

"What're you waiting on, Christmas?"

She didn't want to appear too eager to hear his voice, sounding desperate, especially when her heart was screamin' and hollerin' for him. When Troy arrived, exercise had kept her mind off Bryce and on her tired muscles. "I've been busy. Workout this morning, hard. I gained two pounds."

"How the hell did that happen? Screwing burns calories. Of course," Galaxeé said, "unless you've been doing the lollipop thing. That could add a few ounces." She burst out laughing.

Rio's jaw went slack. Oral sex had not been part of her repertoire. Ever.

"Hello-o," Galaxeé sang.

"Stop it." She really needed to ask her a few intimate questions. Toying with the food on her plate, Rio poked a hole through the wedge of tomato with a stick of celery. How does one ask about . . . "Can you come by? I need to talk to you."

"Hour. I'm still in jammies. Want to give me a hint?"

"Don't you already know?"

"Sometimes my intuition needs rest, Ms. Saunders."

11

"Ooh, shit. Even *I* haven't done that."

Rio groaned. Now she'd put her business in the streets, but Galaxeé had always kept her mouth shut on personal issues.

"I'll ask Ellie. She probably has. The tramp brags about everything, like tramps do."

Why did she have to use that dramatic tone? "Don't you dare. She'll know you're talking about me. Just forget we had this conversation."

"What're you gonna do?" Galaxeé's face contorted. "Let him? I mean, it happens. Some folks like it. Guys especially. Gays really do. They don't have much choice if they want to poke and probe and only *one* tight tunnel to work with."

Lord. Was she trying to convince her or scare the devil out of her? Rio shuddered. "Forget I brought it up."

Setting the glass of grapefruit juice on the breakfast counter, Galaxeé tilted her head to one side and asked, "You guys do use protection, don't you?"

"Yes, of course. Well, sometimes we forget."

"Ah, hell, nah. Uh-uh. You . . . Jesus . . . Puh-lese," Galaxeé sputtered. "Girl, I need a drink. What've we got in here that's hard? It's after the noon hour somewhere in the world. Got any tequila? Ooh, shit, Rio."

"Calm down." She slid off her stool and went to a cabinet, pulled out the bottle of 1800 tequila. Nerves shot, she needed a strong elixir to tame her emotions. "Get a lime and slice it. I've already made up my mind about the situation."

"And that is?" Galaxeé questioned. Her eyebrows shot up like missiles.

"Guess, Miss Know-It-All."

Bryce shook hands with the tenth-grade teacher, then with all sixteen students. He'd herded the group to the front door to see them off, but two young girls hung back, kept asking silly questions. Personal ones. Finally, their teacher beckoned them to the waiting school bus.

The day had gone well so far.

The motherboards were in good shape, Galestone was happy, the tour was a success and Maureen had delivered payroll checks.

Except, he still hadn't heard from Rio.

He'd carried around his cell phone, anticipating a call from her. Twice, he'd escaped Galestone's boring conversation for privacy. Twice, the caller had been Maureen, reminding him of the tour. And twice, he'd hung up on her without even a "good-bye" when she admitted no calls had come through from anyone, in his opinion, worthwhile.

Bryce ducked into the men's room and tried Rio's number again.

Voice mail answered. Angry, he snapped the phone shut. "What the goddamn hell are you doing?"

"I'll be out in just a few seconds, sir. M-my zipper got stuck."

Bryce swung around. Seeing no one, he bent over slightly,

glimpsed a tattered pair of tennis shoes under the stall's door. Pete the Sleeper. A rumor had floated through the office, hinting that somebody had caught Pete in a stall one day. He was standing; his sandy-haired head was balanced against the wall, dick hanging out, sound asleep. Pete was one of two excellent software programmers. Evan Campbell was his competition.

"Talking to someone else, Pete. Take your time."

Bryce turned back to the sink. He splashed cold water on his face, wiped it dry with a paper towel and stared at his reflection. Good God, man, get a grip. Readjusting his striped tie, he drew in a cleansing breath and went out the door on the exhale.

He stopped at Maureen's desk outside his office. "Have I had any calls?"

"No, sir. Anything wrong, sir?"

Damned if she didn't make him sound and feel like a grumpy old boss. "No."

"Good. Meeting in five minutes."

Bryce snarled. "If I get a call, buzz me."

The meeting shouldn't take more than thirty minutes. Once adjourned, home to catch a few winks and run through a hot shower before the retirement party.

At quarter after six, Bryce was madder than a three-legged tortoise flipped on its back. He'd followed Pete, Evan, and Maureen across the small parking lot.

Traffic *was* a parking lot, but he finally strode into the party at five after seven and found the head table.

He acknowledged sixty-five of the sixty-six employees under his regime, some with spouses, some with significant others. The turnout was great, an expensive get-together for a true friend. Fortunately, Frankie was a new employee and Maureen had forgotten to invite her. From Maureen's cool tone when asked, she'd left her off the guest list intentionally. Thank you, he'd thought.

"Sorry I'm late," Bryce said to the guest of honor and pulled out a chair next to Oscar Berman. Each guest had an embossed nameplate. An astute planner, Maureen's talents extended far beyond the norm. She sat three chairs away, in conversation with a tech and his wife.

"Not late at all," Oscar said. He introduced those people Bryce didn't know at the circular table. "Rosalind, my lovely lady, is somewhere looking for her daughter, probably in the ladies' room. Can't keep these women away from a mirror. Most everyone else is here from what I can tell. Real nice of the company to put this together, Bryce."

Oscar had started work at Thorobred when his former employer had downsized and laid him off, back when Bryce had opened the doors to his company. He was the best electronic technician working.

"Sure you want to retire? There will always be a place for you at the company."

"If I don't, Rosalind won't give me her hand." Oscar laughed. "She's got a few plans for our future, traveling and all, and she's hell-bent on taking a romantic cruise for some odd reason. Frankly, I don't much care for floating in more water than a bathtub."

"Why not plan a vacation you'll both enjoy?"

Oscar looked back at Bryce as if he were crazy. "You don't know my Rosalind, or you've never been struck by love. I aim to please her, been courting her going on ten years. Here comes my sweet Rosie now." A mischievous twinkle glowed in his eyes. He patted his jacket pocket. "Gonna surprise her and ask her to marry me tonight. Picked out a ring. Got it right here."

"Have you seen my daughter yet?" She surpassed *lovely*.

A classic beauty, she flaunted stylishly combed snow-white hair and a smooth caramel complexion against the sparkling cream-colored cocktail ensemble. Not one wrinkle marred her skin.

Both men stood. "No, sweetpea. She'll be here, don't worry. Maybe she's hung up in traffic," Oscar replied, seating her. "I want you to meet Bryce Sullivan, my boss. This here is my beloved. Rosie to me, Rosalind Barnett to others."

Why did that name sound so familiar? Why did she look slightly familiar? "Pleasure," Bryce said, shaking her hand. He cocked his head to one side. "Have we met?"

"I don't believe so, unless you went to school with my daughter, but I think you're much younger than she is. Wouldn't you say so, Oscar?"

"She's got a few years on him. Most everyone here does. Boy knows his stuff, though, got it together."

If he knew so much, and had everything together, why wasn't Rio sitting beside him right now? Why hadn't she called? He would've asked for a date, their first real date.

"I try," Bryce said. "Thanks for the compliment."

"Well, Mr. Sullivan, I think it's time to begin," Rosalind said. "Cecilia, as usual, is late, but our guests are fidgeting."

Pushy, with a familiar smile. "No time like the present. I'll make it short and sweet."

"Please do," Rosalind replied. "People want to eat, and the big to-do is after dinner."

Damn. Bossy just like Mother and someone else he knew. "By any chance, is Galaxeé Barnett related to you? Is she Cecilia?"

"Why, yes. Do you know her? Of course, you do. Goodness, such a small world." She actually flapped her hands, shooing him away. "The podium?"

He could certainly see where Galaxeé got her good looks *and* her bossiness. Bryce nodded politely, smiled. He reached into his pocket for the . . . Ah, hell. He'd forgotten the damn notes Maureen had typed, left them locked in his briefcase, at home, on the bed. Nothing like an impromptu speech to keep his mind off a woman.

Since Galaxeé—rather, Cecelia—was due to arrive, maybe she'd have some answers about her best friend's disappearing act, maybe tell him why she'd forgotten to call, or hadn't wanted to call.

Bryce went to the podium and blew on the microphone, which squealed and whistled obnoxiously, gaining the crowd's attention.

"It works," he said, smiling. "If it didn't, I'd have to call the man of the hour up front to fix it like he repairs everything at Thorobred. Ladies and gentleman, we're losing a valuable employee and good friend from our company. Tonight, Oscar Berman is hanging up—"

And then he caught a glimpse of her.

Rio tugged at the bodice of her indigo-blue strapless dress. "Lord. This thing is tight. I should've worn an outfit already in my closet instead of letting you talk me into buying this one, Galaxeé," she whispered.

They'd gone shopping after tipping the bottle back for three shots. Each had bought a new outfit and accessories, had foolishly spent a bundle in a pricey downtown boutique not far from the loft. They'd dressed for cold weather and walked the distance.

"How am I supposed to eat when I'm squeezed tighter than a girdle's suction?"

"You look great. Doesn't she, honey?" Galaxeé said. Randy nodded. "Quit pulling at everything. Pick at your food. You're dieting anyway."

Rio stuck her tongue out. "It's cut too low, too much cleavage showing."

"So a big ear peeks out. Cute. If your nipples were pink, I'd worry, but they're not," she replied, giggling as Randy opened the door. "We have to get inside. The speaker—Wuh-oh."

"What?" Rio followed her gaze. "Oh, shit." Bryce was staring right at her, hard. Heart beating in a romp, she tore her eyes away and glared at Galaxeé.

"I didn't know, Rio. Truly."

"Save it." Galaxeé never could lie very well.

"Maybe something came to me this afternoon, but I got too busy and forgot about it."

God, what was she going to do? She couldn't turn tail and run out of the building. Bryce hadn't said another word. The audience had followed his gaze, spectators all staring at the three of them.

Rio squared her shoulders. She readjusted the faux fur over her arm and switched the evening purse to her left hand. "We're here now, seen by everyone. Let's find the table and sit down, for God's sake."

"It's at the front," Galaxeé whispered, looping her arm into the crook of Randy's.

"Oh, this is just real dandy. Lead the way."

Good lord, this is worse than walking a gauntlet when my feet are tortured.

She followed behind the couple, head held high, back straight, teeth grinding the enamel away from pain. Bryce had finally begun talking again while they wove a snake's path around chairs and white linen-draped tables. Waiters served salad and filled water glasses.

Rio refused to stare back into Bryce's eyes, but she felt his hot gaze burning her skin.

Momma Barnett flagged them down with a small wave, a frown firmly in place. "Where have you been?"

"Traffic, and we picked up Rio."

"Hi, Momma, Oscar. Sorry we're late, but you know your daughter." Galaxeé had never arrived anywhere on time.

Randy pulled out chairs for the ladies. Galaxeé sat beside her mother, Randy beside her, and Rio sat next to a thirtyish black man who whispered an introduction. Evan Campbell, software programmer for Thorobred Computers. He did have an intriguing design razored through the top of his short-cropped hair. Actually, Mr. Campbell had introduced himself to her breasts. Shameless devil.

Rio turned a little to the side in her chair. She crossed her legs, then uncrossed them, grimacing. The split of her dress parted to the thigh. She should've worn her trusty navy standby, covering her body from neck to ankle in the loose-fitting sheath. She concealed the gaping length with the new satin purse that matched the new high heels biting into her tootsies. Alcohol must have dulled her sense of pain when she'd tried on these kicks. Sexy or not, cute or not, the long pointy style had put the hurt on her feet. And Galaxeé had talked her out of wearing hose tonight, which made her toes feel more cramped.

"... and enjoy your meal. We'll get to the main event afterward," she heard Bryce say.

No, he wasn't, she thought, when the audience clapped.

Yes, he was, heading straight for their table, to that one empty seat opposite her.

"So," she said to Campbell, wishing he had a spouse or girlfriend instead of a young fellow sitting beside him, eyes closed. She chuckled, though. He'd fall facedown into a salad laced with Thousand Island dressing if he nodded one more time. It was rude not to wake him. Campbell continued eyeballing her rather than rescuing the man beside him. He finally nudged the sleeper awake, only because she'd nodded toward him. Poor guy. "You do what?"

"Programming, as in computers. You do own a computer."

"Of course. Doesn't everyone?" She hated the thing and it despised her.

"How do you know Oscar?" Campbell asked. "Friend? Relative? He didn't mention he had a daughter as fine as you."

Get out. Tired line. "Friend of a friend."

She wished he'd direct his gaping eyes somewhere other than her breasts.

"Is that a tattoo or your—" Campbell began a little too loudly.

Someone bumped the table really hard. Startled, Rio snapped her head around.

Bryce. Scowling Bryce.

"Mr. Sullivan," Rosalind said, glaring at Campbell. "Have you—"

"Yes," he replied. "We've met."

Rio heard the bass chill as their gazes collided. She looked over at Galaxeé, who grimaced.

"Well, good. Shall we eat?" Rosalind said and passed the bread.

Thank you, Momma Barnett.

Rosalind winked and smiled as if she'd read her thoughts. Probably had. She was every bit as perceptive as Galaxeé, if not more of a mind reader. And, right now, she stared at Bryce, one eyebrow curiously arched toward the ceiling.

Dinner was going fairly well, except Rio had to endure Campbell's blatant stares. She ignored Bryce's icy glare as much as possible, but at inopportune times, she caught it, hard as stone, usually when bug-eyed Campbell leaned toward her too closely. Steam seemed to spew out of Bryce's devil-red ears.

Galaxeé slanted over Randy and whispered, "Momma says we should go to the ladies' room."

Rio shot Rosalind a glance and received a curt nod. "Let's go."

"So, Mr. Sullivan."

He watched Rio's swaying hips until she reached the doorway. The goddamn slinky dress looked airbrushed on her body, clung to every curve. Worse, he noticed Evan Campbell tipping back in his chair for a thorough examination of Rio. The son of a bitch.

Bryce glowered. Campbell might see a pink slip in the near future if he couldn't keep his goddamn eyes in his head or his dripping tongue in his mouth.

"Mr. Sullivan?"

"Bryce." Oscar nudged him.

"What?" His temper hung on the fine edge of explosiveness.

"I think now is the right time," Rosalind replied.

He frowned. "Time for what? The ceremony?"

"No, no," she said casually, dark eyes twinkling. "There's plenty of time for that during dessert."

"Then what?"

Rio had skipped calling him today, never answered her phone, only to show up at a function he was presiding over, flirting with his employee, and ignoring Bryce as if he didn't exist in her life. "Highly pissed" was too mild a term for the emotions searing his brain. Rosalind's riddles were not what he cared to hear or solve.

"It's time for you," Rosalind said, lacing her fingers together. She set her elbows on the table, rested her chin on her hands, smiling. "To go and get her."

Oh, shit. His mouth went dry. Licking his parched lips, he looked around the table at the guests. Had everyone noticed his agitation since Rio's arrival?

"Go and get her," Rosalind repeated.

Oscar chuckled. "Better do what she says before Campbell decides to make a break for the door."

When Bryce scraped his chair back, the noisiness drew everyone's attention.

"Let's go to the one down the hall," Galaxeé said. "Too many women in line here."

"What's the rush?" Rio asked.

The longer they stayed away from their table, the better. Imagine Bryce coming out of his chair if Campbell showed too much more of his silliness. He carried an unbelievable jealous streak. She'd witnessed the flash of jade-green and vibrant hazel in his eyes and shuddered. For sure, Bryce would never hurt her, but he might try to put the hurt on Campbell, who was far from big and muscular, much slighter in stature. Would he really fight another man over her? Could she convince Bryce not to hurt him, that it was all a mistake, and protect the man some way?

Galaxeé looked over her shoulder and grimaced. "I saw big sparks flying in Bryce's aura. Mama said she saw explosions. Why didn't you call him today?"

"When did I have time? We got stupid and went shopping, remember, and spent too much money? Let him cool off. He has this nasty little jealous thing going on." A small smile crossed her lips. She'd always liked seeing a man's possessiveness. It made some women feel special. Devon had never given her a reason to enjoy the privilege.

"Well, you're gonna wish you had." Galaxeé pushed the door to the ladies' room open. "Get in here."

Rio hobbled to the mirror. "I'll contact him later, after the party when I get home." She checked her reflection then found her lipstick and applied a fresh coat of shimmering red.

"It's too late for—" Galaxeé started to say.

The door burst open and hit the stopper with thunderous noise.

The tube of lipstick clattered into the sink, marking the sides with squiggly red lines. Rio jumped back from the mirror and her breath caught.

"Wuh-oh."

Rio thought the very same thing. She was in trouble, and cornered. "Galaxeé, don't—"

"I'll see you later." She tiptoed around Bryce and said,

"Don't you dare hurt her, or you'll wish you'd never met the Barnetts."

Oh, this is just great, Rio thought, when the door clicked closed behind her friend, buddy, and partner.

She wanted to scream, "Don't leave me alone with him!"

12

He stripped her naked without touching her.

Rio didn't know what to do with her hands while Bryce's narrowed gaze raked over her from head to toe.

There was no place to escape without running into him. He filled the space on this side of the narrow walkway. And there was no place to hide, except the stalls. From the vicious look in his eyes, he'd rip the swinging door off the hinges.

When he took the first step swaggering toward her, lips flattened razor-thin, she chanced it anyway. She didn't make it far. Two steps. Bryce surrounded her like white on rice in a tight squeeze. Rio shuddered.

"You want to tell me what the hell's going on?" he asked in the deep, deep tone that mimicked a bass drum.

She swallowed. "What do you mean?"

He spun her around, pressed her against the cold tile, chilling her back down her spine. Ironing his big body against hers, he wedged his knee between her legs.

"We're in a ladies' room. A ladies' restroom. Someone might come in," she said, frantic.

"I don't give a goddamn if they do. What the hell are you doing? You came in this goddamn place and treated me like fucking bacteria."

"No, I—"

"Tits hanging out for everybody to see."

"Bull—"

"Flirting with an employee of mine."

"Employee of—" Had she heard him correctly?

"You didn't bother calling me today, never mind saying you were coming here tonight."

Well, damn. Was he expecting a reply or not? Did he have to holler, too?

"Answer me, goddamn it."

"Answer what?" she demanded hotly. "You haven't asked a damn question."

"Don't get cute with me, Rio."

He all but snarled the words and she was truly nervous now, feeling his erection swell. "Bryce, please, step back. Take a deep breath and relax. There's no need to argue." She had to talk fast. His penis was hard, his face harder, and he still held her imprisoned against the wall. "I had no idea you were coming tonight, and today I was really busy. I planned to call you w-when I got home. As for Evan—"

His knee came up and Rio heard a slight tear in the dress' fabric somewhere, probably the split up her thigh. Oh, Lord. Prickly sweat spread across her scalp.

"I talked to everyone sitting near me at the table. How could I begin to ignore him w-when he's sitting right there next to me?"

"You sure as hell ignored me."

"If we'd tried to talk, we would've been hollering at each other." Oh, God, she'd told a lie to keep this blaze under control.

"But he was close enough to slobber down your tits in this goddamn designer washcloth you call a fucking dress."

Bastard. She slapped him hard enough to snap his head to one side. "Get out. Now."

Flame-broiled red, fire engines had nothing on the color of his face. "Not until I'm finished with you."

She tried to stop his hands, but he shoved her dress up to her hips and hoisted her off the floor to ride his bulging thigh. "Don't do this," Rio panted. "Please. This is rape."

"Consensual." To prove it, he slipped his hand inside her panties, gliding his fingers into her heat, and smiled an awful demonic grin. Eyes glassy, pupils dilated, much of the stormy gray had disappeared. "See?"

She squeaked out a groan, felt her insides click on meltdown, dripping wet. "Please, Bryce, don't."

"Is everything all right?"

He stiffened, withdrew his fingers, lowered her to the floor and readjusted her dress. "Fine, Rosalind. We're just having a conversation. Weren't we, Rio?"

She knew she should disagree. Knew it. "Y-yes, Momma Barnett. Talk is all."

"All right. Mr. Sullivan, the waiters are serving dessert."

"Thank you."

The door clicked shut and silence followed, but their gazes stayed fixed on each other's. Air rushed out of Rio's lungs in short pants.

Bryce broke eye contact first, shook his head and stepped away. He huffed out a breath that sounded—tortured?

His Adam's apple bobbed erratically and his lips moved, but he said nothing. Then, he raised his hands toward her, except he changed his mind. They fell to his sides in clenched fists.

"I-I'm sorry," he finally said. "I'm so sorry."

Spinning on his heels, he left her where she stood, left her dazed and trembling.

* * *

Bryce shifted one arm over his eyes.

Flat on his back, he lay diagonally across the bed. When he arrived home, he'd trudged up the stairs, feeling old, wasted, sickened.

He'd showed his ass but good. Blew it and lost her forever. And damn, if it didn't hurt like a son of a bitch.

He had no one to blame but himself and an uncontrollable jealousy—well hidden even from himself—beneath the surface of his guarded heart. A trait so despicable, it blinded his eyes, saturated his brain and burned his soul. He'd managed to drive away the only woman he'd desperately wanted in his life.

Reaching across the bed, he dragged the pillow Rio had rested her head on when she'd slept beside him, inhaled the sweet, dominating scent of her and closed his eyes. He had nothing but this one part of Rio that she'd left behind.

He would resign from Killer Bods, no point in staying, no reason whatsoever except to torture himself. But Rio would mail him a pink slip, probably tomorrow morning if she hadn't already. How could she allow a jealous beast to work in her establishment?

You are fired.

The words droned in his ears. Only this dismissal had ended their relationship permanently.

The telephone rang. Bryce rolled across the bed to answer the summons, prepared to beg if necessary. "I'm here," he said and held his breath.

"Ooh, you don't sound so good." Catherine.

A reply was worthless. Useless. Unnecessary.

"Sounds like you need company."

Yeah, he did, and a way to get his mind off what he could never have again. "Not tonight."

"Tomorrow?"

Long seconds went by. "I'll call you." Why couldn't he just tell her he didn't want to see her? That she wasn't the woman he wanted? It was so male to keep a standby—a dangler, a pinch hitter. Only in the game when necessary.

"You've said that before. Can't expect me to sit around and wait until you decide, Bryce. I do have a life that doesn't revolve around you."

"Why don't you just live your life and leave me out of it?"

"Hmm. Snippy tonight. Could it be woman problems?"

He wrinkled his nose. "I've got work to do."

Bryce snapped the phone shut. No point in hanging around here. He re-dressed, grabbed his gym bag and started for the garage.

Damned if his cell phone didn't ring again. He was tempted not to answer, except the number display wasn't working right. God forbid if the caller was Galestone or another client in need of his assistance. He had no choice but to answer.

"Guess who I just finished talking with?"

Bryce wasn't in the mood for a conversation with his mother, no matter how excited she sounded. "What is it this time? And, Mother, don't start in on me about—"

"Frankie!"

Goddamn her.

Rio and Galaxeé stayed inside the building while Randy dealt with valet parking attendants. Snow fell again, covering walkways and streets, but a noisy snowplow went by, getting a head start on the storm. Steam percolated through manhole covers. People huddled together by the curb while waiting for their cars or taxis.

"Want to talk about it?" Galaxeé asked. When someone opened the exit door, a cold blast of winter blew inside. She pulled the full-length mink tighter around her body, dancing a little jig on the marble floor. "Momma and I knew something was wrong and you haven't said a word since. He didn't hurt you, did he, sweetie?"

"No," Rio said softly.

"No, he didn't hurt you or, no, you don't want to talk about it?"

"He didn't hurt me physically."

"Okay," Galaxeé replied and slid her arm around Rio's shoulders. "Want to stay at my place tonight? We could do a jammie party. Just you and me. Get shit-faced. We don't have to go to work until Thursday."

"Bryce doesn't know where I live, Galaxeé. You saw him leave right after the ceremony. He won't look for me anyway."

"Oh." A few quiet seconds went by. "Do you want him to?"

Her emotions dubious, Rio wasn't sure what she wanted anymore. "We'd better go. Randy's waving."

They held on to each other's arm and hurried in mini-steps toward the Lexus.

The ride home was quiet and subdued. Rio had nothing to do but pick at the new color Galaxeé had polished on her fingers and toes today, sit and watch the snowflakes falling from the cloudy skies above Denver and think about what had happened.

"Warm enough back there?" Randy asked.

"Perfect."

Why couldn't her life be as perfect as Galaxeé and Randy's, where she'd feel grateful for a loving relationship, caring and devoted, a once-in-a-lifetime opportunity?

When am I supposed to get mine? Did I already miss the chance? Or is it still hanging in the wind?

"Here we are." Randy opened the car door.

"Stay there," she said. "I can make it on my own. Thanks, you guys. I had a good time."

"Sure you don't want to come by?" Galaxeé asked, peering

between the bucket seats. "You can bring the 1800. I've got rabbit food, too."

"I'll pass tonight. Rain check?"

"Anytime," Galaxeé said and smiled. She blew Rio a kiss. "Call me tomorrow or sooner if you feel like it."

"We'll wait here until you get inside," Randy said as Rio climbed out of the car. "Good night."

She waved and stepped quickly through the few inches of snow to the heavy, metal door leading to her loft.

Inside, Rio kicked off her heels, tromped to the closet, and hung her fur. The floor was cool on her bare feet. She wiggled and curled her toes, grimaced from the achiness.

Unzipping her dress on the way to the bathroom, she had it peeled off before closing the door and stripping out of her panties. She took a hot, hot shower to clear her brain and warm her chilled bones.

When she was finished, the fluffy white robe wrapped around her skin in soothing warmth. She shoved her feet into a pair of rabbit-eared slippers she'd left by the door.

She tried to think of what work needed tending tomorrow, or sometime. The invoices at Killer's had been paid already, inventory completed, new stock put away and they weren't expecting any shipments for another week. Newly waxed hardwood floors were the prettiest picture. Stools had been re-covered and the coolers cleaned and disinfected. Luanne had spotlessly sanitized everything in Killer's small kitchen.

She wouldn't need to go in for anything, except to check if the break-in had caused a problem. Galaxeé had already filed a report with police and called their insurance company.

Rio went to the kitchen to keep her hands busy.

She filled the sink with soapy water and Clorox, scrubbed down the counters, wiped each appliance's surfaces, did the same in the three bathrooms and replaced the towels. Only time prevented her from starting a floor-wax job.

At one o'clock in the morning, she poured a glass of wine, moseyed toward a window overlooking Denver and sank into the plush cushions on one of two tan suede eight-foot sofas.

Between the pair of picture windows, the saltwater aquarium bubbled gently. Some of the exotic fish darted from plant to plant, corner to corner, in a hide-and-seek chase. The bright orange clownfish hovered at the waterline, looking for more to eat as usual and the royal-blue Siamese Betta glided elegantly in its own area, secluded, without companionship. Exactly like she had lived.

Running her fingers over the picture window, Rio cleared the dew, watched each droplet stream down the glass. Snow continued to fall at an odd angle, blurring the streetlight's glow like her emotions seeking solace from the pain tearing her heart in two.

Her cell phone chimed a jazzy tune. Rio knew it was Bryce, or possibly Galaxeé. No one else would call this late. Galaxeé knew better, knew Rio needed time alone.

And she was afraid to answer when it chimed again. She stared at the unit lying on the table, then she sneaked a peek out the window, ensuring Bryce's Cadillac wasn't parked on the street and he waiting by her door. She would not let him inside her safe haven to disrupt her well-being again. Except, he hadn't known where she lived anyway.

He'd called God knows how many times today, and she'd ignored the recorded messages. Why answer now? Why hadn't she turned the noisy thing off?

It chimed again. Cautiously, she leaned forward, read the display. The number was unfamiliar. Pay phone? Surely he hadn't foolishly bought a temporary cell, expecting her to answer?

Lord knows why, but she picked up.

"Did I wake you?"

"Marcus!" Excitement coursed through Rio at the sound of her brother's voice. "Where are you? Stateside?"

"D.C. for now. I'm flying into Denver in a few days. Is that same room still available to put up a tired-out preacher?"

And dread sprinted up her spine.

"What's the problem, snookums?" Randy asked.

He lounged in the oversize, tufted chair near the fireplace, watching Galaxeé wear a trail into the carpeting. Sampson and Delilah, the Borzoi hounds, sat on each side of the ottoman watching her as well.

"You've been pacing and cooking ever since we got here," Randy said. He puffed on his pipe. The sweet vanilla aroma wafted through the living room, mixed with the delicate scent of yeast bread.

"Rio," she mumbled.

"What about her? Come sit. You're making me and our pups tired."

Sighing, Galaxeé grabbed the side seams of her rainbow caftan, lifted the fabric, climbed over Delilah and onto Randy's lap. Settling, she said, "Did you notice how quiet she was at the party and when we drove her home?"

"No more quiet than usual. She's not as talkative as you or as aggressive, but that's what I like about you."

"I like everything about you." She pressed a chaste kiss to his lips. "But I'm worried about Rio. She wasn't herself after what happened."

"What did happen?"

"Some drama."

"Uh-oh. Don't get involved in anything you'll regret."

"Too late." She grinned, showed teeth.

"Cecilia." Randy rarely called her by her birth name, but this time his tone sounded reprimanding, as if she'd cursed.

"Rio and Bryce belong together. What's wrong with helping things along? Wouldn't you want somebody to help us stay together?"

"Cecilia."

"Oh, pookie. I won't do much, just give them a little push," Galaxeé cooed. She planted a sloppy kiss on his smooth lips. "With Momma's help, of course."

"Oh, brother." Randy emptied the aromatic tobacco from his pipe into a crystal ashtray. "Why can't you let nature take its course and quit meddling?"

"Because Mother Nature's busy sometimes." Galaxeé wrapped her arms around his neck, nuzzled his cheek. "Afterward, we can celebrate with a little champagne. Oh, never mind, maybe wine."

His hand slipped under her caftan, found its way between her thighs and she spread a little for him, gave him better access. "Why not champagne if this is so important?"

"I forgot I don't have any pretty flutes. But wine will work, just not with strawberries. Maybe some plain old cheese and crackers. How about that?" She shifted positions, straddled his thighs, began unbuttoning his shirt, following with kisses down his smooth chest.

"Whatever my baby wants."

"Your baby wants a lollipop." Galaxeé scooted farther down his legs.

Rio rapped on the door and rang the doorbell.

It was cold today, freezing with a light breeze blowing snow in miniature tornadoes. The sidewalks were ice-covered beneath a layer of fresh drifting snow, the streets were slick, cars rolling their way slowly from stoplight to stoplight. Every snowplow had been out all night, trying to keep up with the storm. As predicted, eleven inches had fallen.

By nine this morning, the sky was clear, sun shining brightly, the air crisp and clean—free of the brown cloud constantly marring Denver's airspace. Farther west, heavy snow had painted the majestic Rocky Mountains glistening white against a sparkling blue sky. Few scenes were as breathtaking or beautiful as this masterpiece on display. Soon, Rio knew, she'd journey to her mountain cabin surrounded by a winter wonderland. She could hardly wait to vacate the city.

Galaxeé opened the door. "Hey, girl. Took a while, huh? Bet the roads are slick as snot on a doorknob."

Grimacing at the sound of that statement, Rio stomped her booted feet on the carpet remnant. She shed her wool street coat and Galaxeé hung it in the hall closet. "About right." She traded her boots for a pair of slippers her friend kept for visitors. Safeguarding the new plush, white carpet took great effort. "I got a call late last night."

"Not from Bryce."

Frowning, Rio wondered just how Galaxeé knew he hadn't rung her phone. At all, when she'd thought he would. She'd stayed up until three this morning, expecting one. "No. Marcus."

Galaxeé screwed up her face. "What now?"

"He's in D.C., back from Somalia."

"And?" she asked flatly.

"He's coming to Denver in a couple days."

"Just fucking great."

"Stop that, Galaxeé! He's my brother, a preacher who has never, will never, appreciate your foul mouth."

"He's a self-righteous asshole who preys on the struggling. He also steals from the stupid and keeps it for himself!"

"He does not," Rio said, stomping her foot, "keep any money for himself, except to survive on."

"Survive, my ass," Galaxeé shot back, planting small fists on her hips. "*If* that were true, why does he drive a damn Rolls-Royce, wear diamond and ruby cufflinks, have all them damn old-ass women, young ones, too, kissing his stinky feet? Do you truly believe he was in Somalia? I'm thinking he was in Monaco or some other pricey-assed locality! Marcus doesn't

have the balls to go to Somalia or any other war-torn country
and put himself in harm's way."

"That's not true. He wouldn't lie to me, he's my—"

Galaxeé threw hew her hands in the air. "Yeah, he's your
brother, in blood only. And he didn't learn shit from the Rev,
who would be appalled seeing what his son has turned into
after all these years. Girl, don't you think it's about time you
took off the blindfold? Marcus is as wicked as wicked comes.
Unfortunately, he's also damn smart. Slick. Way slicker than
Carson ever thought to be."

No doubt, Rio had shielded her eyes from the obvious as
her mother had quietly walked around, day in and day out,
blinders firmly in place, believing the best in every person on
the planet. Was that so wrong?

Was Galaxeé right about Marcus? She was right more often
than not. But, Rio had still refused to lift the blindfold very
high.

A few years ago, Galaxeé had jumped dead in Marcus's face,
had accused him of the treachery she was articulating now. For
a few tense seconds, Rio thought he was capable of using his
fists against her. She'd intervened before a knock-down, drag-
out fight broke out. Galaxeé was never one to back down. At
the time and for someone her small size, she would have
brawled with the best of them.

"How long is he planning to upset your life this time?"

Puh-lese. "He doesn't upset me."

"Bullshit. If he didn't, you wouldn't be peeling my twelve-
dollar polish from your nails."

Rio wrapped her hands behind her back. "Two, maybe three
days."

"At your place. Great. Just great."

"I didn't say—"

"Not a problem," Galaxeé mumbled. She said something
else unintelligible. "I need tea. And we can talk about *any*thing
different."

Fine by her. Arguments had become all too familiar these days. She was tired of them, sick of them. Everybody seemed to pluck at her last assailable nerve. Well, no longer. As of today, times were changing. A new Rio would finally emerge. Stronger, confident, bolder.

"Where're the children?" Their arguments never lasted for very long and neither held a grudge against the other.

"Sampson and Delilah are at the hairdresser's. They needed a bath and cut. Randy dropped them off after lunch on his way back to the office."

Two huge animals, white carpeting, mostly pastel-colored furniture and delicate crystal. Rio shook her head. Galaxeé was lucky to have Randy, his giving ways and his insight for maid service.

"Coffee? Soda? Hot tea since it's freezing outside?"

She nodded, followed Galaxeé to the formal dining area and stopped at the china cabinet. "When did you get these?" She popped the glass door open and withdrew a fine crystal flute.

Galaxeé turned the flames higher under the teakettle. "Lunchtime."

"How? You're not dressed yet." She wore the African-print caftan Randy had brought back with him last month—a gift from an ambassador's wife he'd met.

"Randy."

Rio studied the inscription on the stem's base. "Baccarat? Bet it's way too pricey for me. I'm lucky to have a few pieces of Waterford."

"Those are Les Deux Palm Miers. They were out of the Dom Perignons. He didn't want to wait for them to be shipped."

"How much?"

"You don't want to know."

"More than Dom's?" Rio didn't have the faintest idea what those cost, but if Randy bought them, a bundle.

"Triple."

"You need to quit," she admonished and set the fragile flute back into its place. She closed the glass door gently. "Or he should."

What sort of hint had Galaxeé dropped this time? Rio wondered more how long Randy would continue financing her penchant for the extravagant. Galaxeé had the overseas investment banker, one of the most eligible bachelors according to *Ebony* magazine last year, wrapped around the first knuckle of her pinky after their first date.

"Got a set of eight," Galaxeé said. "I just haven't unpacked them."

Was that a blush she saw from this distance?

"I'll give you a couple."

"Who would I drink champagne with?" A low whistle from the teakettle gained strength. "Besides, I couldn't afford the bubbly those flutes require."

Galaxeé flashed a disgruntled sideways glance and lifted the kettle from her six-burner industrial stove. She loved to cook as much and as often as Momma Barnett.

"Hell, Rio, you can put Kool-Aid in them if you wanted, or tap water, but I'll give you a bottle of Dom with them." She put a tea bag into each fragile china cup set and poured hot water. "Let it steep for three minutes. Tibetan steeps well. Speaking of celebrations."

"We weren't."

"We are now," Galaxeé replied, frowning, shoving her bottom lip out in a pout. "Oscar asked Momma to marry him last night. Remember?"

He was so cute and nervous when he'd asked for her hand while at the podium. Momma Barnett didn't answer right away and Oscar's forehead spontaneously erupted into a sweat. Rio had never seen him in such a fluster, like a teenager asking for a first date, expecting rejection.

"And?"

They moved to the living room, choosing to sit in oversized chairs, color matching an evening winter sky.

"I suggested we have a little engagement party for them, a small, intimate function. She agreed as long as she gets to do all the cooking. Momma doesn't trust a caterer."

"Sounds good. We can use the loft if you help me wax the floors."

Galaxeé screwed her face up. "Like hell. Call a floor company, have it replaced."

"Girl, you are too lazy," Rio said and laughed.

"We're talking what, three thousand square feet? Shit, not a chance. No, we'll do it at Momma's place. How does tonight sound?"

"Tonight?" she questioned.

"Yeah, why not?"

"Last minute, but fine." More like last second. "I don't have anything planned. What do you want me to do to help?"

"Just come. No gifts. They don't want any gifts, said they have too much shit now. Card. Eightish. Calls have been made."

Rio narrowed her eyes. "When did this plan go into action?"

"This morning." She showed a mouth full of teeth. "Barnetts don't waste time. Life's too short. Momma knew whom she wanted to invite. Close friends of hers and Oscar's. She said their friends needed to get out or shrivel up and die. You know how she feels about getting old. She's not ready to start yet, even if her friends have."

"She's a timeless beauty," Rio said, "as is her daughter."

"Get out." Galaxeé cackled. "Just don't let anybody see my bony toothpicks and knobby knees. What I wouldn't give to have your shapely legs."

What she wouldn't give to have a man to love as Galaxeé had been blessed with Randy. Utter devotion. But we can't all have everything.

What do I have with half my life over? A job, roof over my head, a car and brilliant, saltwater fish for daily companionship. Plus, Galaxeé for a best friend. What more can I ask for?

She smiled at that, but it faded just as quickly. One day, her friend would marry, spend her spare time with a husband, and travel with him as he did so often. Randy hadn't proposed yet, but Rio was absolutely convinced he would one day. She and Galaxeé would stay friends and, if they still worked together, which was doubtful, do lunch occasionally and maybe shop for an afternoon.

What would she do in her spare time?

". . . tonight?" she heard Galaxeé finish.

"Hmm? Tonight what?"

"What are you wearing tonight?"

"Haven't thought about it. My trusty navy?" Rio asked. Her jaw went slack. "Don't give me that look. It's ugly."

"So's your trusty bedsheet. You need to burn it, or use it for a rag. To wax the floors?" she said and chuckled.

"What're you wearing?"

"A sexy outfit for my babycakes. Might be a couple singles invited." She sipped at her tea, staring over the cup's rim. "I remember two or three suave, good-looking friends of Oscar's."

"Quit trying to set me up, Galaxeé. I'm not in the market for a good-looking friend."

No, Galaxeé thought. Not a friend, but a permanent lover. And she had exactly the right one in mind.

Rio tried on six different outfits and none looked worth a darn. She dragged out her trusty navy, held it to her body and dropped it on the floor, hanger and all, groaning.

It was ugly, put the "u" in the word, and outdated. Disgusted, she balled it up and tossed it to the trash can beside the vanity. On second thought, grabbing the ankle-length cloak that looked more like a twin-bed sheet, she could use a few cleaning rags.

Galaxeé had said she was wearing emerald green tonight. Rio bet she meant stylish attire to go with emeralds. The woman had more jewelry than a department store's showcase.

Oh, well, if you've got it, flaunt it. She snapped on the tennis bracelet laced with zircons, hooked her mother's diamond pendant around her neck, and fought with the diamond stud earrings she'd bought herself on a whim—the day her divorce was final—in celebration. Devon had only purchased one diamond piece of jewelry, her engagement ring. The stone in the ring he wore now was bigger than her one-third carat stone.

Now, what to wear?

The hangers screeched on the bar as she passed up old dress after passé outfit. She looked over at the clock and groaned. Seven-thirty, and she went back through her wardrobe. She should've gone by the club on her way home, picked out a teenybopper number.

No, no, the guests are older, more sophisticated folks.

She stomped her bare foot. And it was too late to call Galaxeé for help and way too late to stop by Cherry Creek Mall on the way to the Barnett condominium.

She yanked out a knee-length black skirt. Flipping through tops, she found a wraparound black knit threaded with silver strands. This would have to do. Black heels. And some stupid hose.

By the time she found black hose without a snag, hole or run, she'd emptied the drawer and the time had moved to quarter of eight. Galaxeé was going to kill her for being late. Or Momma Barnett would.

With one shoe on and carrying the other, trying to switch purses at the same time, Rio hobbled to the phone and dialed the Barnett residence.

"I'm running late."

"Girl, hurry your ass up," Galaxeé ordered. "Everybody's here."

"You said eight o'clock."

"Oh. Momma told everybody else seven thirty. Sorry. Get the lead out." Galaxeé hung up.

"Darn her," Rio breathed. She tottered to the elevator and got her shoe on before it started its descent.

The roads were a mess and traffic was backed up for a mile, according to radio reports, after a stupid fender-bender that caused a twelve-car pileup. She took the first exit off the highway and maneuvered through city streets.

It was twenty after by the time Rio arrived at the high-rise. And there was no place to park except on the street. She hated leaving her Benz out in the open, unprotected. But this was Cherry Creek. Cops patrolled regularly.

At the Barnett door, she heard chatter, music, and laughter. The engagement party was in full swing. Nobody would notice her late arrival. Or care.

Rio tried the doorknob. It was locked. She rang the bell and waited, smoothing her skirt at the last second.

"Somebody get that," she heard Galaxeé holler.

Expecting to see Momma Barnett or even Oscar, Rio lifted her chin and put a smile on her face.

But when the door opened, she thought she would faint.

13

"Rio," Galaxeé yelled from across the room. She looped her arm through her mother's and dragged her to the door. "What took you so long?"

She looked like she was ready to turn tail and run, hop over the first fire escape no matter that they were five stories above the frozen ground.

Galaxeé and Rosalind each took hold of an arm, led her inside and helped her out of the black waist-length jacket defining her shapely figure.

"Cecilia, put this in the master," Rosalind said. "I'm so glad you made it, Rio. You remember Bryce Sullivan, don't you?"

"Stricken" couldn't describe the expression on her face better. Bryce had trouble forming a simple "hello."

God, she was as radiant as the first day he'd met her. Seemed so long ago and, yet, only twenty-two hours and thirty-odd minutes had passed since they'd faced each other last. Yeah, he'd counted every minute of his miserable life as it ticked away.

Last night, the chat with his mother had flipped his guts inside out. He had no way to contact Frankie and no way to stop her from invading his privacy or his mother's. She hadn't gone as far as mentioning his second gig, but she'd hinted at a possible get-back-together scenario. Claudine Berardi was ecstatic.

Sleep-deprived, Bryce made it to work this morning much later than he'd ever arrived. Maureen had left six frantic messages on voice mail, wondering where he was, wondering if everything was all right. By the time he made it into the office, she'd called every hospital in Denver, the police station—911, no less—and called Mother, who had left a dozen messages. Bryce just didn't want to be at the office or talk to anyone other than Rio. And she'd not called once, not even to bitch him out for his stupid behavior.

As for Frankie, Maureen said she'd called in sick. Yeah, she was all right. Bryce figured he'd deal with her later and none too delicately.

Oscar had dropped by at ten thirty to invite him to the engagement party tonight. Bryce declined, but then Rosalind called and refused to take "no" for an answer. Persuasive. Bossy. He was glad to get out, though, away from Rio's scent permeating his household. Or was it just his imagination?

Now she was here, standing three feet away, and he couldn't take her into his arms, couldn't kiss her sweet lips, couldn't tell her how much he wanted her in his life.

The same knotty ache started in his chest, worked its way to his throat, nearly blocking his air passage.

"Rio, would you care for a cocktail?" Rosalind asked, breaking the silence. "Rio? I'm sure Mr. Sullivan . . ."

Gazes locked, Bryce had no idea how long they'd stared at each other when she broke eye contact and acknowledged Rosalind.

"Yes, please," she said with a ghost of a smile. "I'll get it myself." She hurried toward the kitchen, dodging guests, hips swaying a seductive rhythm.

Bryce sighed. How long could he stand to be in the same room with her and not talk to her or touch her?

"Give her time," Rosalind said. "She'll come around. Only this time, you had better be a gentleman. Come now, join the party."

He had trouble forcing his legs to move. Did she just say what he thought she'd said? She'll come around? Not a chance. Rio wanted no part of him, not as a lover, maybe not even as a friend. The ache in his chest intensified.

He followed Rosalind to an interesting group. The sexagenarians were as lively as any band of rowdy twenty-somethings, laughing, talking and drinking. He moved beside an elderly, baldheaded gentleman and vaguely listened to the conversation. They were discussing the old days, a period Bryce knew nothing about.

From this vantage point, and adding his height, he had a clear view of the kitchen, a commanding view of Rio. Odd, he'd always seen her sipping wine, but tonight she held a tumbler of dark liquid with cracked ice. When Galaxeé tapped her shoulder, the tumbler nearly slipped from Rio's fingers. Nerves. Or fear.

He'd leave in the next instant, if he'd caused her to fear him.

But Galaxeé said a few words to her. She ran her hand down her friend's arm and Rio looked up, made eye contact with him.

Talk to me. Please. I never intended to hurt you, would never hurt you.

She blushed. She actually blushed. New, profound emotions gave him more hope than he'd wished for in a lifetime and, at that moment, Rosalind laid her fingers on his forearm.

A warm tingling spread through his body like wildfire, one like he'd experienced somewhere before, and calm settled over him, the knotted ache ceasing its torment. Rosalind smiled.

Leaning toward him, she whispered, "A gentleman never keeps a lady waiting."

An instant later, Bryce wove his way around guests in a desperate rush, heart pounding, blood pumping, mind swirling with anticipation. And hope.

Rio stepped back into a corner when her partner left her side, eyes wide and glorious.

"Don't make me regret this night and don't make me come after you, Sullivan," Galaxeé grated as she marched away.

He swallowed, frowned. "How are you?"

"Fine," Rio replied, eyes shifting as if looking for a way out.

He knew he blocked the doorway from any attempt at escape or of anyone's intrusion unless she took a chance at vaulting through the food-service opening. She looked ready to leap. "I didn't know you were going to be here."

"This," she said, waving her hand between them, "wasn't planned. At least, not by me."

Knife-sharp, the words pierced his heart. What little hope he had embraced, fizzled. "I-I want to apologize again for last night. And anytime I've ever hurt you, Rio."

"No big deal."

"It is a big deal. To me, it is. I've done some stupid, childish things before, but last night . . . last night," he said and swallowed again. "I made an ass of myself and now . . . now I've lost—"

Her cell phone rang. Nervously, she upended her purse, dumping everything on the counter. Bryce watched her beautiful face, saw the change while she talked, and knew something was terribly wrong.

"I have to go," she said hurriedly, stuffing her purse again. "Have to find my coat."

He caught her arm before she fled passed him. "What happened?"

"Alarm. Killer's. I have to—"

"I'll drive you."

She shook her head.

"Rio," Bryce said, "You can't drive when you're shaking like this. Your coat, it's in the master bedroom. I'll tell the Barnett family."

"I don't want . . . Galaxeé's too . . . tell Randy."

Cops swarmed Killer's perimeter.

"They didn't get in, but somebody pried the hell out of the back door enough for the alarm to lose contact," one officer said. "Isn't this the second time we've been called here in recent days?"

"Y-Yes, S-Sunday night it w-went off. Break-in," Rio stammered, cold and shivery. "We've had additional locks added."

"They held, but somebody sure wants to get inside this place pretty badly," the officer replied.

Bryce wrapped his arm around her shoulder, pulled her closer to his side. Heat radiated through his suit jacket and into her body. She snuggled even closer. The lightweight coat she wore wouldn't melt an ice cube.

The policeman's shoulder unit crackled. He moved away to answer the summons.

"Get inside the car and stay warm," Bryce said, putting his keys in her hand. He wrapped her icy fingers around them and opened the Escalade's driver door. "I'll deal with the cops, fill out the report and bring it to you for a signature."

Grateful, Rio nodded. Her feet were freezing. Killer's was last on the snow-shoveling list from the looks of things. The parking lot was still socked in and, with gusting winds, deep drifts edged up the side of the red brick.

She climbed inside, started the engine and turned the heat on full blast when Bryce closed the door. Sitting there shivering, she wondered why someone wanted to get inside Killer Bods.

The club really had nothing expensive or hockable. Except the new computer. And thieves would play like the devil getting the gigantic safe out; four workers fought to get it up the stairs. They'd bolted the fireproof steel box to wall studs and the floor. To open its heavy door required a key and combination that no one knew other than Rio, Galaxeé and Momma Barnett.

Bryce opened the driver door. "Your signature."

She scribbled her name. "What about the back door?"

"They pounded it back into place and Brinks did a test. Everything's A-OK. Cops said they'd cruise by more often. They don't expect a return visit tonight, though." He gazed into her eyes, smiled. "I'll be back in a couple."

Comforted by his nearness, Rio watched him while he dealt with the officers. She'd missed being with him, missed the gentleness she knew lay beneath his jealousies. Could she deal with that one emotion? She didn't know, but she wanted to try if he was willing to work on his behavior.

They talked little during the ride back to Cherry Creek. She had no idea what to say to him and, evidently, he was at a loss for words.

When the elevator doors parted, Rio said, "This isn't five."

"I know," Bryce quietly replied. "Will you give me a few minutes to talk to you? Just a few. Please. I promise I won't touch you."

She stepped out of the elevator into a glass-enclosed solarium. Frost covered the windows, but the air was warm and humid enough for lilies, roses and African violets among a multitude of beautiful vegetation, displaying a springtime rainbow. Momma Barnett had said condominium owners tended the garden for relaxation.

She bent over a brilliant peach-colored lily, another aromatic vine, gardenias, inhaling their sweet fragrance, when she heard Bryce call her name. Rio spun around.

"I put money in the pot it came from, handpicked. It's for you." He held a single red rose that touched her heart more than any bouquet would ever please her.

She looked down at the perfect bud, a flowering specimen, then at the stem. He'd shucked every thorn, his fingers scratched and red. Rio accepted the blossom. She held it against her drumming heart while tears burned the backs of her eyes.

"A small price for the terrible things I've done, things that drove you away from me," Bryce admitted, holding his arms out. His hands vibrated, but he kept them suspended, kept them off her. "I fell in love with you, Rio, and—"

"Don't," she said on a sob and leapt into his arms, clung to him as he embraced her.

Bryce buried his face against her neck, struggling with the powerful, first-time emotions. He'd denied having the mounting feelings for Rio, had quarantined what should be romping testosterone and sheer lust. No longer. He did love her.

"I will never hurt you again. Ever." He squeezed tighter, wanting to absorb her to keep from losing her again.

"Bryce?" she said, chuckling on a suffocating noise. "You're hurting me now."

"Oh. Sorry," he said. He touched his lips to hers, a gentle peck, but went back in for more, deepening the kiss. She responded. The tongue duel kicked his pulse into overdrive, raced to his loins.

Not here, he told himself. He would not treat her so callously. Backing off, Bryce lowered Rio to the floor in vibrant contact with his body.

"We really do need to talk about last night," she said.

Talk? He wanted to make love to her.

But, okay, talk was good. They did need to converse, a private dialogue rather than a screaming match in the middle of a party. "Can we go home first? To my place or—"

"Yours," she said a little breathlessly. "I'd gotten used to being there with you."

He wasted no time. Bryce grabbed her hand and dragged her along. They'd leave now, talk in the car, and get home in twenty minutes, making love in twenty-five. Twenty-one. Somehow, he'd make sure they got to the bed first.

She dug in her heels. "In an hour."

He came to a dead stop, groaning.

"We can't just sneak out," Rio said, pulling at his hand. "I wasn't at the party long enough."

"What difference does it make? You showed up." And he was so thankful they both had.

"Etiquette," she snapped, frowning.

Women always had this thing about proper decorum. Men never gave a goddamn, and never would. How the hell was he going to stand there with her and keep his hands off her for a whole freakin' hour?

"I'll meet you in an hour and a half or so."

"What are you saying?" Was she planning to . . . That's a guy thing! College years, Bryce sent chicks home while he stayed out to play. Hell, no.

Rio smoothed her hair into place. "I'll go downstairs first. You can follow in five minutes."

"What?"

"We can't walk in together."

"We left together, remember?" he said, temper on the verge of a rolling boil. "Stop that." He grabbed her busy hands into one of his.

"Look," Rio said, "it's different. The Barnett guests are different. They're an altogether different generation."

"Exactly what the hell does that mean?" He held on to her hands, though she tried to free herself.

"Can't you just do this for me? Please."

He chewed on it a moment, came to a decision. "All right, fine. One hour tops, and we're out of here." God, he wanted to get inside her panties. "Go. Now. Hurry." He checked his watch as she dashed inside the elevator.

The party was still in full swing. One couple danced a jitterbug and a suave older guy moved his partner gracefully across the floor in what Bryce guessed was a two-step.

He looked all over for Rio. When he saw her and winked, she looked away. Never did smile. The next time Bryce approached, she walked off. The final insult, Rio deliberately shrugged away from his touch and engaged in conversation with some old dude about trimming damn flowers.

What in the hell was going on now?

Yep, they needed to talk and soon. Fuck an hour.

He went up behind Rio and whispered, "Get your coat. We're leaving." Her shoulders drew up, but she didn't budge. "Or I make a scene. Right here in the middle of the room."

Rio stomped off.

He slammed the garage entry door with enough force to make her teeth grind away enamel.

They'd argued from the time she finally stepped into the elevator until they reached the lobby. Rio was mad because of his childish ways; Bryce was angry because she wouldn't walk out the door with him and because she'd made him wait in the hallway an extra five minutes.

Electing to drive her Mercedes instead of riding with him started a brand-new quarrel. Rio shut the car door while he complained.

They made it to his house at the same time because he'd followed her, staying dead on her bumper. Was he thinking she'd take off in a different direction and dodge this argument? Not today, not the way her mood had darkened.

Rio followed him up the stairs, listening to his grumbling and complaining. Men. This was another emotional outburst he needed to tame. Jealousy, threatening to make a scene, whining for no reason and slamming doors—oh, yes, they were going to talk about this mess before anything else.

In the bedroom, he yanked his tie off and tossed it. Just

tossed it. Rio snatched it off the floor and hung it on the armoire. She unzipped her tight skirt, wriggled free of the fabric and draped it across the armoire's seat.

"You really need to get control of yourself, Bryce."

"Control? How the hell can I get control?" he asked, unbuttoning his shirt. He stripped it off, kicking off his shoes at the same time. "When you treat me like a damn virus."

She unwrapped the knit top, pulled it off and hung it next to his tie. "I don't treat you badly. We just can't—" She fought with the darn pantyhose and tore a gaping hole in one leg before she got them down her legs.

"Can't what? Be seen together?" he snapped. He dropped his trousers, including his boxers, to the floor, stepped out and kicked them aside, then pulled off each sock.

"Not yet. Not—"

"Why the hell not?" He advanced on her, spun Rio around, unhooked her black lacy bra and snatched it off, tossed it and spun her back to face him.

"Because, darn it," she said, stamping her foot. "Because you're too young and I'm too old. Because you're too handsome for an old woman to be hanging off your arm. Because I'm black and you're—"

He kissed her, lifted her off the floor and delved his tongue way down her throat. She kissed him back, her arms circling around his neck, molding her body to his, loving how he felt against her. The penetrating heat, the need would always be there.

Rio threaded her fingers into his hair, enjoying the feel of his dark waves covering her hands like fine silk. He slanted his mouth over hers, deepening the kiss, and she melted as liquid fire set her body aflame.

He lifted his head. "I want to make love to you. Make real love to you. Slowly. Intense. Will you let me do that?"

She kissed him hard and bit his bottom lip. "Yes."

He slid her down his body and she tried to crawl back up. "Slowly, Rio. Otherwise, I'll lose it too soon. Hurt you. Don't want to hurt you," he panted.

"I want you to lose it now. Waited too long." She clamped her fingers around his erection, squeezed, and Bryce groaned, deep and rumbling.

Sliding her hands back and forth along his length, she watched the head swell, veins engorged, pulsing. Heavy and smooth. And all of this beauty would soon be inside her. She rubbed the tip against her belly and a tiny orgasmic spasm caught her off guard. She tightened the muscles in her legs, whimpering.

Bryce ran his hands up her arms to her shoulders, cupped her cheeks. "You're gonna make me lose it just by watching you," he whispered. "Just feeling your hands on me makes me frantic." His shook, vibrated against her face.

Rio nuzzled her way through the dense mat of hair on his chest, kissed his nipples, sucked one bead into her mouth and bit gently. Bryce sucked in air between his teeth. She continued onward, trailing kisses over his chest down to his abdomen. Hard muscles twitched. He hissed out the next breath. She continued down, down, sank to her knees, pressed her lips to his hardness, ran her tongue over the bulging head.

She took him into her mouth, sucked at the tip and glided her lips a little down his length, teeth grazing his hardness. He was too big, too stout, and she drew back.

But Bryce shoved his fingers into her hair, forced more of himself into her mouth, drew her back away. Again, two more times.

Above her, Rio heard the roughness of his panting. He was on the brink of combustion. She wanted him needy, wanted to give him the same erotic pleasures he'd given her.

Bryce tugged her free. "Enough! Damn it."

He dropped to his knees, knowing this had been her first attempt at oral anything other than kissing. She was awkward and clumsy and . . . and awkward. Inexperienced teasing, but willing to please him. A delectable mouth and body unused to any primitive sex, a mouth so dangerous to his sense of composure she'd strangle if he let her continue.

"I won't let you do this."

"Why?"

Jesus. He ached. He hurt. "No, you can't," Bryce replied and straddled her over his thighs. "Never do anything just to please someone else and not yourself. Jesus, Rio, you're killing me." He'd die if he didn't get inside her soon, or lose the load all over the dark-blue carpeting.

"If you won't let me taste you with my mouth, I want to taste you inside my body." Lifting, she tugged her panties aside and sank down full length, engulfed him on a small cry.

Christ Jesus. She was sopping wet and still tight as hell. When she lifted her body again, he tore the panties away, shoved his hands beneath her butt cheeks and moderated her descent. He'd seen the pain on her face. Saw it now. Why did he have to be so damn big, expanding each time she slid down his cock?

"I'm sorry, kitten. Didn't want to hurt you." He kissed every inch of her face, finally kissed her lips and thrust his tongue into her mouth, tasting the essence of himself.

Holding her tightly with one arm, he leaned her back onto the thick, plush carpeting. Her long legs came around his waist, squeezed. Bryce slipped deeper inside, so very deep into tightness. He withdrew by inches, thrust again, slowly, intensely, holding back from driving recklessly inside her. He would make love to her and give her pleasure to forget the pain he'd caused.

She climaxed, a quick spike, and dug her nails into his shoulders, whimpering. The sound was as sweet as she was, but only the calm had begun, before the tempestuous storm sure to brew. Passion lay in her hazel eyes—a glassy shine of sparkling gold. She would give herself completely.

He increased the tempo. "Take me with you, kitten."

Undulating, she writhed beneath him, the tremors sparking a new beginning. He sat up, dragged her hips onto his thighs, never missing a beat, thrusting. Harder, fast and furiously, sliding out wet, glistening from her juices, and disappearing inside her again, retreated, vanished again.

He kneaded her breasts, then tormenting, used his thumbs on her sensitivity, rolling the swollen little nub, his fingers smoothing the satin skin around the opening where their bodies had joined. She was almost there. So was he. Bryce pounded harder, plunging into her, shoving her farther across the carpet. He had reached his limit. Steaming sweat poured down his face and splashed onto her belly.

"Now, Rio," he ground out. "Goddamn it, now." Unable to hold back, he burst, opening the floodgates that blurred his vision with blinding light, and lost track of reality.

And she reared up screaming his name, wrapping all her limbs around him, and viciously clamped his cock in a sizzling inferno.

Incineration.

He let loose a bellow loud enough to split logs and lifted Rio, shoved her body down hard, repeatedly, emptying every fluid gram of his loving inside her.

Shuddering and panting, Rio pressed her face to his throat, holding on to Bryce for dear life, unable to catch her breath, her senses bombarded with unmerciful chaos. The violence of their lovemaking had sent white-hot lightning through every fiber of her being. She tried not to move again. Each one tripped another quiver that shook and rattled her soul.

"You turn me inside out," she finally whispered. "I hate you for doing it so easily."

His hand slid over her backside, up her spine, down again. "You leave me open, raw with brutal pleasure, and wanting you more. But I don't hate you for it."

He kissed her shoulder, but when he moved his hips, another quavering shook her. "Don't move. They haven't stopped completely. God," Rio said, squeezing her eyes shut, sinking her nails into his muscled shoulders.

"Even at half-mast I can feel a pinching sensation. Damn, kitten," Bryce said. "Tell me when you're ready and I'll take you to bed."

Minutes later, Rio rested her head on Bryce's shoulder, her hand on his chest, curling soft hair. He drew lazy, finger-teasing circles over her hip.

"We were supposed to talk, before you seduced me," she said.

"We seduced each other."

"Whatever." She looked up into his eyes. "Bryce, what happened last night? What made you s-so upset?"

Frowning, he pinched the bridge of his nose and sighed audibly.

This didn't look easy for him, but he gathered her closer and launched into a speech that unfolded yesterday at dawn's arrival. She let him talk without questioning, without interrupting.

She should've called him as she'd promised. How was she to know he'd react this way? She'd know better next time, but she hadn't flirted with Evan. Yeah, he lost his cool, over nothing. Well, okay, she had ignored him. For good reason, but he had no right to barge into the ladies' room on a freight-train vendetta.

"I fell in love with you, Rio," Bryce said.

There was that word again. Love. He couldn't love her. Infatuation with an older woman, nothing more, ever. Didn't he realize that by the time he turned forty, she'd join the retired community and probably need detailing? A face-lift, boob job, liposuction. Just to keep him hers, and most likely the high-dollar events wouldn't help.

Of course, there's the male midlife crisis. Nope, couldn't go through that drama again. Not as a seventy-year-old hag, or even at sixty.

"I'm a guy who's never shown a jealous streak before," he continued. "Never knew I had one, and you bruised . . . you trampled my ego when I wanted you so badly."

Because there was no future in their relationship.

"I want us to go places. Do things. Be together as a couple."

She tsked to herself. *And look like Aunt Jemima with a Chippendale's calendar boy, holding hands and strolling down Larimer Street? I don't think so. What in the world was Galaxeé thinking?* What was going through her own mind?

"Let's enjoy right now," Rio said. She rolled on top of him, gyrated her hips, nipped at his lips. "Let's not think about tomorrow or any day after."

14

Rio combed her fingers lightly through her damp hair. She grabbed her designated toothbrush from the holder and spread a hefty layer of paste on the bristles.

Bryce had awakened at dawn. He'd made sweet love to her, slow and sensuous, so tenderly. Afterward, they'd cuddled until she shooed him from the bed and into the shower. No, she wasn't showering with him. He'd said he had to go into work today and get some business completed for a change. Showering together, they wouldn't make it out of the house.

She sat on the counter, swinging her legs rhythmically to the music playing from the CD, watching Bryce while she brushed her teeth.

The bathroom was still steamy and damp, but the mirror was clear. He'd wrapped a big blue towel around his waist, matching the one she had covering her body.

Barefoot on the heated floor, sable hair slicked back off his forehead, small droplets of water slid over his skin while he lathered shaving cream across the dark bristly shadow. The new growth had chafed her skin this morning. Everywhere.

"Shit." He'd nicked himself.

Rio giggled. "Need help?"

"No."

"Does my watching make you nervous?"

He ignored her. By the time Bryce finished carving his face, he had three tiny pieces of tissue attached to his chin and two on his thick neck.

"Maybe you should try an electric shaver," Rio said, thinking how many times she'd cut her legs and knees before switching to a less painful hair-removal method.

"Are you trying to brush the enamel off your teeth?" he asked. "Or are you afraid to spit in front of me?"

"Neither." She hopped off the counter, turned on the faucet and rinsed away the residue. "Three-minute brush job twice a day. No cavities, no silver and no gold. Got all thirty-two. Originals." She smiled brightly, then bent over and splashed her face with water. "Can you say the same?"

While she patted her face dry, he gave her a good, hard slap across the butt. Rio yipped and stood straight. Bryce soothed the sting with a gentle caress. He encircled her in his arms, her back flush against his chest.

Staring into her eyes through the reflection of the mirror, he said, "Three times a day. Crown. Got two teeth knocked out during football, chipped another. You'll call me today, won't you? We can do lunch."

She had no plans for the day. None. Zippo. "I've got a ton of work at Killer's."

"An early dinner?"

She looked away, folding the hand towel. "I'll let you know if I can."

"Call me anyway and make sure your cell's on," Bryce said with a smile, "or I'll come looking for you."

She refolded the towel and hung it on the rack. "I'll phone later on."

"Promise?"

Sighing, she said, "Yes."

Sure as the devil, he'd search for her at the club to drag her into public, and she had no reason to be at the club. She'd call him. Late. Too late for dinner. No, early, then again later.

"I'd better get dressed and out of your hair so you can get to work." She wiggled free of his embrace and sashayed toward the closets.

Bryce caught her arm and pulled her right into his arms. "Work can wait after that little hip action." He kissed her hard, bending her backward over the counter.

When his towel fell away, or maybe he'd yanked it free, Rio naturally spread for him. Sex with Bryce felt so right—all the time. She wrapped her fingers around his hardness, guided the pulsing head over the lips to her waiting heat, teasing, and refused him entrance.

"Open," he ordered.

"And if I don't?" She ran her tongue across her upper lip.

"We'll work on alternative methods later, and work on your technique," he said and chuckled. "Now, let me in." His noisy cell rang. "Shit."

Rio grinned. "Apparently, not everyone believes work can wait."

Probing her sensitivity, he said, "Fuck the phone."

"That's exactly what you'll have to do because you're not getting any from me now. Mood swing, and I don't do quickies." She shoved him backward, hopped off the counter and marched into the closet.

"Damn you," he mumbled darkly and went to get the phone.

As she drew the blue bikinis over her hips, she heard him say, "Hey, Boo." Rio straightened and her jaw went slack. *What?*

She strained to hear the one-sided conversation and couldn't catch a single snatch of his words, but his tone was as good as a caress. Rio huffed. Why wasn't she surprised? She'd seen him at the club, up close and personal with Frankie. Was she the caller?

Rio glanced in his direction. He had the same expression on his face when a woman was on the phone line.

She yanked her lightweight skirt off the hanger, shook it out hard enough to move furniture and dressed quickly.

"I'll be there in fifteen minutes," Bryce said.

Was that for her benefit? "I'll be there in fifteen minutes," Rio mimicked silently.

She stalked out of the closet. She grabbed her purse and keys from the nightstand. From there, she headed directly for the stairs in a stiff-legged stomp. Since she was leaving, he could do a get-together in five minutes. And stay there. Too bad the carpeting muffled her indignation.

She didn't get as far as the bedroom door.

Bryce wrapped around her, hauling back against his hard body, and he wouldn't let her loose. Both arms held her securely in a straitjacket embrace. But then, one hand slid over her breast, squeezed gently, moved down her belly and between her legs, cupping her mound. Rio hissed, squirming.

"Are you sure?" he said into the phone. "All right. Call me later. Where do you think you're going?" The cell phone landed on the bed.

"Home."

"It's not what you think, Rio." That big hand moved up, down and circled in a teasing motion, fingers pressing, while his heat penetrated her backside.

"Really," she said flatly. Darned if she'd ask who, what or where, and give him the upper hand. The hound. "What you do and who you talk to is your business, not mine."

He released the button to her skirt. Rio squirmed. The zipper disengaged. "Don't you dare!"

But his fingers skillfully delved inside the boundaries of her sagging skirt, then bikinis, and touched one special place that always sent her on an express-ride into orbit.

"Okay, the system's up and ready," Randy said.

He and Galaxeé had retrieved the club's videodiscs for viewing at his plush downtown office.

Galaxeé had dressed for cold weather in her fox jacket, highheeled boots, kicky suede skirt and silk blouse. She stared outside the gallery of plate-glass windows overlooking the Denver skyline. So much energy filled the planet and she wanted to absorb her share.

"Tell me when there's something worthwhile."

While Randy searched through the videos, she held her arms out, closed her eyes.

"Well, now," Randy said and chuckled. "They're making good use of the storage room between performances."

"I knew it." Galaxeé moved to his side. "What the hell?"

"Isn't that Orlando?"

"And Jason." She leaned forward, squinting. "That's Frankie! Ooh," Galaxeé said on a long note. "I don't want anybody to know about this, babycakes. Let me handle the situation."

A few minutes later, she squeaked out an "eww."

"Quiet, now, sugar cakes." Randy drew her down to his lap. "To each his own."

"But, booty—"

"Hush."

He depressed the floor button with his foot, engaging the locks to his office doors. Immediately the quiet signal went to his personal secretary. His clever fingers inched under Galaxeé's skirt, began to toy and play.

Before the pornographic show on video ended, Randy had Galaxeé facedown on his conference table.

* * *

He called at ten thirty, right after Rio sent Troy out the door. Bryce said just to hear her voice.

He called again at half past noon, wanting to do lunch, as Rio climbed into the Mercedes. Declining, she went by the club. Galaxeé met her in the parking lot.

After another walkthrough, they found that nothing seemed to have been stolen, nothing was broken, nothing in disarray.

"Why would somebody break in, not take anything, and try a second time?" Rio asked, folding her arms.

"Maybe they escaped before the cops got here, didn't have the time or the chance," Galaxeé replied. She went behind the bar and poured Perrier over ice. "Want anything?"

"Pass."

"Maybe they thought to steal some liquor and the lock to the storage room kept them out the first time. Good thing we bought that iron door."

Rio agreed. Liquor costs had recently increased for some name brands. She and Galaxeé had balked at raising drink prices for now. But if a thief broke in and stole or destroyed all of their liquor, they had no choice but to raise prices. "Can't imagine the same idiot trying again."

"Have you thought about buying a pistol?"

"Don't want to. I don't like guns."

"Well you need some sort of protection if you plan on staying in this building late at night. I'm sure as hell not going to stay here alone." She grinned. "Of course, there is Bryce, your shining knight."

Rio gritted her teeth. Although Bryce had easily enticed her back into bed this morning, he hadn't elaborated at all about the phone call. She was still stung. Just a bit. "I'm not planning on him being here. Remember, they didn't get in the last time. The locks held up."

"What about when you leave? What about when you walk

out the door, snap both locks and go to your car at three o'clock in the morning? What then?"

Her jaw went slack. Fear bred more unwanted fear. "I'm not trying to think about that, Galaxeé. For nine months I came and went without worry; I am not going to start worrying now."

"We can hire a security guard."

"We have bouncers for security and don't need to spend more money."

"I'll pay for it out of my own pocket."

"You mean out of Randy's wallet," Rio replied, settling her hands on her hips. They'd run this club without assistance. Why start asking for help now? "No."

"Sometimes you really piss me off."

Rio turned her back and walked off. Not today, no arguments today, but Galaxeé always found a way to start one. "Damn it, do you have to pop that gum?"

"Just goes to show your nerves aren't made of iron like the door. I think you beat your record this time, jumped a whole foot off the floor."

Since Rio had other obligations, Bryce arranged to meet his sister for lunch.

Twenty-five-year-old Angelina strolled into their favorite French café. The shade of her hair matched Bryce's, but tumbled past her shoulders in a messy array of curly waves. Behind the oversized dark sunglasses, her eyes—though not gray—sparkled a brighter green from the tinted contacts. She was truly a little angel as a child—well mannered, tiny like their mother, smart. Until she turned fourteen. Peer pressure, illegal drugs and Mother Claudine caused the change back then. The male population resulted in the alteration now.

Fortunately, Angelina had sense enough not to drag Jason along and she was smart enough not to mention the scumbag's name. He knew too much, had listened in on their conversations a few times, Angelina had warned.

"Hey, Boo," Bryce said and placed a chaste kiss to her cheek.

He'd given her the nickname after the first time his mother let him hold his half sister in his arms for a family photograph. Claudine had scolded him for the ugly frown on his face and trashed the picture.

"How's it going?" This morning she'd refused to admit there was a problem with her boyfriend. Bryce had noted an odd tone in her voice at the time.

"Could be better." She slid into the chair.

"SS?"

"Part of it."

The waitress came by, filled the water glasses and set a basket of breads, crackers and flavored butters on the table.

"Give us a minute," Bryce said before she asked for orders. He cocked his head to one side. "Problems still?"

Angelina snorted, threading her fingers through the mass of waves. She flipped it over her shoulder. "The usual. Lost another dancer, thinning crowds, liquor prices, among a few other things. And, of course, your mother."

"She's your mother, too."

"You invited her to visit."

"Wrong. Claudine Berardi invited herself and, as Maureen quoted, two of her dear friends. Nothing like having a house full of bickering broads."

"Well, they're not staying at my place. I don't need the headache. Got enough problems without a bunch of New York society hens telling me how to live my life. God. Just the thought makes me want to puke." She sipped on water.

"Chill. They'll stay with me."

"Where?" Angelina snickered.

"The spare bedrooms," Bryce replied, sarcastic. "I've got

time to clear everything out of my crib. Found a warehouse to rent this morning, not far from . . . near here."

Angelina hadn't heard about his affair with Rio. No one—except Galaxeé, Rosalind and Oscar—knew for now. Bryce wanted his sister completely out of touch with his personals because of one man. On the other hand, the relationship with Rio was certainly a conflict of interest.

"I'm meeting the guy who owns the building Friday afternoon," he continued. "It's pricey, but I think a little bartering is in order. The place is perfect for my needs. Evidently, the space above it is occupied, but I'm only planning to use the warehouse for storage."

"Why not buy the building, kick the tenant out, sell your place and move in? Bet our accountant could save you lots of taxable money."

Angelina had a good head on her shoulders until some male scrambled her brains.

Eyebrows lifting, Bryce replied, "Could."

Rio looked through her ledger, then at the computer screen again, wondering if she'd dreamt about these same calculations. Anyway, it gave her work to do for part of the day.

Her cell phone rang. Thinking the call was from Bryce, she picked it up and said, "I'm still here."

"I've never wished you dead."

"Oh." She set the ledger on the desk and tapped her pen. "Devon."

"Your voice rings of disappointment."

He rarely called and only when he wanted something. She'd hang up if he started whining again about alimony. Last month, he'd tried to talk her into skipping the payment for unspecified reasons. Six months before, he'd threatened to take her back to court to cut alimony since she had income from Killer Bods. Threats only, her attorney had said. Victoria would make sure he lost and paid more than Rio had asked for during negotiations, said she deserved much, much more.

"What do you want, Devon? If it's about alimony, call Victoria." She heard the muffled c-word he saddled on her. Rio bristled. "Say that foul mess again and *I'll* contact her. Better yet, I'm hanging up."

"Wait."

"Think slander, Devon. You're an attorney."

"Why is it every time we talk begins a new argument?"

"Maybe it's because you always manage to start one." She'd given him eleven years of her life and he'd dumped her. "Just like you did when you started playing with your she's-just-a-secretary girlfriend. How is Tiffany?"

He quieted.

"Don't tell me," Rio said, chuckling. "She found a new boss? Is he older or younger than you?" It really didn't matter. Tiffany, obviously, had kicked him to the curb and, now, at age fifty-two he was alone, probably lonely.

"That's not why I called."

"Younger. Hah!"

"Not very becoming of you, Rio. You've changed a lot."

Galaxeé came through the doorway. Rio motioned her to listen in on the conversation. She mouthed her ex-husband's name, knowing the partner couldn't resist.

"For the better," she said as Galaxeé plopped her butt against the drafting table, leaning in ear to phone.

"You didn't use to . . . now you sound like a cuffy."

"Excuse me? I don't believe I recognize that old saying." She covered the mouthpiece when Galaxeé cackled. Rio could just imagine Devon's square, clenched jaw grinding the bone away. "Is that good or bad?"

"Real cute, Rio. You're not that far behind my age."

"But I'll never catch up." She and her partner high-fived.

"You've been around Cecilia too much, starting to talk like

her. I never did like the influence she had on you. If it wasn't for her—"

"Eleven years of *my* life would have been boring and miserable." Another high-five.

"This is going nowhere."

"You're right. Let's just cut the BS and hang up."

"Wait, Rio, I called about business."

"And that is?"

"Can we discuss it over dinner?"

Galaxeé shook her head, hard.

"You're buying, right?" Rio slapped at her partner's hand, then rubbed her pinched skin.

"Of course. Name the restaurant."

Without hesitation, she said, "Morton's."

"Should've known you'd pick one of the most expensive eateries," he muttered.

"Well, we could do the Brown Palace's famous cuisine." He'd taken her there once during their marriage, on their first anniversary.

"Never mind. Seven thirty."

"I'll see you there," Rio replied and clicked off her phone. She looked at Galaxeé, smiling. "That certainly was—"

"Stupid."

"—beneficial." She screwed up her face. "It was not stupid."

"Was, too. He's slick. You shouldn't be around him unless Victoria's there to keep him in line. That's why he hates her."

"Devon doesn't hate Victoria."

"His aura radiates devil-red when she's around. Surprised he hasn't sprouted hooves and horns. You should cancel, call Victoria and let her set up an appointment with him to be on the safe side."

"We're only doing dinner and talking. I won't commit to anything." She swiveled the chair around and grabbed her ledger.

Galaxeé leaned over her shoulder. "The last time you had lunch with Devon he talked you into giving him the Cancún timeshare."

"I couldn't afford the maintenance fees or to fly down there every year anyway."

"The last dinner you had with him," Galaxeé whispered in her ear, "he got you to trim your monthly alimony. That's why you couldn't afford the timeshare."

"He'd fallen on hard times."

Galaxeé straightened. "Quit defending that mongrel when his hard times took Tiffany on a three-week vacation to your timeshare."

"He's not with her anymore."

"Stop it, Rio. You don't have the snot to deal with a man like him. I mean, sweetie, he knows how to win, how to persuade you. He's an attorney, for God's sake." She struck a get-real pose. "Don't snarl at me; save it for Devon. You'll need it. Speaking of baring fangs, what happens when Bryce calls?"

"I've already talked to him today. Twice."

"So?"

"He knows I'm busy." Rio closed the ledger, stuffed it inside her black handbag. She'd planned to call him a little later to re-iterate that dinner was, in fact, out.

"Oh. You still better think of a clearer way to tell him, just in case." The popped gum sounded like shotgun blast.

Rio's cell phone rang.

"Better hurry, too," Galaxeé said. She sashayed out of the office.

"Make me sick," Rio mumbled. "Thinks she knows every-thing. Hello?"

"Hey, kitten."

She fumbled the phone as Galaxeé's laughter echoed through-out the club. "I was just thinking I should call you. But I was so busy." Oh, lord. Fibbing again.

"Need a break. All work and no play makes me worry about you. Dinner?"

"Can't." She tucked the phone between her ear and shoulder.

"Why?"

She grimaced. "I still have some errands, a business meeting, and I don't know what time I'll be finished." Okay, a business dinner with Devon was not a complete lie. No telling what Bryce might do or say if she told him about meeting her ex, even if it wasn't a social get-together.

"All right. We could meet at your place. Say, ten?"

Oh, shit. I mean, shoot. "Bryce, the meeting could run late. Later," she recanted hurriedly. "Why don't I come by your house when I'm finished?"

Silence dominated the phone line.

"A meeting after ten at night?" he asked.

Rio swallowed. "Probably not, but just to be safe."

"Call at ten and not one minute later."

He didn't sound the least bit convinced. Darn him. Not one minute later. Just who did he think he was? "Time permitting." Was that a growl? Oh, this is just too silly. "Look, um, I've got some things to do."

A few silent seconds went by.

"Fine," he said. His tone was etched with anger, or jealousy.

"Don't flex on me, Bryce."

Another few seconds flew by.

"Rio?"

"What?"

"Ten."

He had the damn nerve to hang up on her. She looked at the cell phone and clucked her tongue. "Don't hold your breath."

Bryce dropped the receiver into its cradle.

In a freak moment, he'd forgotten to ask where she'd planned to have her goddamn meeting and with whom. Hell, she'd never told him where she lived. He looked over at the digital clock sitting on his antique desk.

Five hours until she was supposed to call him.

Five hours not knowing whom she planned to be with until ten at night.

Five frigging hours to stew over this shit.

Where the hell had all this jealousy crap come from anyway? He really needed to get a grip and not allow an innocent meeting to change his frame of mind.

Things were going well with Rio, weren't they? She knew his feelings, knew how much he cared. He'd admitted loving her— Shit, she sure as hell hadn't admitted the same, goddamn it.

"Mr. Sullivan—"

"What?" He caught himself just as Maureen charged toward the door faster than a frightened rabbit. "Come back here, Maureen."

She came to a halt and turned. "This can wait. Nothing important."

"What is it?"

"Uh, contract," she stammered.

"Contracts are always important."

"Not when you're in one of your moods."

"I don't have moods." Bellowing was a rare phenomena and Maureen had never been the target of his anger. He pinched the bridge of his nose, then dropped his hand to his side. "Leave the contract on my desk. I'll look it over later."

She stayed frozen in place, eyes wide, face drained of what little color she had, clutching the papers with both hands.

"Maureen, I'm not angry at you." She took one tentative step forward. "I'm not angry at all."

She ran partway over, sort of tossed the clipped papers to the desk and hurried out the door. Bryce shook his head.

Moods.

* * *

She ordered a vodka martini, a top-shelf brand. While contemplating an entrée selection, Rio chose a bottle of her favorite chardonnay at the Brown Palace, knowing she was doing seafood tonight. Devon had called back. He'd said the Palace was a good choice after all. She'd wondered about his change of mind.

"You do have champagne taste," he said.

He was still devilishly handsome and debonair. His hair appeared grayer at the temples than when she'd seen him last. Smooth chocolate complexion, perfectly trimmed mustache, even manicured nails. As usual, he wore an immaculately cut, pinstripe tailored suit, crisp white shirt and silk tie; his shoes had been polished to a mirror-gloss.

"You taught me well," she said. The waiter poured a few tablespoons of wine into her glass.

"Still look good, too," Devon added quietly.

His gaze, a pair of midnight black eyes, traveled down to an abundance of cleavage she'd deliberately flaunted in an off-white clinging teaser. Tiffany had little in comparison. But, she'd had stealth to steal Devon from a devoted wife.

"I keep fit."

She sipped the wine, rolled it over her tongue, purred and nodded acceptance. For an appetizer, Rio ordered escargot swimming in butter, wine, garlic and two or three thousand calories with fresh French bread. The ex declined a starter.

"That look on your face," Devon said. "You always liked wine better than sex."

She gave him a sideways glance, deciding not to spare him a reply. Not anymore, she thought, noting the time. Seven fifty. In approximately three hours, she'd coax Bryce into spreading his big body all over hers, working every inch of it in a wild frenzy.

No, sex is much better than fine wine with the right partner.

They engaged in idle chitchat—weather, mainly—until the waiter returned. He bragged about the restaurant's famous Caesar salad prepared tableside. Rio was game. Since the salad was a two-person deal, Devon went along with the order. Even he suggested Maine lobster with drawn butter. The entrée came with saffron rice laced with almonds and baby asparagus tips on the side.

Troy the Trainer was sure to have a conniption and Rio thought not to write the information into her notebook. Friday was two days away, plenty of time to exercise the excess calories off her hips. With Bryce.

"About this business," Rio prompted as the waiter set her appetizer on the table.

Devon readjusted his tie and launched into his usual attorney tirade for nearly an hour. She remembered all the years he'd practiced his closing arguments on her, boring her to tears while she stayed attentive, rarely disputing his techniques. Nothing had changed, either, except he ate his meal during the spiel.

"You want me to sell my home back to you?" Rio asked, setting the fork aside.

"And make a very tidy profit, enough to pay off your equity loan and still have enough money to buy a new house, mortgage free. Look. The warehouse is empty and property taxes are increasing. My expenses have reached a maximum. Four other attorneys and I want to start a new firm. I can turn the place into an office building, cut costs—"

"It's always about you, isn't it?" A mortgage-free lifestyle had piqued her interest, but she absolutely loved the loft.

"Not just about me, Rio." He wrapped his fingers around her hand and squeezed. "I'm looking out for you, too."

"Bull." Who was he kidding?

Devon huffed, but he sat more erect while the waiter cleared the table and brushed debris from the linen. "Just because we're divorced doesn't mean I don't still care for you. We had a lot of good years invested in our marriage, quality years. As good as you look now," he said, "I was a fool to let you slip away."

She looked down at their joined hands, his thumb smoothing over her fingers. Once upon a time, she had enjoyed his caresses.

"Ah," she said, pulling her hand free. "I see the dessert cart moving in our direction. Mmm, banana flambé sounds really good right now."

By ten-oh-seven, Bryce had learned all about moods—unsettled gloominess, mild outrage, and another round of uncontrollable jealousy. He'd broken the small crystal paperweight by accident. Thumping his fingers on the paperweight, he'd knocked it to the floor, broke it into a million glittering pieces.

He sat at his home office desk, holding the cell phone, willing it to ring again. Coop had called shortly after nine. He and Shannon had worked out their problems. The wedding was on schedule as planned.

Since Coop's call, Bryce had simply sat there, swiveling the executive chair side to side, waiting. He tapped a pen, really banging it, on the hard wood desk.

Setting the phone aside, he got up and circled the room. "Fine. Don't bother calling. No problem. Eight more minutes and I substitute my pinch hitter into this game."

At ten thirty, he stepped into a cold shower to chill the anger scalding his blood, to douse the humiliation. He'd dialed Catherine's number. He just couldn't bring himself to punch the "send" key.

As he braced his hands against the slate tile, the overhead sprayer's icy water pelted his body along with his bruised ego and, most of all, his heart. Rio had tromped on it again. How much longer could he take this punishment?

The doorbell chimed.

He knew it was Rio. Bryce rubbed his eyes, knowing he should ignore the summons. Let her leave, kick her out of his life permanently, and rid himself of the torment.

When he stepped from the shower, he wrapped a big towel around his waist and stared at his reflection in the mirror, focusing on the dark sliver of anger in his hooded eyes. An indignation so volatile and pernicious from this woman's rejection and blasé attitude . . . but he was more ticked with himself for simple lack of control, for allowing her to bring him to his knees, brutalizing his heart, leaving him raw and, goddamn it, bleeding. No, he had to let her leave for her own good, for her own protection. Otherwise, he might hurt her when he'd vowed he never would.

The doorbell chimed back-to-back, nagging melodies.

Smoothing his hair off his forehead, Bryce crinkled his nose as his anger increased and each millisecond ticked away.

15

"Rio!"

She heard him, ignored the warning in his tone, and pulled the door open to her Mercedes.

"Rio!" Bryce called out, louder.

She took her time, shut and locked the door and strolled around the long end of the car. As she started up the wide side-walk, she said, "I wondered if you were home. Were you in the shower? Why are you standing out here barefoot as cold as it is? Go back inside."

She looked away because the shimmering darkness in his eyes, reflected by the porch light, gave her pause. Maybe this wasn't a good time to be here. Maybe she'd waited too long and should've called first. Maybe her intentions had backfired. Just maybe the other woman had found her way back into his life and now he wanted to gloat while the hussy lay spread-eagled in his bed.

Bryce clamped his big hand around her arm, ushered her inside and back-kicked the front door. The *boom* was loud enough to wake a neighborhood in Boulder, thirty miles away.

O-kay. She looked down at his hand. He still had a mighty grip on her arm, but she refused to cower and stuck her hands into the leather coat's pockets. "Want to tell me what the problem is?"

Water droplets had frozen on his powerful chest. They melted now, steamed and dripped down to his rippling six-pack followed by a tiny river pouring off his drenched hair. The towel soaked up the wetness. Beneath the terrycloth, the serpent lurched.

A lusty rush flared through her belly.

She drew her gaze slowly up his muscular body, met the pair of sword-gray daggers glaring into her eyes. "Are you going to answer me tonight or continue this stare down?"

He stripped her naked without really touching her again. Clenching her hands into fists, she resisted the nervous urge to wring hands or pick at her nails. This was exactly what she had expected from him, a show of temper.

Boldly, Rio lifted her chin. "Well? I didn't drive this far to stand here and—"

"Upstairs." His lips barely moved. He had yet to blink. Something sinister glowed behind his piercing eyes.

"What?"

Had she heard him correctly, issuing an order? When he released her and started for the staircase, she stayed rooted to the floor, folding her arms beneath her breasts. "I don't know who the hell you think you're—"

One death-mask glare over his shoulder and Rio clamped her mouth shut. Well, shoot.

Fine. She followed. So what if it was after eleven? For that matter, she hadn't given him an exact time of her arrival. Obviously, an argument was brewing over her tardiness. They might as well get it over with so she could get on with seducing him.

Devon had tried to talk trash to her, tried to get her to go home with him. She didn't want him and all but told him so.

Burn me once, shame on you. Burn me twice, shame on me.

When she'd left the Brown Palace, she was hornier than a bitch in heat. Devon had a smooth way of talking dirty without talking dirty and her juices readily flowed, but not for her ex-husband.

By the time she had arrived at the loft, peeled out of her clothes and packed a small overnight bag, she couldn't wait to get to Bryce. She'd planned the tardiness to get him in the mood. Now he wanted to argue when she was needy, ready to wrap her body around his—until he implied she'd better get her butt in gear.

Like Galaxeé had said, it was time to take the blinders off; time to step up to the plate and take complete control of her life.

Rio stomped up each hardwood riser, dead on Bryce's heels, bristling with righteous indignation.

"Upstairs," she mumbled and clucked her tongue. Oh, yes, she had a thing or two to tell his young behind before *anything* else.

They marched into his bedroom. She slammed the door. Leaning back against the wall, Rio stuck her finger out.

"Let me tell you something, Bryce. You don't order me around because you don't run my life. I don't answer to you or anyone else on this planet. I go and come as I please. And if you don't like it, then . . . then learn to deal with it." There. That should set him straight. Simple. Plain. Straightforward.

"Are you finished?"

She thought again. "Yes."

"Now, let me tell you something."

He'd said the words so softly she strained to hear them. Rio blinked, blinked again. And he was right there, trapping her before she took a breath. She smelled his anger, the raw male power of it, and every DNA strand quivered inside her body.

Leaning closer, he whispered, "Don't ever fuck with my head, Rio. You won't like what happens when you do."

She stared at his lips and, God help her, she wanted to feel them on her body. Everywhere. "I can hold my own," she challenged. "Anytime. Anywhere. With anybody."

Five seconds passed in dead silence.

"Can you?" His voice snapped crisp as the night air.

With one hand braced against the door, blocking any escape, he released the top button to her coat, and the next one, and the next . . . His nostrils flared as the leather fell open, her naked breasts spilling out, nipples on display like dessert on a smorgasbord. Taut and peaked.

Another five seconds passed.

"Where were you tonight?"

Her breaths turned into pants, her flesh sizzling as his fingers brushed against her sensitive skin while freeing two more clasps. "Out."

"Alone?"

Rio swallowed. "No," and the threads snapped on the last button. Sweat sprouted spontaneously on her temples, drizzled, cooling her heated face. His harsh, hot breath reheated her skin to scorching.

His gaze slid up her body, locked with hers. "Take it off."

She waited, knowing defiance provoked him further. She finally let the leather slide off her shoulders, down her arms and into a pile at her feet. Standing nude, the cooler air and Bryce's fiery glare caused her breasts to swell. She ached for his touch.

Staring at her breasts and all the way down her body, he said, "Did he put his hands on you?"

Automatically he assumed she'd accompanied a male, assumed she'd had sexual contact, the reason for her lack of communication and tardiness. She'd purposely *not* called, and she'd taken her time getting here. They'd shared an uncanny need for each other. Addictive sin.

Tonight she wanted more of him, wanted him to prove how much he did need and want her. A frenzied reunion. She came prepared to taunt him, literally in naked provocation.

"Why?" she baited.

"Did. He. Touch you."

As he shifted his weight, the towel fell away and the serpent reared up—on the prowl—within striking distance. Throbbing heat pulsed against her belly, sent an electric surge of lust-driven currents charging through her system.

"If he did," Rio replied bravely, "I'd never—" He spun her so fast she lost her breath.

Plastered against the wall, surrounded by him, she felt the full length of his body, every hard inch of angry male flesh. The next shudder blazed a wildfire's path from her toes to the top of her head, one molecule at a time.

"Say it now," he demanded. "Say it."

She knew better than to open her mouth. He was angry, he was jealous and he had her pinned—a dangerous combination for any woman. "You don't—"

Bryce yanked her wrists high on the wall above her head. "Lesson number one, don't jack with me or expect to win. Number two," he said, pressing the engorged length of that stout serpent between the cleft of her buttocks.

The heat of him penetrated her core, flipped her internal switch to meltdown.

"You'll regret breaking rule number one."

"Rules are made for breaking. All rules."

"Not mine. Never break my rules."

"I will if—"

In one quick motion, he spread her feet apart, dipped and shoved inside her full-length. A strangled scream left her throat as she came off the floor, impaled, suspended. He reached around her body and caught hold of her sensitive nub, squeezed.

She clawed at the wall, but this was what she'd wanted. Blistering, rough sex.

His mouth went everywhere, in her hair, ear, and he sank his teeth into the tendon down her neck. She wouldn't fight him, didn't want the sweet torture to stop. He slid his hands beneath her thighs, lifted her to the tip of his bulging heat.

"This," Bryce said on a snarl and let her drop down the length of him as he plowed upward.

He raised her. "And this," dropping her again.

He lifted. "For breaking my rules."

On the bitter edge of a turbulent orgasm, nothing could stop her from coming apart. She climaxed, nearly raked the paint off the sapphire-blue wall on the plummeting descent, shrieking a high-pitched sound.

He held her in place, arms wrapped tightly around her, kneading her breasts while the riotous tremors skated across her nerve endings to completion, leaving her stunned and a little dazed.

"We've only just begun," he whispered savagely in her ear. Still fully embedded he swung her around and marched toward the king-sized bed.

He did things to her she'd never conceived, turned her every which way but free. He cursed her, tormented her, teased her, even hurt her once or twice, only to soothe and coax her to the next feverish plateau.

If this was his revenge, she wanted it and welcomed the predatory violence of his powerful thrusts, smacking against her with brutal force, awakening a tide of pleasures from every imaginable angle.

But he had yet to give in to a climactic finish.

Straight-armed, Bryce withdrew from her body. The loss was so sudden, Rio panicked, urged him to continue, tightening her legs ineffectually, writhing beneath him while on the fine razor's edge of mindless insanity. But he would not return.

"Damn you," Rio breathed. "What do you want from me?"

"Everything," Bryce replied, pressing that big, bulging head to her slick heat. He pulled away. "And nothing."

Torture. Evil, retaliating torture. He intended to make her suffer. "You son of a bitch. I hate—"

He rammed into her, buried himself to the hilt, lifted her from the bed, held her steady and nearly pulled out only to ram again.

She gulped in air, filled her burning lungs to capacity, and the gasps burst out of her with each pillaging stroke. Each time he touched a new place, each time he sent new sensations spiraling out of control. He worked her relentlessly, triggering a mind-blowing sequence.

But he had not reached his peak.

On the threshold of obliteration, she had one chance to force his hand before she slipped into oblivion, into uncharted territory. He plowed into her one more time and she viciously clamped around his length, would not let loose. The shock on his face was palpable as realization hit him.

He sank deeper, deeper yet, swelling, then burst on a mighty roar and pitched forward. Rio helplessly gave in, eyes rolling back as a sudden hot surge erupted, wave after tidal wave consuming her, boiling her blood, and finally detonating. A joint release so powerful, so beautiful, so brilliant . . .

"I love you. I love you," Bryce chanted, burying his face against her throat, rocking against her, prolonging their tempestuous orgasms.

Those simply declared words shattered Rio, released a dam of tears she'd fought valiantly to hold back. Shaken, she stroked his smooth hair, his strong back and his broad shoulders as tears poured from her eyes, soaking the satin sheets.

He'd stripped her of everything she'd held on to, everything she'd vowed to contain since the first time he'd touched her. He was too young, too handsome, too different for a woman of her age and background.

I love you, too. I love you with all my heart and soul, but we can never be a couple.

Stunned by the poignant revelations, she broke down with heart-wrenching sobs.

Long minutes passed with just the sound of her tormented sobs.

"Please don't cry any more, kitten," Bryce said on a ragged whisper. "You're tearing me apart."

She'd drawn her legs up, wrapped her arms around them and buried her face against her knees until he persuaded her to unfold while he cleansed her body with a basin of warm, soapy water and a washcloth, hoping to ease the pain.

Bryce dragged the sheet up and over them, soothing her. He spooned her body with his own, ran his hands up and down her skin, whispering words of comfort to no avail, ashamed that he'd hurt Rio and tortured her much, much too long.

Her sweet revenge catapulted him instantaneously to the sky's limits and he emptied his heart and soul, gave all he owned to her, and still she wept.

Bryce squeezed his eyes shut from the gut-twisting ache inside. He'd promised—promised!—that he'd never hurt her, then lost his head and complete control of his body.

My God. What have I done?

"Please, darling," he begged, pulling her closer, wanting to absorb the pain that caused her tears. "I can't bear to see you like this."

She quieted, shuddered, sniffled. Minutes later, she slept soundly, her breathing deep and even, except for a catch on occasion.

He kept her securely in his arms all night. Sleep was elusive.

At dawn's awakening, Rio shifted, turned toward him, slipped one arm around his waist, one leg over his thigh and nuzzled his throat. Bryce kissed the top of her head and smoothed his fingers through the shag of her hair.

If only he could wake every morning like this—Rio in his arms, snuggling closer. But those days would never come. Not after last night, not ever again, leaving him with so little time to enjoy her nearness.

He felt the wet teasing of her tongue on his skin. Searing heat coursed through his veins, snatching his breath away. He flexed his fingers into her skin, but then he relaxed. A figment of his imagination, a selfish wish that would never materialize. Drugged from lack of rest.

"Your heart rate sped up," Rio said quietly. She flattened her hand against his chest. "I can feel it pounding."

He swallowed, willing his beater to slow. "Startled."

"By this?" She licked a ticklish path down his chest, bit at his budding nipple and pressed her belly against his growing erection.

Bryce sucked in air when she nipped twice more. "Kitten."

"I need you."

She still wanted him, after everything. He hadn't lost her to immaturity or stupidity. Unbelievable, when he loved her to no end. She wanted him, but she didn't love him. He'd settle for desire alone for the chance to spend time with her, to prove he never really meant to hurt her and never would again, needing her in his life.

He tipped her chin up, stared into her glorious eyes. "You've had enough for one night."

To his undoing, she wrapped her fingers around his sudden arousal, stroked ever so gently, squeezed while his cock swelled as hard as the Rock of Gibraltar. Pulsing in her hand, his cravings meant nothing now, curbed, shut down. Only Rio's needs mattered.

"I want you inside me," she said. "Love me again."

Love her? He'd love her for all time, but only her desires

concerned him from here on. He would take her on a slow sweet journey to the end of the universe and give her the sun's rays, the moonbeams, the planets and the stars.

Bryce rolled to his back, lifted her to straddle his chest. "A painless loving. A gentle loving for all I've foolishly done to hurt you."

"How—"

"Hold tightly to the headboard, kitten, and let me take you riding a lover's waves."

"Galaxeé, have you been messing around with this darn computer?" Rio asked. "This is the third time I've put this stuff in here. And, the totals are way off from my ledger." At four-thirty in the afternoon, she needed a little downtime before the club opened.

"You know I don't touch that thing if I can help it. Maybe you forgot to do a save."

She quickly looked through the file cabinet. Where's the Gamble file? And the— "I always do a save!"

What in the world was going on? They were due for an audit at the first of December, thanks to the cheating accountant they'd fired. Everything had to be just right. Perfect.

Too bad perfection and pragmatism hadn't claimed her brother. He'd shown up at the loft this morning, when Troy was still there. Marcus was undone because she'd had a man in her home at that time of day, any day when she wasn't married to the man in question. He'd resented the fact she'd divorced Devon. In his eyes, women had their place, like children, seen and not heard. Live quietly. Catering to your man without question fit his ideas best. She'd walked out on his tirade before the subject of her work came into play. Once he heard about Killer's, he'd soar past ballistic.

For a thirty-seven-year-old preacher, he, who dressed in Italian-made suits and shoes, was as uncompromising as an eighteenth-century slave owner. Marcus had always loved to jump sharp, dazzling young women. Obviously, he'd used clothes and slick words to his benefit.

"Have Bryce look at it. He's a computer nerd."

"He is not a nerd."

"Glad to hear you're doing better." Galaxeé dropped into a chair, crossed her legs at the ankles. "Maybe it's time we went out on a double date."

"Not." She'd said it too fast and grimaced.

"Why?"

"Just because. Can we not talk about this? I'm too busy for an argument with you. Argue enough with him," she mumbled.

He'd been hounding her about going out to dinner, going anyplace together. She'd made excuses and bowed out. The tension between them had mounted. Their lovemaking had become just as hot, just as intense. Torrid.

"Grow up, Rio. The boy's in love," Galaxeé said. "So are you."

Damn her. She didn't need reminding.

They'd spent time together when neither was working, cooped up in his house, making mad passionate love, talking, learning about each other and making more passionate love.

One day soon, it would all end. They'd go their separate ways and forget they'd ever had a relationship.

"Why do I get the feeling you want it to end?" Galaxeé asked.

She did. She didn't. Knew it had to end. Knew it would. Eventually.

Bryce would find a younger woman his age and fall in love, marry, live happily ever after with a dozen children. That's what his mother wanted. Grandchildren. Caucasian grandchildren from a beautiful Italian daughter-in-law, Rio suspected. Bryce had neglected to admit he wanted the very same things.

"Our relationship can't go anywhere. It's a temporary—"

"Bullshit."

Rio narrowed her eyes into a glare. "Temporary meeting of the bodies, a little longer than a one-night stand."

"Where the hell do you get off talking that crap?" Galaxeé flicked her braids over her shoulder and leaned forward, braced her elbows on her knees. Her gold bracelets jangled together and four gold necklaces slipped out from under her shirt. "Have you completely lost your mind? He's laid his heart at your feet. What are you going to do? Kick it? He can't take much more punishment, Rio. You'll drive him away," she said, frowning. "I realize he's young and has a lot to learn, needs to grow up, too, obviously. But you've had him on a roller-coaster ride from the beginning."

She looked back at the computer screen, although she was unable to focus on her work.

"That's what you're planning, isn't it? You're gonna dump him. Dump on him. Kick him to the curb. That's the lousiest thing I've ever heard."

"I didn't say it. You did." She kept her eyes trained on the monitor.

"You break his heart and you'll break your own." Galaxeé got up and stomped out of the office.

"It's breaking now," Rio whispered.

She'd made up her mind. She would not spend a night with Bryce—not as long as Marcus was in town—no matter how angry or persuasive he became. Besides, the less time they spent together, the easier the breakup.

Rio woke to loud noises after a short night of restless sleep.

Bryce had complained up a storm about their sleeping arrangements. She'd left him in the parking lot. When she arrived home, Marcus started in on her. The argument was long and hard about the work that kept her out into the wee hours of the night. He'd flipped hearing she owned a club for *freaks*, flaunting a bunch of indecent men. Had she lost her mind? She'd slammed the bedroom door in his face.

What the devil is that screeching sound? Metal against metal? Thumping. Beeping. The roar of a motor?

Didn't people understand that folks slept in on Saturday mornings? Were the street crews out again? Lord.

She pulled the pillow over her head, but when the thumping increased, she knocked the pillow to the floor and snatched the blankets off. Jamming her feet into the pair of rabbit-eared slippers, she grabbed her robe and door keys.

The sounds came from below the loft. In the warehouse.

Damn Devon. He should've told me, warned me instead of trying to get into my panties.

She yanked open the heavy metal door and let it slam shut. Tying a loose knot to her robe, she raced down the stairs and the noises grew louder, voices, too.

Great. Just great. A bunch of loudmouth men. Well, she'd give them a piece of her mind.

"Waking me up at the crack of damn dawn," she muttered.

Seemed like dawn to her, even if it was seven fifteen. The sun was barely up; the auto-lights in the hallway were still on. Too early for this racket.

She shoved on the double doors, burst into the cold room where several men carried boxes. Another drove a forklift, scraping the cement floor with the lifters and shifting gears. The whining beeps grated on her nerves.

"Do you know what time it is?" she shouted.

No one paid her any mind.

Rio marched over to a corner, grabbed a metal bar and tossed it. The clanging noise brought everyone's head around.

Fisting her hands on her hips, she shouted, "People sleep at this hour!"

They looked around at each other, looked stupid—eyes wide, their mouths hanging open.

What the devil were they staring at anyway? She followed their gaze and looked down.

Hell. She pulled the lapels to her robe together, tied the belt tighter. She'd all but flaunted her nakedness. Lord, she must look like a disheveled tramp, and Rio ran her fingers through her hair, knowing it stood on end.

Lifting her chin, she said, "I want you to stop all this noise."

"We have our orders, ma'am. The boss—"

"Who's the damn boss?" she demanded. "I want to talk to him. You will not make this racket at this time of day. What are you doing here anyway? Who sent you?"

"He's right behind you now," a baldheaded, fat man said.

Rio whirled around, ready to pounce with all fours, claws and teeth bared.

She looked up and almost fainted.

It was Bryce, and he shoved her behind him. "Get back to work," he snapped caustically at the eyeballers and wheeled around once they had. "What the hell are you doing in this warehouse dressed like that? Where are your damn clothes?"

"I live here. What the hell are you doing here?"

"You live here? Upstairs in the loft?" he asked, incredulous. "Aw, shit. Why didn't you tell me? You knew goddamn well this place was for rent. You knew damn well I was looking for a warehouse."

"I—" She clamped her mouth shut.

"What the goddamn hell are you doing down here half-naked in front of these men?"

Latching onto her arm, Bryce shoved one side of the double doors open, dragged her into the open area, and swung her around to face him.

"Is Devon your ex-husband? Is he who you were with the other night?"

She saw murder in his eyes, and Rio couldn't draw enough spit to swallow.

16

He'd strangle her beautiful neck. Right here, if she lied. "Well?" Bryce bellowed.

"Yes."

"Yes, what?" He needed a hell of a lot more than a simple affirmative.

"He's my ex. And, yes, I had dinner with him to discuss the warehouse. Except Devon omitted telling me that he was renting it out."

"Rent? Temporary leasing with an option. I want to buy this place, the whole damn building."

He'd planned exactly as Angelina had suggested. Buy the building, boot the occupant out of the loft and move in at his earliest convenience.

Rio's mouth dropped open. "You'll do no such thing, not without my written consent. And I have no desire—"

"You're part owner?"

"Yes, I am." She yanked her arm free of his tight grip. "I'll kill Devon. He tried to talk me into selling my share to him, moving out and buying a new place. I swear before God, I'll kill him with my bare hands. No-good, cheating . . . I bet he stood to make a fortune."

"We're still negotiating the price."

"Start un-negotiating. We're not selling yet, and I'm certainly not moving."

Bryce snarled. He'd made plans; he'd talked to a real estate agent to put his home on the market, all without seeing the loft. Devon Wagner had said it was a great living space and Bryce had believed him. From the size of this place . . . whoa. The amenities would fit perfectly into his lifestyle, and the location of a storage building couldn't be better.

"Why didn't you tell me this place was available?"

She wrung her hands. "It really wasn't. It—"

"All this time you've never wanted me to know where you lived. Why? Have you neglected to tell me a few odds and ends that I should know about?" He forced her chin up with his fingers, made her stare into his eyes. "There is, isn't there? What is it, Rio? I want to know right now."

"Hey, boss, got a minute?" the fat man yelled through the glass.

"Hang on," Bryce replied. He looked back into Rio's eyes with those mighty sword-daggers. "I'll be up to your loft when I'm finished here. We're going to have a sit-down conversation."

He left without kissing her. From the tone of his voice, fury had settled in.

Rio raked a vicious path through her hair with one hand. Well, darn it all, she had a right to privacy. How could she live here with him using the warehouse below her? It just gave him more reason to stop by, unannounced. Like he belonged here. Next thing she knew, he'd want a key to her place.

Frustrated, she tightened the belt to her robe enough to cut off blood circulation and marched up the stairs.

I'm going to kill Devon.

She punched in his phone number and waited. Hearing his tired, groggy voice made her feel better, a whole lot better. As angry as she was now, waking Devon from a dead sleep lifted her spirits, gave her the upper hand.

"Wake up, damn you."

"Rio?" His voice sounded rough, grating.

"Your ex-wife, who will no longer do any one-on-one business with you. From now on, Mr. Wagner, you will call my attorney if you have anything to say to me. Is that clear?"

"What in the world is wrong with you? Why are you screaming at seven thirty on a Saturday morning?"

"Kiss my ass, Devon. You should've thought about that before you decided to try and weasel my half of this building out of me. How much do you stand to make off the deal? Three, four times more than me?"

"Listen—"

"I'm not listening to anything you have—" Somebody banged on her door, hard. Shit. "From now on, Devon, call Victoria. Don't ever call me again." She dropped the receiver into its cradle. Hell, now she had to deal with Bryce. Damn men. "Just a goddamn minute." She stomped her way to the door. Flinging it open, she said, "Do you have to beat the damn door down? I'm not fucking deaf!"

"Don't curse me, Rio. Don't curse at all. I don't like hearing it coming from you. You didn't answer the first two times I knocked."

In a numbing rage, she guessed she hadn't heard him. "There is a doorbell."

He barged his way inside. "All right. We're going to talk. Now."

The telephone rang. "Ah, for God's sake." She stormed back to the telephone, answered with less congeniality than ever, prepared to cuss out a telemarketer.

"Rio, this deal was for the two of us. You know how much I

still care for you. I was thinking this might help get us back together."

She dropped the phone like a hot skillet and unplugged the
unit, at a loss for a decent thought.

"Woman, why are you screaming—" Marcus stopped in
mid-sentence.

Good lord. She'd forgotten he was here.

"And who, may I ask, is this," he asked, dropping his suitcase on the hardwood with a loud thump, "inside *my* sister's
home at this time of day?" He had a problem with the general
"white" population.

"Get out, Bryce. I don't have time to talk to you, either."

"Who was on the phone?"

"None of your damn business. Get. Out. Now."

"Rio, what are you hiding from me? My competition? Is
that what you haven't told me?"

Seeing Marcus's eyes glaze over, she believed an exchange of
blows was on the horizon. Fortunately, Bryce had heard "sister" and cooled his jets. "Get out." She went to the door, held it
open and beckoned him. "I will not be intimidated by you or
any man. Get out."

"Rio—"

"Out," she snapped, stomping her foot.

He finally left. Angry, by the scowl on his handsome face,
but he didn't argue this time. Thank God for small favors. She
couldn't handle the emotions brewing inside her like a static-
electric thunderstorm, not with Marcus gearing up to detonate.

"Who in the devil was that talking about 'my competition'?
Have you *completely* lost your mental faculties, Rio? Do you
have any idea what you've done?"

Folding her arms beneath her breasts, she asked, "What,
Marcus? What have I done worse than the crap you've been
doing all of your adult life? Pot can't call the damn kettle black,
damn you. You have no right to badmouth me when you've

been stealing money, *playing* a religious role and screwing every pussy on the streets."

"You've earned a filthy mouth, own a filthy—supposed—business enterprise and you are even more filthy after being with that—"

"Get out," she snapped. "Get out and stay out. I've decided I don't want a brother any longer."

He snatched his suitcase off the floor, glaring. "As weak as you are, you'll need me in your life, Rio. And I'll be waiting to chastise you into submission, a punishment you'll welcome."

"Don't hold your fucking breath."

He yanked the door open and let it slam shut behind him.

Lord, she was tired, drained of energy.

Rio leaned back against the door, but her knees gave way and she sank to the floor.

"You're shittin' me," Galaxeé said.

"I wish I were." Rio massaged her temples.

She'd spent the day in bed, unable to rid herself of a throbbing migraine and somersaulting stomach. Her nerves had frayed into tattered ribbons, emotions tied up in a jumble of knotty twists.

"Don't tell me you're thinking about getting back with Devon," Galaxeé said. Her lips were pressed razor-thin. "Girl, I'll kill you myself."

"I don't know what I want right now, except peace and quiet. Don't start in on me. I can't handle it."

Without a doubt, she loved Bryce, but what were these feelings she still had for Devon after all these years?

"Sweetie, this is impossible."

Yes, it seemed that way, should be that way. She had reason not to continue a relationship with Bryce, though—the usual top three.

Devon fulfilled every aspect of a companion. Except she'd

already married him once and their relationship lacked in so many ways, unlike the connection she'd had with Bryce, who was caring and tender and giving. An excellent lover, in and out of bed. What more could any woman ask for these days?

"You can't," Galaxeé continued. "Think about the past and what your life was like, how unhappy you were. He creeped on you. He'll do it again."

Would he? Times had changed. Devon had matured now, gotten over the middle-age crisis, it seemed. And she had loved him once upon a time. Could she love him again? "I doubt—"

"He will do it again, Rio. Devon hasn't changed." Galaxeé knelt beside her. "At all. He's as devious as any lawyer can get. God, I knew I should've called Victoria," she said and cupped Rio's cheek. "Don't let that snake slither back into your life. He's worse than a damn cobra, worse than any rabid dog. What you need is real-live puppy and not an old, two-legged hound variety."

"Now, just a minute."

"Just a minute, my ass," Galaxeé said, straightening. "You didn't listen to me the first go-round. Damn it, you'll listen this time. Think about it. Look how much good life you lost while married to him. Look how much he hurt you. He'll do it again, and again, and again. Old dogs usually learn one new trick, but not Devon." She paced back and forth over an imaginary six-foot line and swung around. "What do you want to bet he screwed around on Tiffany? Dollar says I win. Hell, you game for ten bucks? A C-note? Shit, I'll bet my new damn set of Doms."

They'd never bet more than a dollar, and Galaxeé had laid down the betting rules. She was probably right on target.

"Girl, you need to really think about this. Don't make any hasty decisions, or you'll make the wrong one. Again."

Rio pressed her fingers to her forehead and swallowed. "Let me be. I need to work this through on my own."

The afternoon deteriorated, from bad to worse than tacky.

Adding to her jumbled emotions, the data she'd entered into the computer was partly incorrect. What had she been thinking about at the time to make so many mistakes? But she knew the answer without question.

Bryce.

She looked down at her bracelet watch. Quarter after seven. Why hadn't he called, or come by the club? Killer's was due to open its doors in forty-five minutes. Bryce had always come in an hour early. Always.

Biting her lip, she knew they'd parted on bad terms. She'd needed the space, time to gather her thoughts and emotions into a less miserable state. Had Bryce understood, or had she driven him away with bitchy evilness?

Evidently, her plan had worked. She drove the little boy away from an old hag. So why was it hurting so badly? Why did she feel like dirt, and so lonely?

Call him, a small voice said. Call him.

"But why?" she whispered. Their relationship had no chance of surviving.

Call him.

A revived relationship with Devon might work better.

Who do you love?

Many seconds passed.

Decide. Decide. Decide.

The word pounded her brain, intensifying her headache.

"I can't," she shouted and buried her face in her hands.

Bryce sat in the Escalade outside Killer's, staring at the illuminated clock, wasting fuel while the engine purred. He had arrived at the usual time, an hour early, but stayed inside his vehicle, contemplating today's events.

He'd kept his vow, had not harassed nor completely lost his temper with Rio today. Yet, he'd lost it completely with the warehouse work crew. Yelling, cursing and badgering anyone for any small complication. To top the list, two workers luckily had prevented a near fistfight. The idiot forklift driver had made a lewd comment about Rio's luscious body. Bryce flipped out. In the end, he fired the man.

Oh, yeah, his equanimity had collapsed faster than a popped balloon the moment Rio gave him the boot and slammed the loft's heavy door. Hearing the noise had bolstered his discontent, knowing she'd shut him out for some unknown freakin' reason.

Was she hiding another lover? How could she? When did she have time? She'd spent most of it with Bryce, except she *had* spent an evening with Devon—a long evening with an ex-spouse.

And what about last night? She'd adamantly refused to spend the night at his place.

Snarling, he pinched the bridge of his nose as a wave of churning jealousy burst hot in his gut. What the hell was he supposed to do, sit back and watch another man take her away from him? Call him out? Bust his goddamn mug?

Jesus. A boxing match. Exactly how an unsophisticated thug handles a problem, and Devon's as sophisticated as royalty. I'd lose her for sure after an immature stunt like fighting over a woman.

How had this emotional crap wheedled its way into existence? Why, after all these years, now?

Bryce raked both hands through his hair, unable to answer his own questions.

He'd stayed away from her today, didn't call and gave her space. She needed room, he'd give her room, whatever she needed. But damned if he'd give her up easily. Chemistry. They had a prescription for it. He knew it and so did Rio. Nothing could destroy the atomic molecules they'd created.

He shut down the Escalade's engine and climbed out. From

the backseat, he grabbed the hangers holding nightly strip clothes, slung them over his shoulder and tromped through the snow toward Killer's front door.

When the door closed behind him, he saw Galaxeé lounging against the bar, sipping on a cocktail—martini, probably—and staring at him. "You're later than usual. Gettin' tired of taking off your clothes?"

He smiled. Why was he still stripping? But he knew why.

"We don't have much time. Come talk to me," she ordered.

She led him down the long hall into the very storage room they'd caught on video and flicked on the light switch.

Spinning around, Galaxeé said, "Close the door."

How was she going to tell Bryce that he was losing ground, that she could only do so much to help him? He had to find a way back into the forefront of Rio's heart.

"You have to curb your damn jealousies and grow up."

"What?"

"You're losing her, Bryce. Rio needs a reason to believe that you belong together. So far, you haven't given her that reason."

"Like hell."

He tossed his clothes across the back of a chair, the same one Frankie had bent over to get her jollies and to give a few back. Galaxeé contained the derisive snort threatening to leave her lips.

"Sex isn't everything, Bryce. She needs more than just a good fucking."

He stepped back.

"She wants—needs—a man," Galaxeé said, hands riding her slim hips, leaning toward him. "Someone she can depend on. Someone she can trust with her heart. You're young and virile, but to tell you the truth, that's the problem. Most of the problem."

"How so?"

Did she have to spell out Rio's insecurities and his inability

to understand older women? "Where do you see the relationship going?"

Just as she thought, he shrugged his wide shoulders.

"Figures. Have you ever thought that Rio might see that
shitty-looking shrug in her mind?"

"But—"

"Have you ever thought that she believes the relationship's
not going anywhere, except to a damn Select Comfort mattress?"

"How did—"

"Why would any grown woman continue a relationship,"
Galaxeé harped, "with a youngster like you when chances are
damned good that you'll find some young bimbo your own age
and hightail out of there?"

"I'm not into young bimbos, never have been."

She huffed. "Why the hell should Rio continue a fling with
you, Bryce? Why the hell would she risk getting her heart broken by a dumbass again?"

"I'm not a dumbass. I love her." It came close to sounding
like a shout.

Galaxeé grunted. "I didn't think you'd go as far as to admit
it. Good. But think about it, since you say you love her. Think
of all the times you've been with Rio. What have you done together besides engaging in frantic monkey sex?"

"It's not like I haven't tried to get Rio to go out."

"Don't pout. Hell. Sometimes you just overdo things." This
boy could fluster a damn rag doll. "Sometimes you push it too
hard, Bryce. What have you done to make her see the light?
What have you done for her? Not to her, for her. Something
worthwhile, to prove you love her."

Galaxeé watched him, could almost see his brain working.
He didn't find an answer. "See what I mean? Hell, you don't
know shit about good women. I don't know why in the hell I
got involved in this mess."

He folded his arms in such a defensive posture, Galaxeé almost laughed. "I've told her I loved her."

"Words are as cheap as the air we breathe, especially in the heat of passion, but it's a start," she mumbled and walked circles around Bryce, lips pursed.

"All right. There's some sort of problem going on with Killer's computer. I'm not exactly sure what it is yet. Can't quite come up with a clear . . . Damn, I should've talked to Momma about this. Too late now. But I think somebody working here is tampering with it or we have a hacker. You see, we have our first audit next month and Rio's worried. I think the same person who tried to break in is messing around with the computer. Could be anybody. Dancers, bartender, though I doubt Luanne would step so low, janitorial folks, yada, yada," she said, flinging her arms. "We have to find out who's the culprit, and you have to be the shining knight since you're the computer ner . . . uh . . . expert. Rio will see you in a little different light. Get my drift?"

"What will that prove to her?"

Jesus. "It'll prove you'd do just about anything to make her happy. You do want to make her happy, don't you?" She didn't give him time to answer. "If you don't, fine. Get the hell out of here. You're fired."

He had the common decency to appear exasperated, maybe even appalled. "Her happiness matters to me. Matters a lot."

"You make sure it does," Galaxeé commanded. "I won't let anyone hurt my best friend and get away with it ever again. Got it?"

He nodded, and he didn't look away.

She liked sincerity. Had Bryce not continued to hold her gaze, she really would've handed him walking papers. "Before I forget, a situation has come to my devoted attention, and for unspecified reasons I think you need to know about it."

Galaxeé omitted Jason's and Orlando's name, but she laid out the dirty details of Frankie's menagé à trois.

"I want that disc," he ordered in a no-nonsense tone.

"Not a chance, bud. But," she said, grinning. "When you're ready for cleanup duty . . . that is, if she can sit and listen. God knows I—Just let me know. I'll be your explosive ammunition."

Galaxeé chewed on her bottom lip. Those details were a tiny fracture in the ice, had nothing to do with Killer Bods' current problems or Rio's distress about the audit.

"Now, back to what we talking about earlier—Rio. The situation won't be an easy job, Bryce. I sense a very rocky road ahead."

"I can handle it."

"You sure as hell better be ready. It's gonna be pretty damned bumpy. In comparison, a spiraling roller-coaster ride is as tame as a merry-go-round at a standstill. So here's what we have to do."

For a weekend night, Killer's was packed, crawling with women on the hunt. With its closure during the holidays next week, these ladies wanted action to hold them for the extra days. The last Bryce had heard bouncers were turning customers away at the door. Ideally, the stranded "cats" had decided to head for Smoothly Silk. Angelina needed the business.

He'd followed Galaxeé's recommendation and stayed away from Rio. He spoke to her once, just before his first dance set, with a simple one-word greeting. She didn't look happy and it took every ounce of strength to keep from pulling her into his arms to kiss away the hurt he saw on her beautiful face.

With the evening coming to a close, Bryce wondered if Galaxeé was plain crazy. Or maybe he'd lost his mind for going along with her ridiculous plan. So far, nothing had happened and no one had approached the office. He knew one day he'd catch the idiot tampering with Killer's computer and ease Rio's worries. He'd do anything to make her happy, even if she didn't love him.

Galaxeé came up beside him at the bar. "Have you been watching?" she yelled over the blaring music.

"Yeah. Nobody's been up there. Where's Rio?"

"Checking liquor. Luanne, honey, get me a drink when you get a chance! Poor child has been running her butt off. Guess we'd better think about getting another bartender to ease her job. Got a hell of a mixed crowd tonight."

A pretty, long-haired blonde waltzed over to Bryce's side. She leaned in, rubbed her breasts against his arm and said, "Hi, I'm Brianna."

Galaxeé rolled her eyes just as Luanne set a martini down on the bar. She sipped on the cocktail, eyeing Bryce.

"You dance really well," Brianna said. He didn't answer. "Care to dance with me?"

"No, thanks. I don't break rules and dance with customers."

"Bravo," Galaxeé muttered.

"Some of the other dancers do," the young woman said, sounding indignant.

"I'm not the other dancers."

Just then, Rio came through the swinging doors behind the bar as the music wound down. From the look on her face, Bryce should've keeled over. She had a way with her eyes that made a man lose inches off his height.

"Besides," he said, watching Rio ignore him. She bent over the cooler, tooted her ass right toward him. "I've got a good woman."

"Bastard."

"Hey," Galaxeé snapped. "One more snotty remark like that, sister, and I'll eighty-six your butt." The girl stomped away. "I hope you didn't say those words for my benefit."

"Not a chance," he replied, still staring at Rio's derriere, wondering what color panties she had on tonight. "I do have a good woman and I intend to keep her." He set the glass of ice water down and started around the bar.

"Hold up," Galaxeé said, grabbing his arm, laughing. "Remember what I said? You have to make her want you, make her come after you." She went slack-jawed and let loose of his arm. "What the hell?"

Bryce swung around, followed her gaze and caught a glimpse of the office door closing.

"Come on," she said. "It's showtime."

He cleared a path through Killer's rambunctious crowd. Galaxeé stayed hot on his heels. At the top of the stairs, she said, "Give 'em a chance to get started. I don't want any mistakes. We'll nail 'em."

While they waited, Bryce looked down at the bar. Rio stared up at him.

"Now," Galaxeé ordered.

Bryce tested the knob. Locked. He shouldered the door open.

"You son of a bitch," Galaxeé snapped.

Frankie hopped a good yard backward from the file cabinet, her eyes wide, her mouth hanging open like a trapdoor.

The chair rolled away from the computer. But Bryce marched toward the man who spun around. He curled his fingers into Jason's shirtfront, dragged him to a standing position, and shoved him against the metal cabinet, closing the open drawer with a big bang.

"Man, get off me!"

"What are you two doing in here?" Bryce asked, glaring at Jason, then at Frankie.

"Nothin'," Jason said.

"Nothin', huh? Why's the computer on?" Galaxeé asked, moving closer. "It's been you all along, hasn't it, you and this trashy bitch? You're the ones messing up Rio's work, trying to destroy our club."

"I've only worked on the website," Frankie said quickly. "Ask Bryce. He's hiring me to work as a web designer for Thorobred. I had no idea what Jason was doing here."

"In your dreams. It'd be a cold day in hell before I'd ever put you on my payroll."

"Oh, but you will. Claudine—"

"My mother will never hear one malicious word. However, *your* mother might have something to say about your backroom jaunts. Let her have it, Nitro."

Galaxeé laid down the laws of truth, which had Frankie dazed, cowering and tearful. Finished with one weasel, she clamped onto Jason's arm. "Why, Jason?" Her eyes grew larger. "You stole the files!"

He had a mean glint in his eyes.

"Answer the question," Bryce ordered, "or I swear I'll bust your ass."

Jason chuckled nastily. "You oughta be glad, Sullivan. I was finishing the job you'd planned to do for your sister. Why tear into my ass when it was all your idea?"

"That's a lie," Bryce said in a savage voice.

"Y-Your s-sister?" Galaxeé sputtered.

"Yeah. Didn't you know?" Jason continued. "Angelina Berardi of Smoothly Silk is Sullivan's half sister. He was helping her out, set up the whole job to save her club."

"Job?"

Bryce looked over his shoulder. Rio. Christ.

"You planned this? You used me to get at Killer's?" she whispered. Stiff-legged, she moved toward him.

"Rio, no, that's not true. He's lying."

"Is Angelina Berardi your sister?"

Her breathing was short and choppy, but he'd never seen a frown like this one on her face. A sickness coiled in Bryce's gut, sprang free as he let Jason loose. He couldn't lie. "Yes, she is, and at first . . . before I met you—" He swallowed. "But I didn't. I promise you, I didn't."

"How could you?" Rio burst out. "I trusted you. I gave . . . I gave—" Her glorious eyes swelled with angry tears. The dam broke suddenly and a river washed over her cheeks.

Bryce raised his hands toward her, but she stepped out of his reach. "Please, Rio, believe me. You know me, know I'd never hurt you."

She drew her hand back, tagged Bryce with a powerful roundhouse left and ran out of the office.

"Boy, you got a lot of damn nerve," Galaxeé snapped. "Jason, Bryce. You are both fired. Pack your gear and get the hell out of our club. Now, or I call the cops. And Frankie, I suggest you lead the way before I help you out of here."

"Son of a bitch," Bryce said. He stared menacingly at Jason as Frankie made a fast dash for the door. "I ought to break your goddamn neck."

Smug as hell, Jason said, "Bring it on, cowboy."

He did. Bryce flattened him.

17

On Sunday afternoon, Randy hung up the phone for the fifth time since eight o'clock. "You really should talk to him, snookums," he said. "I believe him."

"You would," Galaxeé replied. "Males stick together like stink on shit, no matter what the truth is."

"Cut it out, Cecilia. You know me better than that."

She poked out her bottom lip in a pout. "Oh, pookie, how could I have missed all this? Why didn't I know he was up to no good?"

Randy wrapped his arms around her body, squeezed gently. "I wouldn't put it past Jason to lie, but Bryce," he said and sighed. "I've checked him out, didn't find anything untoward. Hard for me to believe a businessman of his caliber and success would resort to this type of dishonesty. Corruption crosses the desks of even the best of men, but that doesn't mean they'll all follow the scent of deceit. Money talks, doll. Bryce is a very talented young man for his age, and he pursues the scent of honest business."

"True, but Killer's competition, Smoothly Silk, is owned by his sister. He didn't bother telling us."

"Would you have hired him if he had?"

"No, but—"

"You knew Bryce would love her when you hired him."

She poked out her lip again and Randy nipped at it. "I know, but—"

"You know he truly loves her now, don't you?"

She nodded, staring over his shoulder.

"Do you honestly believe Bryce would hurt her this way?" Randy cupped her chin, forcing her to meet his gaze.

She wished she had lashes like his, thick and lengthy, permanently curled. Eyes showing sincerity like Bryce's glittering grays. "No," she replied in a little girl's voice.

"Call him and listen to what he has to say. It can't hurt no matter what happens later."

"Rio will strangle me if I do."

"Baby girl, that has never stopped you from meddling before and you're still breathing."

When the doorbell chimed, Rio was sorely tempted not to answer. She knew Galaxeé was on the other side of the door, even though she'd told her not to stop by.

The melody played again and, mumbling filth, she tightened the belt to her robe and went to answer the noisy summons. On second thought, the ringer might be someone she had no reason to see.

"Who is it?"

"It's me, sweetie."

"Galaxeé, I said I didn't want company."

"Well, you got company. Open up the damn door. It's cold out here."

She unlatched the metal lever, then turned around and walked off, grumbling, "Can't get any damn peace and quiet."

"It's so friggin' nice to know how close I am to my best friend," Galaxeé said, slamming the heavy steel. She followed

Rio and tossed her fox jacket onto the chair next to the sofa. "You look like shit."

"Thank you very much."

"You haven't taken a shower or combed your hair. Have you eaten?"

Rio knew she looked awful, felt worse. "Yeah," she replied, staring at nothing in particular outside the snow-dusted window.

"When, and what?"

Her nose started running again. She found a crumpled tissue in her pocket. "Earlier," she lied.

"Ah, sweetie." Galaxeé climbed onto the sofa, wrapped her arms around Rio and rocked her. "I talked to him today. He's been trying to call and stopped by—"

"I don't care," Rio said and sniffled. The telephone had rung at least fifteen times today. She'd answered Galaxeé's call and one other first thing this morning. "It's over. The bastard."

"Rio, what Jason said was a lie."

"Yeah, right. Angelina's not Bryce's sister?"

"Well, that part is true."

"That's the important part. Nothing else matters. He lied to us. Which means, he lied about everything."

"He didn't lie. He just didn't tell us. We didn't ask, either."

Rio pulled free of her arms. "You're supposed to be my best friend and you're siding with him?"

"He loves you, honey," Galaxeé said, reaching for her hand. She huffed and drew away.

"Look in the mirror. You love him, too." When she shook her head emphatically, Galaxeé clucked her tongue. "Then why are you still crying?"

Rio blew her nose louder than a honking goose and her friend made a sour face. "Caught a cold."

"Get out. You are lying." Galaxeé slipped off her leather boots, leaned back into the deep cushions and crossed her legs

Indian-style. "Let me tell you some things that'll change your mind about him."

"Nothing will change my mind, so I don't want to hear it."

"I'm telling you anyway." She poked her bottom lip out and Rio sighed. "First of all, the boy's got a hell of a right hook. He knocked Jason out."

"Why? Because he put his business in the streets?"

"No," Galaxeé said. "Let's order delivery first. You need to eat. You look like—"

"I know, I know. But Galaxeé, don't try to play games with me. If he comes to my door instead of a deliveryman, I'll strangle you first. I don't want to see him ever again."

"I rehired him. You can't fire him without reason."

"I already have." She sniffed again. "I'm meeting Devon Tuesday night for dinner, to talk."

Galaxeé's face altered faster than a lethal virus, eyes narrowed to slits thinner than plastic wrap, lips flat-lined. "No, you're not. I'll put you out of your own damn misery right now. Desperation is so unbecoming on you," she said, drama in her tone.

"I'm not desperate."

"You must be. Hooking up with that mongrel again?"

Rio had no plans whatsoever to hook up with her ex, or with any species of the male population. But, if she spent enough time in public with Devon, other hounds would keep their distance.

"Believe what you want," she replied. "I just need to get out of town."

Sitting in the Escalade outside the warehouse, motor running, Bryce kept the cell phone in hand, waiting for Galaxeé's coded call. What would he do without her help—camp out at Rio's door since Killer's was closed through the holiday weekend? She wouldn't have to leave the loft.

He checked the clock. An hour had gone by.

"What's taking so goddamn long?"

He activated the windshield wiper, turned down the heat and upped the defogger fan.

Light snow fell and a brisk wind blew dry flurries into little tornadoes, sweeping the sidewalks clear. Overhead, gunmetal gray, cloudy skies looked as gloomy as he felt inside. The weather had turned cold, frigid and icy as the glare he'd seen in Rio's eyes last night. Bryce grimaced at the memory. From that horrible moment on, he knew Rio loathed him more than she despised the devil.

He realized that rubbing his chest hadn't stopped the nagging ache inching its way through his body. Only one person could stop the pain and she wanted nothing to do with him.

Someone banged on the passenger-side window and Bryce jumped. Oh, hell.

"Unlock the door." Climbing inside, Galaxeé said, "Cold out there."

She didn't look at him. Shit.

"Wind's really chilling. The weatherman said a low pressure moved in."

Bad news. Straightforward Galaxeé was trying to avoid the inevitable.

Icy tentacles of despair squeezed Bryce's heart, slithered to his throat and threatened to cut off his air. He turned away, stared blindly at the blowing snow. "Shitty news, isn't it?" he rasped.

For the first time in his adult life, he felt completely powerless, helpless and downtrodden, but Galaxeé's warming hand on his arm relieved a little of the building pressure in his chest.

"Bryce, honey," she said and popped her gum. "We need a new game plan."

✳   ✳   ✳

Thanksgiving morning, Rio dragged out one soft-sided suit-case.

The last four days had been the worst of her life when lone-liness had wrapped numbing aches around her. She needed time away. The mountain cabin provided solitude and calm that would allow her to gather her emotions into some semblance of order.

"Men," she muttered, yanking open the dresser drawer.

Devon had canceled their dinner date at the last minute, saying something had come up. Yeah, she bet his dick jumped stupid after another woman. Fine with her.

She grabbed a pile of underwear, tossed it on the bed, and slammed the drawer. Next were heavy socks, sweats, and flan-nel jammies.

Jammies. Galaxeé hadn't called since Sunday. Rio sighed, guessing she'd pissed off her best friend enough to steer clear.

"Not even a damn birthday present from her after all these years."

Another birthday. God, forty-one. Nine years short of a half century and still without decent company on the occasion. Rio smiled grimly.

"Alone and grieving."

By now, Galaxeé and Randy had left for an exotic paradise island somewhere to enjoy warm, sunny weather and each other. Rio had no one; not even a best friend to help her through the grief and aching pain of her shattered heart.

She lowered herself to the bed, buried her face in her hands, and let the tears flow freely again, sobbing quietly. She really thought she'd emptied herself of tears days ago, but they still came so very easily.

"Stop it," she said, sniffling, drying her eyes with the backs of her hands. "This is exactly what you wanted, isn't it? It's the best way, the best thing for him. He's moved on now. He'll find a nice Italian girl his own age and live happily ever after."

She stuffed her clothes inside the suitcase and zipped it shut. "At least somebody will be happy."

Bundled for an arctic trek, she made five trips to the garage loading the Mercedes.

Yesterday afternoon she'd gone to the grocery store and outlet mall for last-minute supplies. She'd bought a cute black snowsuit, heavy boots and gloves to lift her spirits, just in case she needed to get out of the cabin for fresh air and a walk. The powder-blue snowsuit she'd bought last year was too cute to get wet.

Yesterday morning she'd called Mr. Landers, the small-business owner and property caretaker of the Breckenridge one-bedroom log cabin. He agreed to plow the road leading to the cabin before her arrival. His two sons were on notice to deliver enough kindling and a mixed cord of firewood to last through the winter. They would also do a maintenance check and make any necessary repairs. And, yes, he'd have the snow shoveled from the deck and drop off the portable hot tub, have it bubbling hot before her arrival.

Landers had said snow was two and a half feet deep and they were expecting another storm Thanksgiving night. Was she planning to stay a while? A week.

"No blasted woman needs to be alone up here in these hills during winter, so bring plenty of supplies and one of them cell phones for emergencies," Landers had said pointedly. "Prepare to get snowed in. I can feel it in my old bones. Got a helluva blizzard comin' from way up north."

Perfect. She had novels, magazines, CDs of her favorite music artists, lots of food and excellent wine—enough commodities to satisfy an army. The cabin's pantry still contained canned and dried goods left there from Labor Day weekend. Plus, she'd bought extra candles in case the power failed. What more would she need?

Sutures might help, to mend her heart.

Rio fed the pet fish their vacation standby. They didn't need her any more than the next person. Maybe Galaxeé was right. A puppy would need her, greet her happily and love her unconditionally. She made a mental note to stop by the Dumb Friends League as soon as she returned to Denver. Wished she'd thought about it before now. She could use the company.

She closed and locked the loft's door, grabbed her new snow boots from the cement floor and hurried down the stairs to the garage.

"You did pick up everything, didn't you?" Galaxeé asked.

Far more than she knew. "Yep," Bryce said into the cell phone. "Think this plan'll work?"

"I'm always right about these things. Let me know when you pass Old Chambers Road. You'll make a left on a blind curve. There'll be a huge boulder—"

"Old Chambers Road."

Bryce could've easily used the navigation system, but Boss-woman Galaxeé had insisted on guiding him in and giving final instructions. She and Randy were catching the second leg of their flight out of Houston.

"Okay, slow down. Do you see the rock? It's about five feet high. Turn right."

He swerved onto the snow-covered trail. "Done."

"Just stay on it. About two miles and you'll run dead into the cabin."

"Thanks, Galaxeé, I owe you one."

"Make the best of it, Bryce. Momma and I took care of everything else and we can't do any more for you. Gotta go. We're loading. Damn lightning storm, too. Good luck."

He needed more than luck. At the very least, he needed a miracle. Ever since that horrible night, he'd drowned in loneliness, heartache and misery.

Early Monday morning, he'd instructed Maureen to cancel or postpone everything on his calendar for the next week.

She'd seemed to recognize his listless behavior and had hovered over him like a mother hen all morning.

"Is everything all right?" she'd asked.

At the time, Bryce sat in his brown leather chair, his back to the office door, staring blankly outside the frosted window.

"Mr. Sullivan? Is there anything I can do to help?"

He pinched the bridge of his nose, his emotions in worse condition than he could ever imagine, ego obliterated. But when Maureen came around his desk, he spun his chair away from her and said, "Let me alone, Maureen."

She stayed behind his chair, laid her hands on his shoulders, kneading the tight muscles there. "I've never seen you like this before, but I have seen this type of despair. My son. Last year. Remember the wedding you attended this past summer? He's so much better, so much happier." Maureen sighed. "Take some time off from work and evaluate your life. There's nothing urgent on our calendar."

He was fortunate to have Maureen. Bryce left the building a few minutes later.

The next night, he stopped by Angelina's condominium, needing to be around a friendly face. His sister was just as miserable. She'd decided to close Smoothly Silk's doors permanently. Bryce would absorb the financial burden, but money was the last worry on his mind.

As for Jason Simmons, Angelina had said, "The Beamer's in his name, not mine."

"Did you pay for it?"

She hemmed and hawed, twirling a lock of dark brown hair around two fingers—a habit she'd had since childhood.

"Did you, Boo?"

"He still has two years' worth of payments. All right? That

woman I caught him in bed with can take over. Or the dealership will simply repossess it. We're finished."

That *woman* was likely Frankie Perino.

Angelina signed a quitclaim deed to her condominium over to Bryce and packed her bags. He'd purchased a first-class seat to New York for her this morning. She planned to enroll in college again. All expenses paid from her brother's deep pockets.

So happy, Claudine Berardi postponed her trip to Colorado. She wanted to find her daughter a fiancé by Christmas since her eldest child had no plans for marriage.

"Why didn't you come home with your sister?" Claudine had asked.

"Busy."

"I found just the right young woman for you to meet. She's very lovely. Cooks Italian, too."

"Mother—" He sighed into the phone. "Maybe I'll see you at Christmas." Bryce hung up.

He didn't want to spend the Thanksgiving holiday alone in the big house. He wanted to spend time with Rio, and somehow Galaxeé and Rosalind Barnett had made it happen.

Almost.

Bryce was on his own now, and nervous.

Darkness had moved across the sky and over the mountains. He switched on the fog lamps, dimmed the driving lights to hide his approach. Snow glistened from the yellow glow. In the not-too-far distance, a small cabin appeared, a single window illuminated by soft lighting.

Rio's black Mercedes was blanketed with snow. Flakes had been falling since three o'clock and snow-packed highways were slick, treacherous in many areas. The Cadillac hugged the road well in these conditions as snow crunched beneath twenty-two-inch chrome wheels.

Whoever had plowed this obscured trail had done it earlier in the day. The weatherman predicted two feet of fresh powder by morning. A heap had fallen already, from the looks of the surrounding terrain. According to the Highway Patrol, most of the mountain roads would be shut down long before midnight.

Bryce parked far back on the side of the small cabin and cut the engine. He climbed out, inhaled the woody-pine scent coming from the chimney, and went around to the passenger side of the car.

He lifted one decorative box from the seat and tiptoed to the front door. There, he set it down, knocked and hurried around the corner of the cabin to watch Rio from safely out of sight.

The porch light came on and she stepped outside dressed in a sweatsuit and slippers, as beautiful as the first time he'd laid eyes on her.

"Galaxeé?"

Bryce melted into the shadows.

"Stop playing and come inside before you freeze to death." She stooped to pick up the white box. The sky-blue bow on top jiggled and the lid moved. "What in the world?"

Rio lifted the top. A little black-and-white ball of fur panted, scratched, yipped and begged for her, then toppled over.

"Oh," she said. "Oh."

Even from this distance Bryce saw her tears spilling, glistening on her face, and his heart split in two while he watched her gently take the puppy into her arms, nuzzling the mixed breed he'd gotten from an employee of his. Wearing a matching blue bow around his neck, the pup licked the wetness from her face, whimpering.

Rio sniffed, wiped the remainder away. "What's your name," she asked and looked underneath the dog, "little boy, huh? Do you have a name?"

"How about calling him Bryce?" He came around the corner, heard her sudden gasp and stayed where he stood under a shower of heavy snow. "Only, I think he's got more smarts than this little boy."

Rio swallowed back the threat of more tears. He was the last person on Earth she'd expected to see tonight, any night. "What are you doing here? Where's Galaxeé?"

He didn't move from the spot so far away. "I've missed you," Bryce countered softly. "And no matter what you think of me, I still love you, Rio. Always will."

"No, don't. Don't." She couldn't stand another wave of unwanted tears. "You can't." The dam broke and a river gushed free.

"Hey. Don't cry. God, please don't cry," he said and rushed across the porch in three long strides. He enfolded her into his embrace, buried his face against her neck, swayed to an unheard song.

She couldn't help it, couldn't stop the raging flow. Even though he'd lied and hurt her, she still loved him. Her deepest wishes had been granted, wishes she had no right to hope for at all.

And Bryce was here, holding her in his strong arms, soothing her, giving Rio all the love and comfort she'd secretly prayed for during the last few days.

He tipped her face up, kissed the wetness from her cheeks and pressed his lips to her forehead. "Happy Birthday, kitten."

She smiled tremulously. Galaxeé had told him. Had she mentioned the exact number of years of her age? Did he realize that well over a decade separated *their* ages?

"Can we try again? Will you take a chance on me one more time? Let me keep loving you through the next ones," he whispered and planted a light kiss to her lips.

Yes, she thought, enjoying the feel of him surrounding her and the sensuous warmth of his kiss. Just for a little while longer. She melted, like the snow dripping from his silky hair, into the heat radiating from his big body.

Moments later, he lifted his head. "Better get you inside. You're shivering and wet."

"I'm dry," she replied, sniffling. "You're wet."

Bryce stepped back, held out his arms and looked down. "Junior here peed on me."

She laughed through the tears.

He'd brought so much stuff with him. A fifty-pound bag of dog food, toys and a car carrier for her new puppy and a small bed to keep the puppy, now called Durango, off the furniture and bed.

No way. Rio thought the puppy should sleep in her bed. Durango was too young to be without his mother and needed loving comfort. Bryce didn't argue. He went back to the Escalade and brought in food, gift-wrapped packages he said were birthday presents, and finally a case of her favorite wine.

"Done," he said, setting the box on the counter.

"You didn't bring clothes?"

He blushed. "I wasn't sure if you'd let me stay."

With Durango draped over her forearm, she stepped toward Bryce, stroked his smooth-shaven cheek, concerned. Beneath his sparkling eyes were dark shadows. "Of course, I will."

He gripped her wrist, pressed a kiss to the center of her palm.

"Besides," she teased, "I don't have enough room in my car to get all this stuff home."

He dragged her arm around his neck, wrapped his own around Rio and lifted her from the floor. "Whatever you ask of me, consider it done. Whatever you want or need, I'm here to provide. I'll give you everything, complete devotion."

She frowned a little, swallowed as a shudder raced through her body. He'd make some lucky young woman very, very happy. "Have you eaten?"

"Chef, too." Smiling, he set her down. "Since it's late, steak okay? Tomorrow, turkey and all the trimmings." He reached into his pants pocket and pulled out a small notebook. At her frown, he said, "Recipes." Galaxeé had given him the works.

"You're kidding, right? You don't really plan to do all the cooking."

"Devotion," he replied and placed a chaste kiss to her cheek, then stroked the puppy's tiny head. "Durango and I will take care of you. So, while I cook, you have birthday presents to open."

Bryce watched her from the corner of his eye.

She kneeled beside the hearth. The fire's brilliant glow brightened her face and sparkled through her shiny hair. Nuzzling the whimpering little dog, she cooed and Durango quieted, curled into a perfect ball when she set him in her lap.

Bryce popped the cork on a bottle of '03 Silver Oak and set it aside to breathe while he prepared dinner, smiling, seeing Rio's lips move while reading a card.

She untied a blue bow, peeled the tape from the box, careful not to tear the matching, glossy paper. So meticulous. So cautious. A woman of sheer perfection.

His smile broadened when he heard her gasp. Rosalind and Oscar had selected a pale-blue cashmere sweater ensemble.

Galaxeé and Randy's gift called for a squeal. The champagne flutes must've cost a fortune from the way she handled the fine crystal, as did the bubbly.

She'd set his three presents on the hearth. Was that gesture a good omen or a bad one? Would she accept his gifts?

Her hands trembled, lifting the first box. The long thin one.

She read the card as he repeated the words he wrote in silence. *With this blossom, I give to you* . . . Shit. He should've gone to the library for poetry.

Finally, finally, she removed the lid and lifted a perfect red rosebud. As perfect as the woman holding its stem. She sniffed its sweet, delicate perfume and clutched the flower to her breasts.

Minutes passed as Bryce seasoned the steaks and unloaded groceries he'd brought with him.

She was staring at him, picking at her nail polish. The second card had read: *To my heart* . . . Inside the box laid an old-fashioned gold skeleton key.

Bryce turned on the broiler. Two potatoes went inside the microwave. After shoving the steaks under the burners, he tore lettuce apart, chopped tomatoes and arranged their salads. He filled their wineglasses and set the small table for dinner.

But his nerves were shot. She hadn't opened the last gift, hadn't said a word or made a sound. Why was she waiting?

He gulped down a full glass of wine, refilled it and held on to the bottle's neck, staring outside the small window into the snowy night.

Darkness had settled over the mountainside. Small beads of ice and snow rapped against the window as the blizzard moved in with full force, blanketing the terrain once more. No doubt, they'd be snowed in, but what better place to spend time alone with Rio.

He heard a door click shut. Bryce spun around and the wine bottle crashed to the floor, unbroken, but cabernet spread across the linoleum in a bloody river.

She'd left the small box sitting on the hearth, card untouched.

And his too-vulnerable heart shredded into a gazillion pieces.

18

Rio couldn't bring herself to unwrap the last present, fearing what lay inside the ring-size box, dreading what she needed to say. When Durango whimpered, she stole a few minutes of reprieve and took the puppy outside.

Durango scampered clumsily to the edge of the porch. He went a little too far and sank into a snowdrift.

"Oh." Rio hurried over to her most precious gift and rescued the soggy little pup. He peed on her.

She laughed, holding him away from her body. "Naughty little boy. Shame on you. No wonder Bryce wants you to sleep in your own bed."

The front door opened swiftly.

"I couldn't find you." He sounded frantic. "I thought you'd left."

"You thought I'd what? In this weather?"

"You're wet."

"Durango again."

"Thank God."

"That he peed on me instead?"

"No, no," Bryce replied and let out a long, long rush of air. He stepped outside, gathered her and the puppy into his arms, sighing. "I made a mess in the kitchen, but I'll clean it. Oh, shit, the steaks."

Rio burst out laughing until she saw smoke filtering out of the cabin's front door. She followed him inside, waving her hand to clear the smelly cloud, clutching Durango protectively to her chest. But then she saw the kitchen floor. To make matters worse, the baked potatoes suddenly exploded inside the microwave. Bryce cursed and punched the off button.

"Get out of my kitchen!"

"I'll—" He stepped back when she scowled an intense I'll-kill-you-where-you-stand.

"Out. Out!" She handed Durango to him and shoved him from the room.

She wanted to scream. On the bright side, Chef Bryce's disaster had saved her from opening the gift wrapped in gold paper.

He'd done it now, messed up everything.

Bryce sat on the sofa with Durango in his lap, watching Rio attack the linoleum with a cleanser, mop and bucket. The smoke had cleared, but she had yet to deal with the microwave catastrophe. When he offered to clean a second time, she rewarded him with another deadly scowl, followed by ignoring him.

Damn it all, he wanted her to open the box.

He held Durango up to his own face. "What do you think, big guy?" The puppy whined. "Does that mean I'm looking at sharing a doghouse with you . . . ? As long I don't get sent to the pound, buddy. We'll keep each other company. Maybe we can both keep her happy. How about that?"

He glanced at the one remaining gift left wrapped, then at Rio, then at Durango again.

"I think your chances are better than mine. She said you're sleeping in her bed, which means I get the couch."

Rio finished cleaning the kitchen mess and took a shower. Bryce continued waiting.

She still hadn't said a word, still hadn't looked at him and still hadn't touched the gift. She cooked dinner, though, and the mouthwatering aromas put his stomach in growl-mode.

She'd spent an hour ignoring the wannabe man in her life, but she wasted plenty of dedicated time cooing over Durango.

The puppy ate cooked hamburger, not the expensive dog food. His milk was even warmed. She cuddled him when he whined and rocked him to sleep.

Bryce was as jealous as an old tomcat, more so when she took Durango into her bedroom and left him there.

Without a television, he tried to read, a romance no less. Bored with the beginning, Bryce skipped forward to the book's final pages. Love. Pain. Marriage. Why waste paper on the middle part? Logically speaking, take the shortest route to solve the problem. Who wrote the algorithm for romance novels?

Disenchanted, he worked a crossword puzzle until Rio called him to dinner. First, he added two logs to the fire and it roared to bonfire life.

Half expecting to see dog food on his plate, Bryce went to the table. She'd laid out a spread fit for a king. Smothered pork chops, rice and broccoli looked exceptional.

"Looks and smells really good." He filled her glass with chardonnay, but he couldn't stand her silence any longer. "I apologize for messing up your kitchen, would've cleaned it to your satisfaction."

She didn't respond and Bryce sighed. How could their relationship get back on track if she shut him out?

"Durango agreed to let me share the doghouse, but how long do you plan to leave me there? He peed on you and he's already out on bail."

He didn't appreciate the sound of her laughter. Bryce thought about what he'd said. Jesus. He grinned since the foolish comment had gotten Rio to flash her signature smile again.

Life was definitely on the up and up, soaring.

"There's one more birthday present you forgot to open, but it can wait until after dinner."

And Rio's vibrant smile vanished. "Eat before your food gets cold."

Out of the doghouse, but he'd crashed and burned to a freakin' crisp. He would not press her. Galaxeé had warned him not to push too hard.

Give her time. Give her space. Give her reasons to want you in her life. Act as if you don't need her. And, remember, sex isn't everything.

He scooped a helping of rice and gravy onto his fork.

He'd kept his mind off sex and tamped down his raging hormones. He planned to keep his hands off Rio for the duration. Tonight, he'd suffer through sleep deprivation on that hard couch while thinking about her delectable body in the next room.

Naked, sprawled on the bed, waiting for him. Going all soft beneath his hands and body. He could almost taste her sweet essence and he felt the first twinge of a hard-on.

"There's plenty of gravy," Rio said. "You don't have to lick the fork like that."

Hell's bells. If she knew what he'd been thinking . . . Long night ahead.

Tomorrow, he needed to find a fun activity for them outside the cabin. The cold weather should keep his dick in check and his mind on stuff other than making love to her.

As for the little box, he guessed Rio just wasn't ready to open it yet. He had to give her reason to want him in her life. But how, without pushing too hard? They'd always had a burning need for each other. So now what, put the heat control on simmer, douse the flames completely?

He hadn't touched her since the kitchen disaster, except once, when he happened to slide his fingers down hers to take back a soiled fork while he washed dishes. The hot slick sensation reminded her of the uncomfortable wetness she'd suffered, watching him lick the fork. He'd flipped her switch to meltdown again. The devil. By the look on his face, he really enjoyed dinner. Or had he been teasing her?

Bryce had insisted on washing dishes and Rio insisted on helping to avoid the gift issue.

She just knew what was inside the box, darn him. A piece of bright metal mounted with a gemstone she absolutely would not accept. The problem, how could she turn it down gently without hurting him? Without breaking her heart again in the process? And they were shut inside this tiny cabin for how long?

She switched the back porch light on and glanced outside the kitchen window. "Wow."

"Looks like a horizontal meteor shower," Bryce said.

She felt his heat, wanted to lean back and absorb the warmth.

"I'd better bring in more firewood before it gets any worse."

She watched the storm a little longer. "I'll help." When Rio swung around, he was on his way to the front door.

"Stay put. Durango might need you," Bryce said and smiled. The ski jacket emphasized how big he was. The cap covering his dark hair highlighted his good looks and his hands, covered with thick gloves, resembled a boxer's. "I need to occupy myself since I'm stuck here for the night."

Stuck? For the night?

Rio searched the room frantically, eyes darting to every corner of the small living space. Where was his suitcase or duffel? He hadn't brought one inside!

Panicking, she jerked her head toward the hearth, and the bottom dropped out of her belly. She started to pick at her nail polish, squelched the urge and clutched her hands tightly behind her back.

The pretty little box had disappeared. He'd taken it somewhere. To his car?

Why wasn't she flooded with relief?

Bryce closed the door behind him and stared out into blizzard conditions. Snow swirled around the cabin. Chilling wind gusts were strong and fierce, drifts looked awful deep. The Escalade and Mercedes resembled igloos, not a patch of color visible.

He grabbed the shovel and made quick work of the porch, dug a small clearing for Durango that disappeared in an instant, then shoveled a path to the woodshed, grinning every step of the way.

He'd taken a big gamble with that last remark, and he knew he'd beaten the odds. Shock had spread across Rio's beautiful face, followed by disappointment and finally a worried frown, a snapshot of the one she'd displayed at the club. He patted the coat pocket where he'd slipped the gift inside. Galaxeé had been right after all.

"I made hot chocolate. Want some?" Rio asked. She had Durango draped over her arm again.

Bryce stomped his feet while shedding his outdoor wear. "Sure. Need to warm the chill in my bones."

"Will you hold Durango while I get it?"

"I'll get it myself." *Damn dog won't ever learn how to walk, run or play.* "Spoiled little shit."

"Did you say something?"

"Got marshmallows?"

"I'll get them."

Act as if you don't need her. "Just tell me where they are."

Bryce took a seat in the recliner near the fireplace, found a magazine, flipped through the pages, sipping on his chocolate, and ignoring Rio.

"Snow's deep," she said.

"Um-hmm."

"Roads are probably in poor condition."

"Probably." He folded the magazine, grabbed a pencil and started to work a new crossword puzzle. These things were too easy.

"Snow-packed and icy."

"Got chains." He heard the sigh and smiled inwardly.

He kept his eyes on the magazine, then shot a quick glance at her wiggling toes beside the recliner. She had the sexiest feet and seeing them brought back an avalanche of memories.

He'd kissed and sucked on all ten toes, ran his tongue along the arch of her foot, ankle, up her calf, her thigh and on to that one special place he loved teasing.

Bryce looked away, tried to banish the erotic thoughts to a dark corner of his brain. Why did she have to run her fingers through his hair? Did she have to stroke his cheek, too?

"Is it too warm? You're sweating."

"Heavy sweater." He set the magazine and pencil down to yank it off. "Guess I'd better add a log or two for the night."

He had to put some distance between them and went to the fireplace. He poked uselessly at the blazing inferno when sweat poured down his face. He wiped it away with the body-hugging turtleneck.

Rio went back to Durango and the couch, stretching long and sleek over the length of the furniture. A second later, she curled into a protective cocoon with Durango cuddled against her belly.

Rarely missing anyone or anything worth his undivided attention, Bryce really wanted to watch her body lengthen again, naked. Full breasts waiting for his mouth and tongue, back arched, endless legs pinned over his shoulders, toes curled from his deep, deep thrusts demanding her passionate response.

The sound of his own rumbling groan snapped him out of the fantasy. Get a damn grip.

Turning, he raked both hands through his hair, keeping his eyes focused on the dancing flames, keeping Rio to his back, keeping his throbbing erection hidden from her sight.

This stupid game was killing him. Why not openly admit the obvious?

He had embarked on the subtle chase and they'd found the right path, but they'd veered sideways on separate lanes. Yet, they'd managed to find their way back to each other.

He'd never known real love until Rio. Every moment they spent apart when the chips were down, he'd sunk to the deepest trench and nearly drowned in misery. So had she. And she was as miserable now as he was. He'd seen anxiety written all over her face more than once.

Too many issues. Too much pressure. Too many games and this player had grown tired of the sport.

Bracing his hands against the mantel, Bryce squeezed his eyes shut, gathering his thoughts. The truth had to come out, and honesty would either make or break their relationship.

"I should've tried harder to stay away from you, but I couldn't," he said around a shuddering breath. "You know I love you, Rio, but you have yet to say those three simple words to me. Do you or don't you? I can't keep going like this, not knowing your feelings."

Assuming he'd stunned her into silence, what better time to swan dive?

"I want to spend my life with you, to fall asleep with you in my arms, wake up every morning and see your smiling face. You mean everything to me. Everything. I can't sleep without you, can't work when we're at odds. And I can't stand the thought of you with someone else."

A response never came.

He forged ahead. "Don't you see what's happened? I need you, want a relationship a little more permanent than separate living quarters. What I'm asking," he said and turned around to stare into her eyes.

"Hell."

She lay curled up beside Durango. Bryce listened closely to soft snoring.

"Hell," he said, chuckling. Spilled his guts and she hadn't heard a damn word of his confession.

Fine. Tomorrow morning he'd unload again, if he could find the nerve a second time.

He moved Durango to the recliner, went back to Rio, swept her into his arms and took her to bed. She grumbled and slapped at his hands while he stripped her. When she drew her legs up into a fetal position, he covered her naked body with a sheet, two heavy blankets and a down comforter. He tucked them around her shoulders.

He would not sleep with her tonight, would not make love to her again until the timing was right. Closing the bedroom door, he was surprised he didn't have a hard-on, surprised more it didn't bother him not to sleep with her.

Durango was a good puppy. He managed to take care of business outside and yipped happily when Bryce praised him.

After finding two sheets plus a pancake pillow for the couch, Bryce stripped down. It was too hot for clothes, but comfort was still impossible on a short divan. His bare feet dangled over the edge. Durango didn't seem to mind. He curled up on Bryce's chest and they both fell asleep.

Darkness. Rio scrambled to an upright position and held her breath.

Where was she? She reached for the opposite side of the bed, found it cold and empty. "Bryce?" she whispered, panting. Where was he? Had he really left her for good?

She remembered chasing him, running after his car through snow and over ice, screaming when her legs caught in a deep drift, while his SUV rolled out of sight.

"Bryce?"

Yanking the covers off, she discovered she was naked. Naked and sleeping alone. She tiptoed to the door, seeing a soft glow of light beneath it, her heart pounding. She pulled it open.

"Oh, God."

He was still here, lying on the floor beside the hearth, Durango on his chest, a sheet covering both. The fire had died down. Embers sparked and fizzled, but a chill had settled over the room.

Rio added kindling and shoved two logs on top; immediately flames sprung to life, spreading blazing heat again.

She went back to the bedroom for Durango's small bed and set it beside the hearth. When she put him inside, the puppy yawned sleepily and closed his eyes again.

Lifting the sheet, she slid in next to Bryce, snuggled against his warm, toasty body. His arms came around her. Rio sighed. This was where she belonged. Beside him instead of driving him away. Protected by him, comforted and loved by him.

Christ, he was on fire. So goddamn hot, sweat dripped down his forehead, and so damn hard that he hurt. A wet dream?

Bryce heard his own groan. He cleared the hazy fog of sleep from his brain. His hips were circling, lifting off the floor. He forced his eyes open.

Oh, goddamn.

Rio had her sweet lips wrapped around his cock, her hands working him into a freakin' frenzy. "Stop it. Stop it!"

On the brink of a powerful orgasm, he reached down,

jammed his fingers into the shag haircut and pulled her free of his engorged cock.

"Damn you, Rio, damn you."

Struggling to keep from losing the load, he shook, gritting his teeth, eyes tightly shut, his breaths in harsh shallow bursts.

He let loose of her hair and coiled his fingers into the sheet, riding out the last vestige of near-exquisite pleasure.

Damn her. He hadn't wanted to touch her.

When the tremors finally began to subside, Bryce opened his eyes, angrier than a kicked dog. What the hell? He saw her face, tears shimmering in her beautiful eyes, uncooperative hands working unsuccessfully at covering her nakedness with the sheet.

What the hell is this about?

"Sorry," Rio said, her voice tremulous behind a wavering, false smile. "I-I guess it wasn't a dream after all. I g-guess I did make a big mistake."

A mistake? She'd raped him in his sleep.

With the backs of her hands, she wiped frantically at the tears racing down her cheeks and lifted her chin, sniffing. "I've been wrong before. No big deal." Scooping Durango into her arms, she hugged him fiercely to her breasts, as if only he could make it all right.

A mistake? Bryce couldn't quite get past the comment. "Wrong about what? What mistake?" he asked gruffly.

The false smile appeared again, just for a split second. A fake laugh followed. Then, one big watery tear made its way slowly down a used path on her cheek, hung under her chin, splashed on the puppy's head. Rio whispered, "Love."

"Goddamn you," Bryce rasped.

He couldn't reach her fast enough and grabbed her ankle, dragged her across the floor and into his arms.

"Do you love me, Rio?"

"Yes," she said on a tortured sob. "Yes."

He gripped her chin and forced her head up, forced her to look into his eyes. "Say it, damn it. Say it aloud," he commanded. "And you damn well better mean it. Or don't say it at all."

"I love you. I love you," she chanted. "I love—"

He kissed her, drank long and deeply, thrusting his tongue into her mouth, accepting the sweetness she gave so freely.

She'd finally admitted loving him and his heart exploded with rapacious joy. This beautiful woman melting in his arms had given him more in a few mere seconds than he could ever receive in a lifetime. God, he loved her beyond all reason.

He dragged his lips away from Rio's. "I love you," he said, his voice hoarse with emotion. "Make me the happiest man alive."

Her body turned stiff as ironwood beneath his hands and, as all her lithe muscles constricted, Durango yelped.

"Wait," Bryce said and got to his feet. He strode to the coatrack. "Since you didn't open this earlier."

Rio's throat closed off. She couldn't clear a path to make a sound.

"I'll open it for you." He came back and sat, tore the gold paper off, removed a black, velvet ring-size box from the white box and held it toward her.

She wanted to scream. She'd forgotten all about this one issue. Sure, she wanted his love and companionship. But this? Her heart drummed in her chest, beat harder than a tom-tom, and prickly heat tickled her scalp. God, she hated to sweat. She smoothed her fingers over her damp forehead.

"Open it."

She tried to keep Durango clutched in her hands, but Bryce took him away, set the pup in his lap.

"Open it."

"All right. All right," she replied and took the box from his hand.

Lord, what should I tell him? No? Yes? Maybe? I need time?
Oh, Momma, help me.

She stared at the velvet box for a few long seconds, unable to move.

"Go on, open it," Bryce repeated.

She squeezed her eyes shut and flicked the top with a thumb.

Swallowing past the lump in her throat, heart pounding, Rio opened her eyes.

19

"I don't see why we have to leave so soon," Bryce said. "I've got the weekend at least. So do you."

"Because I've got work to do at Killer's." Rio swept snow from her Mercedes while he shoveled a path around it. She covered up his hard labor. "Don't bother. Mr. Landers is on his way to plow."

The sky was a crystal clear sea of blue, and the air, crisp and icicle cold. She'd donned her new black snowsuit, boots and gloves. They sure came in handy for frigid weather. The chill on the mountain was as icy as the blood circulating through her veins and arteries.

She was so mad she could spit. A damn key to his house. Rio tsked. The nerve of him wanting one to hers. She tsked again.

Bryce was lucky she hadn't scratched his eyes blind. Instead, she'd politely said, "I need time to think about it." Setting the box down, he'd hinted about a key to the loft. The bastard.

When the sky had faded from indigo to paler hues, Rio started packing, claiming she needed to get back and finish entering data on Killer's computer. The auditor was due to come by next week.

"I can have my accountant go over your files," Bryce had said. "Cheap."

She opened the car door. "Like the locksmith? No, thank you," she'd replied.

She climbed inside the Mercedes. When she started the engine, it roared to life, calmed to a kitten's purr, much quieter than her feline hiss.

In the distance, she heard the grating noise of Landers's diesel truck. Thank God. She'd be back in Denver by noon if the roads weren't too bad. Of course, Bryce would have to follow her home since most of the stuff had to go into his SUV.

"Why are you being so goddamn short with me?" he asked and blocked her exit from the car.

Why? Why? Stupid question. He'd led her to believe something stupid and outrageous. Bristling, she shoved him out of her way. "I haven't been. Just in a rush to get home, then to the club."

Bryce stood there, checking out her swaying hips as she went back to the cabin, enjoying how well she filled out that tight snowsuit.

He would've peeled it off her body, used it for a blanket and spread her out in a snowdrift, if they weren't leaving so soon. They'd melt a snow angel all the way down to pine needles and gravel. He would've tackled her if Landers's truck hadn't been heading this direction. Spontaneity, and freeze their asses off, he thought on a chuckle.

His smile slid away and Bryce sighed.

Rio hadn't exactly refused the key to his house, but she hadn't sounded enthusiastic.

Okay, so maybe this was a bigger step for her than he had anticipated. It was a huge one for him. Sharing a household with a lover? Wasn't that like staking a claim?

I need time to think about it. She'd neglected to mention how much time. A week? Day? An hour?

He checked his watch. The hour mark had passed an hour ago. The next interval made a full day. Twenty-four hours. Multiplied by sixty minutes. Fourteen hundred and forty. Times sixty seconds. Eighty-six thousand . . .

Stop thinking like a logical computer nerd. Hell, he'd caught each one of Galaxeé's hints, or slips.

Everything in his adult life had been based on logic, well-thought processes. He had followed his dreams, accomplished a whole helluva lot in a little bit of time. He should be satisfied. He should be contented with what he'd accomplished, earned and had.

But he wasn't. Logic hadn't provided an algorithm for love, or one to figure out a woman's mind, her heart or what she intended to do or say from one minute to the next.

Rio came through the doorway carrying two filled plastic bags in each hand when Landers's rumbling diesel stopped near the Escalade. She put a smile on her face, and Bryce realized she hadn't smiled at him since . . . When was the last time she'd smiled at him?

Two men climbed out of the truck, an old scraggly looking fellow from the passenger seat who must be Mr. Landers and, driving, a younger version of him with sandy-blond hair. Much younger. Thick. Built like a college fullback.

"Let me help you with those," the young guy said.

Bryce hurried around her car. "I've got them." He took the bags from Rio, set them in the Mercedes's backseat. On second thought, he put them in his own vehicle.

"Thought you'd planned to stay up here a week or more," Landers said.

Slamming the Escalade's door, Bryce slid his gaze toward Rio. A week? Why the hell were they leaving so soon?

"Something came up. Business," she replied. "Need to get

back. Sorry you went through the trouble, setting up the tub, wood, plowing. I'll write another check."

"Never you mind," the youngster said. "Bart and me don't mind doing stuff for you. Dad don't mind none, either, since you come up here all alone. Can't be having women up in these mountains without an escort, Miss Saunders. I'll make sure you stay safe and comfortable while you're here."

Bryce reached for his wallet. He plucked out two hundred-dollar bills. "Nothing in life is free, Mr.—" he prompted.

"Miss Saunders here calls me by my first name. Ward," he replied a little too snottily, looking Bryce up and down as if measuring the competition. He didn't take the money. "And who are you?"

"A friend," Rio cut in. "From—"

Friend? His temper simmered. "Denver. Bryce Sullivan." Punk.

"Would either of you like coffee, chocolate, to warm up?" she asked and laid her hand on Landers's arm.

Fortunately, Bryce thought hostilely, not on his son's Pop-eye forearm. Without wearing a coat, the little shit flexed, curled his hands into fists.

"Sure—" Ward began.

"Got half a dozen driveways to plow yet. Thanks anyway," old man Landers said. He stepped up to the diesel's door and turned around. "Come on here, boy. We got work to do."

Ward didn't look pleased as he backed up and bumped into the side-view mirror. "Let us know when you plan to come back, Miss Saunders, and have some chocolate ready."

Bryce snarled under his breath. The little fucker had the goddamn nerve to wink at Rio before he climbed inside the truck. The stare down with Ward, Mr. I'll-make-sure-you-stay-safe-and-comfortable fullback, lasted until he wheeled the vehicle around. Bryce half expected Ward to flip him off. He watched the Landers truck drive away and roll out of sight, spewing dark smoke behind them.

"What's with this friend crap?" Bryce said and spun on his heels.

Talking to the goddamn wind. Rio had gone back inside the cabin.

She sauntered out again carrying Durango's bed and toys, loaded them into her car's front seat. "You can lose that macho, nostril-flaring bit before you take flight with the birds."

Hell. She walked off and Bryce deflated faster than a punctured tire under heavy weight.

When would this jealousy thing cease, when Rio moved in with him? Or did he have to wait until his staked claim was notarized, entered into the books like a goddamn patent or copyright?

Meanwhile, every unattached male had the right—some, the power—to steal her away from him. By the way she was acting this morning, the grass on his side of the fence might not be as fresh to Rio any longer.

How the devil was he going to keep her for himself, keep the wolf packs and her ex-husband at bay, a twenty-four-hour-positioned-at-a-distance bodyguard? She'd have a shit fit if she ever found out.

His heart rate sped up from a logical process of deduction.

Ah, hell.

Marriage? As in the get-down-on-one-knee proposal, the million-dollar vow and promise to be a good husband? Diamond ring. Debit card. He'd made a vow to maintain bachelorhood. But he'd left his nose wide open.

Shit, insert ring.

"How can you sweat when it's so cold?" Rio asked. "You haven't done anything. Can I put this in your car? My trunk is full."

While he stood in place, dripping wet like a stunned fool,

she was carrying the fifty-pound sack of dog food. No telling what else she'd brought out of the cabin since the backseat of her Mercedes was already loaded. Cursing, Bryce took the sack out of her arms.

"Don't lift heavy stuff like this, Rio, you'll hurt yourself. I'll get the rest."

"I'm used to doing things on my own, being on my own," she said, frowning.

"Get unused to it. Go sit with Durango and stay warm." He held the bag with one arm, opened the rear gate to the Escalade, and slid the dog food inside. "This is a man's job, and don't argue with me, damn it," Bryce said, frowning, too.

This whole marriage thing had put him in a funky-ass mood.

How much would an engagement ring cost? Wedding bands? Invitations? The wedding? Rio would probably want a big church wedding with a bunch of bridesmaids like Coop's high-maintenance old lady. Bryce didn't think he had enough friends for groomsmen in a royal-size ceremony. They'd need tuxedos, too. Blue ones, her favorite color.

He went inside the cabin and grabbed the case of wine and four overstuffed plastic sacks, tromped through the snow back to the Escalade.

Couldn't forget the reception afterward: food, booze, or-chestra, renting an expensive, high-class joint to accommodate all the guests. Let's not overlook hotel rooms for out-of-town family and friends, limousines to transport the wedding party. Then, the flowers. She'd want a nursery's worth of blossoming flowers. Most likely, roses. Coop said flower arrangements cost the bride's parents a boatload of cash. Rio didn't have close living relatives, except a brother, wherever the hell he was now. Bryce would have to pay for the wedding, etcetera, etcetera, etcetera. High-dollar stuff from what Coop had said. Thou-sands. Hell, there goes the contract money.

Her suitcase weighed a half-ton and he hoisted it onto his

shoulder. He lifted Durango's travel carrier. She'd packed it full of odds and ends. What the devil had she put in there for it to weigh so goddamn much? She couldn't possibly lift this thing into the car. She'd packed enough crap to last a freakin' month in the mountains. Women. Sighing, Bryce took the load to the Escalade.

When he saw her beautiful face again, his mind started a new race at breakneck speed.

What about the honeymoon? She'd probably want to go to some high-priced destination. Aspen? Switzerland? Scottish Highlands? More money. And, God, he hoped she wouldn't pack heavy. She wouldn't need clothes anyway. He'd keep her naked, in bed for the duration.

But, hell, plane tickets, the hotel, restaurants, for what, a week? Two? Impossible. He had a business to run, so did she, and who would take care of Durango while they were honeymooning? He'd miss them. No way they'd put him in a doggie hotel. He was too young and needed them.

A kennel was no better than a boarding school, and that ugly reminder didn't sit well in Bryce's gut. Their children would not attend any boarding school, not like he had, separated from Mommy and Daddy.

Speaking of, how many kids did she want? Two? Three?

Ah, for crying out loud. Kids meant big bucks.

Babies, diapers, kindergarten, college. Braces, clothes. Cars. Dating? Hell, no. His daughters weren't dating anybody until they turned eighteen. Twenty-one, goddamn it. The young punks hoping to court his little girls had to meet Daddy for approval. First chump who kissed them was in big trouble. The first one who made them cry was dead meat.

Scowling, Bryce slammed the trunk shut and swung around, stared at the cabin.

Rio came outside. She locked the door and started down the porch steps with Durango tucked inside her snowsuit like a little papoose. "I guess I can follow you back."

"I want a half dozen kids. Three girls, three boys. Boys first." They'd help protect their sisters. He'd teach his sons to box, to protect all three of his princesses and his queen.

"What?"

"We'll get hitched at a courthouse today."

"What?"

Shit, that came out all wrong, and he forgot to get down on one knee. Damn it, he didn't have an engagement ring. "Marry me," Bryce said, dropping to both knees now, grabbing her hands. "I'll buy you the largest diamond on the planet. We'll get married in a big church wedding, a cathedral, with three hundred guests and have the reception at the Convention Center. We'll take a month-long honeymoon in Switzerland. We'll charter a jet and take Durango with us so he won't have to fly in the cargo bay."

She looked stricken and pulled free of his grasp. "No."

So she wanted a warmer climate. "Okay, we'll charter everybody to Tahiti for the wedding. I'll rent villas and I'll pay for everything. Flights, food, fun, everything."

"No!"

"I'll be the best husband and father. I promise to love, honor and cherish you and our children. I already do." Her single answer finally sank in. "Why not?"

"Because."

"Because why? Damn it, kitten, I love you, want to marry you."

"But I don't think—"

"I do want children—your children—and a long life together, growing old with each other, watching our babies and grandbabies grow. We'll have a bunch of grandbabies. We love each other. Please, say yes, please. I won't give you up."

"Stop it," Rio said, stamping foot.

Bryce groaned, sat back on his heels and slumped like a beaten-down drunk. He'd lost her already. She didn't want to marry him or even be with him. He'd go crazy without her in his life.

"I'm too old to give you six children."

Bryce looked up, held his breath.

Tears filled her golden eyes and she laid her fingertips against his cheek. "I don't think I can have children. You'll have to f-find someone younger, someone who wants a big diamond and a big—" She swallowed several times. "Big wedding and a honeymoon in Tahiti." Her broken sobs tore a gaping hole in his heart. "I'd ruin all your wedding dreams, your family hopes and your l-life."

"You are my life and my dreams. Without you I have nothing," Bryce said and swallowed around the giant lump cutting off his air. "Justice of the Peace, Galaxeé, Randy, Rosalind and Oscar." Suddenly he realized how Oscar felt when in love. "Honeymoon here at the cabin. With Durango. We'll adopt a dozen children. Two dozen. Whatever you want. Sun rays, moonbeams. I love you."

"I'm still too old for—"

"Women live longer than men. We're even."

She smiled tremulously. "I can't," she said and swallowed again. "We need time together, as a real couple, time to think things through."

Bryce smiled. At least she hadn't said "no" as a permanent statement. Like Oscar, he had years to dance a "yes" from her. He got to his feet and wrapped her into his embrace.

"The only thing you have to think about is how much I love you. And, Rio, that will never change."

Turn the page and
find yourself
DOWN IN TEXAS
with Delilah Devlin!

On sale now!

1
_____

Her daddy had always told her a man's worth wasn't measured by the size of his bank account or the square footage of his house. Rather, it could be seen in the proud set of his shoulders or a gaze that didn't waiver.

Her mama had said a man's strength was in his hands—strong and soothing when an animal or child needed comfort, hot and wild when a woman needed shaking up.

Looking at Brand now, Lyssa McDonough knew exactly what they'd both meant.

If she had any sense at all she'd turn tail and run. Everything about the man screamed heartbreaker.

Only, she couldn't. Instead she settled her shoulder against the fence post, kept her breaths shallow and even, and pretended she wasn't melting inside.

As long as she could remember, Brand had had that effect on her—long before she had admitted, even to herself, how much he moved her. Today, dressed in a wash-softened chambray shirt that stretched across his broad chest, blue jeans that hugged lean hips, and leather chaps encasing thick thighs, he was the embodiment of any woman's favorite cowboy fantasy.

Once again, she wished that she affected him the same way, that just looking at her made him breathless. The sight she presented him at this moment, however, would never inspire lust.

Covered in dust and sweat, with hair straggling from the confines of its rubber band, she was grimy, bloody, and anything but attractive.

Too far away to read his expression, Lyssa watched how he stood in the stirrups as he topped the hill, head turning to scan the countryside. When his gaze landed on her, his back stiffened, he settled into his saddle, and his boots spurred his horse to bring him fast down the hill.

Things could have turned out worse.

The day might have broken with a cloudless, blue sky and a white-hot sun beating relentlessly on her unprotected face. Early summer in southwest Texas could be ruthless, but thick, gray clouds had gathered, shielding her from the worst of the heat. Still, she was thirsty, and her canteen was deep in the satchel of the horse that had to be halfway back to the ranch house by now.

She might not have worn the industrial-padded bra that was the only thing keeping one nasty barb from tearing the tender flesh of her breast like the other that pierced the back of her shoulder. The pointed barb only pricked, a reminder not to take deeper breaths. Vanity had guided her choice. She'd chosen the thick-cupped bra hoping she'd see him today, hoping he'd finally take a closer look and realize she was more than his best friend's little sister.

More than an obligation he'd accepted.

The promise he'd made was the crux of her problem with Brandon Tynan.

Lyssa dragged away her gaze and readied herself for what she knew was coming. Again, she stretched the toe of her boot toward the wire cutters she'd dropped when she'd first felt the tension in the barbed wire ease and heard it "sing" as it snapped from a post farther down the fence.

The wire had coiled so fast she'd had time only to spit out the bent nails she'd held between her teeth. It had snagged her, pulling her off her feet, and wrapped around her. The merciless wire had trapped her arms against her sides and her shoulder against the post to which she'd been securing new strands of wire to replace the cut ones.

When the barb atop her left breast bit deeper, she gritted her teeth and sagged against the post. Brand would have to get her out of her current coil.

Damn. The man loved rubbing her nose in her mistakes.

Hooves thundered closer. She wiped the pain-filled grimace from her face and turned to meet his steady gaze as he reined in his horse.

Brand slipped from the saddle as soon as Ranger slid to a stop, kicking up a cloud of dust.

Because Lyssa couldn't tilt her head higher as he approached, she watched his booted feet eat the distance between them.

He knelt on one knee beside her and tipped his hat off his head to hang from the stampede string knotted at his throat. His gaze raked her body once before locking with her gaze.

Inwardly she braced herself. His expression was darker than the thunderheads building in the sky above them. "Lyssa, didn't I tell you not to ride the fence alone?"

She blinked at the raw tension in his deep, rumbling voice, and then felt her eyebrows draw together in a fierce scowl. "I've been mending fences all my life. I didn't need any help. This was just pure bad luck."

"We're gonna talk about this, soon as I get you free."

"Damn you, Brand." Furious tears burned the back of her eyes, but she blinked them back. "No 'Are you all right? Are you thirsty?' No, you have to start in—"

"Fuck." He scrubbed his deeply tanned face with the back of a leather glove before meeting her gaze again. "Are you okay?"

She sniffed, wishing she could reach up and rub her nose. "Too late."

"I was worried. The hands said you'd been gone a long time. When I found your horse . . ." He took a deep breath, and his gaze slid to the clouds overhead.

Only slightly mollified with his nonapology, she sighed, letting the anger slide away and glaring at the wire doubled around her torso. "Just cut me loose."

"Don't think I can," he said softly.

She shot him an irritated glance. "The cutters are at my feet. . . ." Her voice faded as she stared.

Brand's expression had lost its angry tension. Sure, a muscle flexed along his square jaw, but his dark brown eyes held a tenderness she'd never observed.

Before she had a moment to ponder what it meant, he stood and unbuttoned his shirt, tugging it from the waist of his jeans.

She'd seen his tanned, bared chest before—had drooled over the smattering of black-brown hair that stretched between his small, male nipples and sighed when imagining herself lightly stroking her fingertips along the thick slabs of muscle filling out his masculine chest and shoulders.

Her breath caught, pushing her breast against the barb. Air hissed between her teeth.

He bent quickly. "Don't move, I'm gonna slide this under the wire. Let me know if I hurt you."

Lyssa held her breath as his hand slipped between her breasts and under the wire. Slowly he pressed against the thickly padded material cupping a meager curve, working his way toward the barb, and then he pulled the wire away from her, sliding the bunched shirt under the wire.

Lyssa ground her teeth as the prongs embedded in her shoulder cut deeper.

"I'm hurting you. Where next?"

"Behind my shoulder," she bit out.

Brand crawled over her sprawled legs and circled behind her. "Damn, you're bleeding."

She opened her mouth to deliver her usual caustic "duh" but clamped her mouth shut, not wanting to spoil the tender moment stretching between them. "I'm all right. It just stings."

"I can't pad it. I'll have to cut the wire to get it out."

"Thanks for the warning," she murmered.

He leaned to grab the wire cutters. "I'll make it quick."

"Just do it."

A snip drove the barb deeper. Lyssa squeezed her eyes shut as Brand pulled it out. Two more snips, and he dragged away the rest of the wire before kneeling beside her once again.

Lyssa dropped her head and dragged in deep, trembling breaths. Her shoulder and breast burned like fire, but the ordeal was over now.

A large, broad palm entered her line of vision. "Let's get you home and have a look at that shoulder."

She accepted the hand he extended and almost groaned with relief when another hand gripped her waist to lift her to her feet. She felt weak as a baby, and her legs tingled as blood rushed back into cramped limbs.

"Can you walk?"

Lyssa flashed Brand an incredulous look and shook off the hand around her waist. When the one gripping her hand tightened, she didn't fight him, just let him lead her slowly toward his horse.

"Anyone ever tell you you're as stubborn as an old mule?" he said, reaching for the canteen looped around his saddle horn.

She let go of his hand and accepted the canteen, giving the cap a twist. "You. More times than I can count."

A small, tight smile stretched one side of his mouth as he stared while she upended the canteen and let water spill into her mouth. She didn't care when it trickled along her cheek and down her neck.

"Slow down," he said. "You'll be sick."

Because he was right, and, more so, because a sudden weariness sapped her strength, she didn't argue. She handed back the canteen and waited while he stowed it and his bloodied shirt in a saddlebag and gathered the tools strewn on the ground.

When he came back to her side, he handed her the hat she'd lost. "Hold this." Then he gripped her waist and lifted her gently over the saddle. He settled her sideways, the horn between her thighs, and then stepped up, sliding into his seat behind her.

She'd never been this close to Brand before. The juncture of his thighs pressed against the side of her hip. If she leaned, her cheek would lie against bare skin.

Suddenly she felt unsettled. Her stomach tightened. She hoped the water she'd drunk wasn't getting ready to rush back up. When his arm gently encircled her waist, she jerked at the intimate touch.

"Rest against me," he said, his voice deepening. "I won't jostle you as much."

Lyssa knew he was probably just being kind as she relaxed against him and fought against her rising excitement. She slid an arm around his waist to hold on as he nudged his horse forward; she noted that she felt no softness, just hard muscle clothed in skin smooth as oiled leather.

Snuggling her cheek against him, she enjoyed the feel of the soft, swirling hairs that furred his chest, and she inhaled the smell of the man who'd filled her head with lustful thoughts since she'd reached puberty.

His scent—plain soap and his unique musk—filled her nostrils, calming her thudding heart. Another deeper inhalation, and she let her body rock in the saddle with his body as he kept his horse at a slow, even gait.

Even though her wounds ached, she was over being sorry

that she'd landed in such a mess. She'd wanted him to notice her.

Things could have turned out worse.

Brand gritted his teeth and tried to calm the riot of feelings flooding his body. Every rocking movement made him aware of just what part of his body was rubbing against her slim hip. His cock crowded tighter by the minute against the fly of his jeans.

The way she sat, snuggled up against him, her soft cheek sliding on his skin, her slim fingers clutching his waist . . . he wished he could spur Ranger to race toward the ranch house so he could dump her sweet body on the porch and end the torment.

With one smart-mouth comment, Lyssa could trigger his anger faster than fire licking at dry prairie grass. However, the sight of her mouth tightened with pain had shot an arrow straight through his heart.

Worse, horned toad that he was, the trembling of her full bottom lip—and the tears glittering in her wide, green eyes as he'd cut away the wire—had sent his thoughts straight south.

Not for the first time, he'd wished he could gather her in his arms and soothe away all her worries, ease all her hurts. But he knew where that would lead. One intimate, tender touch, and he'd be a goner, his promise as empty as the wide-open spaces stretching in front of them.

Brand wanted to soothe his own aches while sinking every inch of his cock into Lyssa McDonough's silky depths.

However, Lyssa wasn't a woman he could play with and leave. She was his best friend's sister. Before Mac's reserve unit had been mobilized, he'd extracted Brand's promise to make sure she stayed safe. Watching over the woman didn't include sleeping with her—no matter how tempting her sexy little body was or how much she might want to experiment.

He'd have to be blind not to note how her gaze followed him. How curiosity gleamed in her eyes or colored her cheeks whenever they were together. Over the years, deflecting her interest had become a natural habit.

Brand had learned to use her anger to protect himself from his own growing attraction. He gave her a narrowed glance. "What do you think you were doing, riding alone?"

She stiffened in his arms, eyes flashing.

Brand tightened his grip on her waist, not wanting her to harm herself, all the while acutely aware that his thumb rode the bottom edge of her bra.

"A load of hay's coming. I needed most of the hands to unload the trailer."

"Why didn't you call me?" he growled.

"Who made you my keeper?"

His glare intensified. "Mac did. You know it."

"I don't need a babysitter."

"What happened to the fence?"

She bristled with tension, and he suppressed a grim smile. Lyssa was predictable.

"Someone cut it."

"Third time in a month. Don't you think that warrants a little caution?" She stayed silent so long he knew she agreed but was searching for a plausible excuse for today's actions.

"I'm not missing any cattle," she said.

"Maybe they're scoping out the place first. Or maybe it's not rustlers. We're damn close to the border."

Her head tilted back. "You think it might be smugglers?"

"Could be. Reason enough to take precautions."

"I carry a rifle."

"Oh?" he said, letting his gaze slide over her body. "Where's it now?"

Her eyebrows drew into a testy frown. "With my horse."

Brand sighed. "Lyssa, we've got to come to an understanding. You're gonna take my advice."

"Or what?" Lyssa asked, a new, sultry note entering her voice. "What are you gonna do? Spank me?" Her hip wiggled against him.

Shock at her drawled suggestion had him sucking in a deep breath. A vision of Lyssa, her naked body draped over his knees, made his dick pulse. "Would you like that?" he asked softly.

"Maybe I would," she whispered, lowering her eyelids halfway.

His gaze dropped to her mouth as pink lips opened around a gasp.

"I can't believe I just said that. To you."

He narrowed his eyes. "It slipped kinda easy from your lips. Someone else you been teasing, baby girl?"

"I don't tease."

Brand ground his teeth at the solemn promise in her eyes. "Juanita at your house?"

Her head shook, and tendrils of wild, red hair moved around her face. "She's in town doing some shopping."

He swore softly and pointed his horse west.

"Thought you were taking me home."

"I am. My home."

"But we're closer to mine."

"You want Hector or Santiago cleanin' you up?"

Her chin lifted. "I'll manage on my own."

"What about your shoulder?"

Her breath huffed, but a moment later she whispered, "So you're gonna do it?"

The small, feminine smile beginning to curve her lips had him tightening like a bowstring. "I'll tend your wounds; then I'm drivin' you straight home."

"Whatever you say."

"Now you're all agreeable," he grumbled, pretending an irritation that was totally at war with the anticipation building in his body.

"I'm not unreasonable. Makes sense," she said breathlessly. "You tending my wounds. Nothing Mac wouldn't have done."

Shit. If Mac knew the thoughts running through his mind, he'd string him up by his balls. Brand pulled up to the gate between the two properties and leaned down to unlatch it. "Like I said, after we're done, I'm takin' you straight home."